BROKEN WATER

NICK PERRY

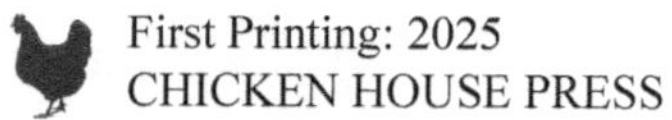

First Printing: 2025
CHICKEN HOUSE PRESS

Library and Archives Canada Cataloguing in Publication
CIP data on file with the National Library and Archives

ISBN trade paperback edition: 978-1-990336-83-6

Okakura, Kakuzō. *The Book of Tea.* New York: Fox, Duffield & Company, 1906. Print, public domain.

The King James Bible, public domain

Cover design by Jes Perry

Chicken House Press
282906 Normanby/Bentinck Townline
Durham, Ontario, Canada, N0G 1R0
www.chickenhousepress.ca

"I want to want to have faith."
Malcolm Lowry

BROKEN WATER

NICK PERRY

CHICKEN HOUSE PRESS

Part 1

ACKNOWLEDGEMENT

Chapter One

*H*ere I am, submerged in uncertainty.

As a recent university graduate, Declan Murphy is looking for a fulfilling start to his career. In his previous roles, Declan has shown a professional level of care in dealing with customers as well as in the execution of his daily duties. He brings a passionate bilingualism that is as equally strong as his fandom for the Montréal Canadiens. Outside of work, he maintains an avid interest in books and paintings as well as a close dedication to his family.

Christ.

Have you ever had your life shown to you and been less than pleased with what it says? I don't mean in a final-epitaph-I-wonder-what-they'll-remember-me-for kind of thing, but an honest assessment of what you've done during your time here. Read that bio over again, please, it's for LinkedIn, and I'm still trying to get this kind of writing right. Would you hire me based on that? Does it look like it was spawned from a high school template?

And if I try something else?

With two languages in his head and two legs on the ground, Declan Murphy is here to help you. (Would an exclamation point be a better ending?) From his previous customer-facing roles at Canadian Tire and JJ Bean, Declan has proven himself to be organized, efficient, and provide a deep level of customer care (Gross, dude). He firmly believes that his skills and abilities would greatly aid any organization in their search for reliable and outstanding employees (Oh? Do you now? Care to tell who the exceptions would be?). With Declan Murphy, you can be sure that your tasks will be a thing of the past! (The attempt at rhyming here is cute, but I don't know that businesses are looking for striving poets.)

This isn't working. I'm feeling too mean to myself.

Or maybe it's not that I'm mad at myself but at the situation of job hunting. Though, even with my minimal expertise, this can't be what a hunt feels like. It's more like a tedious vending machine in which you insert resumes and questionnaires in the hopes of getting a job out of it. The machine rarely answers and certainly does not refund what it's taken. Even if it did spit something out, who's to say it would taste any good? What if the cans have been sitting warm and flat for months and, when drunk, fills you only with the disappointment that it used to taste good and you used to want it.

Mum tried to help me with this mess the other day. I had been pacing and she noticed so she went back to an old strategy, one she used to use on us when we were overwhelmed at making decisions as kids. We'd sit down together and write out all the possibilities we could think of—no matter how ridiculous, outlandish, or impossible they were. Then, with simple patience, we went through the list and crossed off each thing we didn't want to do until only one option was left. The idea being that, whatever we had left until the end, whatever we had saved, must be the thing we wanted most and didn't know it. We had become distracted by our choices and knowledge and needed to clear the mental weeds in order to find our living flower.

While this method had worked before for picking sports teams or musical instruments, something about selecting a career this way settled unevenly. Mum was just trying to be helpful, that's all, and I knew she couldn't see the mismatched wreckage sinking through my torso. Sitting with her, like I was a kid, made me feel like I wasn't really ready to begin my own adult life. I didn't bring it out in any kind of direct scorn but with passive judgements whose edges were coated in venom. They slithered out in the form of sentences like: "Mum, my chances at being a doctor left with my chemistry 11 grades," and "I've seen the guys who went to business school and, trust me, I'm not one of them. Besides, you know that I just never got into *Mad Men* like everyone else."

Grace to her patience, she stuck through the evening's activity until the last scribble. I sat staring at the mess on the page and instantly made the metaphor personal. It must've been visible in the space between because, once that image arrived, so too did her hand on my upper back. Mum spoke in a soothing tone and assured me that things would work themselves out, they always do. I met her eyes as my lips formed into a pursed frown. She supported the moment before sliding her hand away and giving me room to think. There were mutterings between her and Dad amongst the noise of the television but I didn't eavesdrop enough. They were all too tangled to be neatly separated.

Even if that list of possibilities was crossed-out shambles, at least it had a structure. I just don't get what this kind of self-presentation on LinkedIn is really for. Clicking around there is like going through a poorly attempted copy of personal interaction. It's a place of superlatives and empty celebrations—where failure never happens and, if it did, it always ended up leading to something even more spectacular. No one has unhappy endings there, and no one presents as a full person either. Each head floats up the feed like a bubble of perfection. Generous lighting, well groomed, and eyes looking to the centre of the image.

Why can't I just write: This is Declan Murphy. He's a swell fellow who would really love to move out of his parents' place and begin his version of independent adulthood. Yes, he's another arts degree holder and, yes, did not use that time to do a co-op or volunteer or anything, but he'll be a decent employee and probably not make too many mistakes.

I'm not so sure that's the best way to sell oneself; but then again, I'm not so sure of many more things.

If there is a single word that unites me to my generation it is doubt. That's what has all of us Millennials wrapped up in, isn't it? That's a potential source of the anxiety none of us can properly pinpoint. We were raised in a time that was newly beginning to worry publicly about everything. About the air, the water, the soil, the endangered species, the housing market, the cost of tuition, the social unrest, and how many eggs a person should really be eating. We knew people that had one career for their entire lives, and when asked in school what we would like to be when we grew up, it was never presented as a multiple choice question. The sign of our internal times is a question mark, but what we feel the world requires of us is a period. Something definite, something unchanging. The human body is something like eighty-five percent water and isn't our generation acting like it? I wonder if all those people who seem settled today have merely allowed their bodies to freeze.

In that respect, I wish I could've had my dad's life. There's a difference worth a shock to anyone. In his day, so he sings, a kid didn't even have to finish high school to get started at some fishery for a decent wage. It wasn't as great as the ones who went down to St. John's or, as his father liked to say, up to Canada to get their sashes and work in some office, but it was still a decent job. It provided a kind of simple life that supported a predictable family nestled in one house that only felt cramped when company came by. Yes, they worked for someone who probably didn't care one iota for them; and perhaps, after a while, they felt detached from their process as they worked like machines on the same lines, repeating the same actions every day of their working lives. But the alienation they may have felt can't be worse than the anxiety I feel now.

If I may continue speaking for the jumbled

generation, we just don't feel like there's much certainty anymore. To our tastes, the advice of our forefathers has become acrid like spoiled milk. A university degree is seen more as a guarantee of debt than a promise of bountiful employment. What would a child be to this kind of person but a brick attached to an already tired swimmer? And more and more and more. We want to make our acknowledgements for past indiscretions but we don't want to incur the punishments. It's a heaping mess of harm without hope. For any example of the change we can believe in, there is some shrouded and unintended consequence that ends up being louder than the original call. By this account, we should all have given up already, and yet we haven't. At least by all the jobs I'm not getting, someone else must be. And at their level of required experience, they cannot be much beyond my level. Still, despite the dimming glint of future prospects and the reminders of how things used to be better, we continue. The world would certainly become much more boring if we really gave up.

And so I write again.

Hi! My name is Declan Murphy and I'd like to tell you a little bit about myself. As a recent graduate of Carleton University's sociology program—with honours, I might add—I can stand proud of my ability to not only see through difficult tasks to completion but also to do so in an equitable and conscientious way. My studies taught me a lot—including how to write a term paper in three hours!—and I would bring the skills I learned by taking diligent notes, participating in large group projects, and presenting my ideas in a thorough and complete manner. Outside of my school achievements, I love taking walks along my beautiful West Coast, passing time in the kitchen, and engaging with my French-Canadian roots. *Merci!*

That seems… demonstrably unlike me. It's too bright and covers the wrong details. Then again, there doesn't appear to be much punishment for inauthenticity in this place. In fact, the inauthentic folks seem to be doing as well as other categories. All they had to do was make themselves up for one photo and thus present themselves for a permanent image of professionalism. It doesn't matter if, let's say, during their university years (when they earned the base experience necessary for their aspirations) they could often be found vomiting in a low-lit bathroom during unpoetic twilight. Or if they spent all their available time caring for an ailing elder in between classes. What matters instead is the ability to strategically present themselves as capable, passionate, slightly ambitious, and deeply enjoyable to be around. But, even if all the details they choose are true, can one paragraph cover everything a person is?

Maybe I've seen *Good Will Hunting* too many times and tacitly absorbed the idea that there is no work of art that truly encapsulates me. Which is not to say that I think I'm too grandiose to be described, only that Will Hunting is already a fictional character. He only exists to tell a story and show whatever parts of his imagined life are necessary for the purposes of that story. He doesn't have to go to the bathroom or brush his teeth or lose fifteen minutes of his life because he missed his bus. His life is a series of important conversations with life-changing people. My life is not fiction. I don't have the luxury of consistency to myself. It's been only change and experimentation and influence that I can't always recognize when it's happening but might be able to shorten years later. Describing last year's mask is easy because I've had to take it off to wear this year's.

One of the only books I read beyond the required readings of my undergrad was about this kind of phenomenon: *The Presentation of Self in Everyday Life*. Its premise hooked me and its message still lingers. What if we aren't one hard-lined entity, walking through the world, revolving around a base set of immovable, unchanging truths? What if, instead, we are only who we are depending on who we're around? That identity is not a rock-hard casing but the continuous comfort of the anxious, the regular return of the cowardly, and the always amorphous form that provided security for the doubtful. To many of my classmates, this idea was unsettling, and they flung it off like water from a shaking dog. It seemed to be the very definition of a fake person and they must have had some difficulty thinking of themselves in such a shattered way. But who doesn't talk to their mum differently than their best friend—hell, who doesn't talk to their dad differently than their mum? My classmates left that lecture without reference to it again like it was an indecent and dirty idea. I was pierced by it.

It was a book that brought me to my own infinity—something I recommend everyone reckon with. For some, this idea of being infinite is a never-ending freedom. It means multitudes that holler to affirm the existence of the individual life and rebound over all of the other infinite lives of the world. A point of bottomless connection between people. If this were a few centuries ago, that idea would be much easier to fall in love with. In this time, the infinite is nothing to fawn over.

Now, to contemplate the infinity of oneself is filled with questions of doubting and redoubting. It is like standing and looking down on a platform whose point of balance is constantly shifting. If there is no countable number of potential social situations—and it is true, even if only in part, that we alter ourselves to fit those situations—then who the hell are we? Even when I'm thinking, the voice in my head carries on as if it's talking to someone else. My journals—the most private documents I own—contain the recollections of someone smarter, deeper, and more intellectually rigorous. My performance never stops, not even in so-called solitude.

These are the kinds of reflections that a mind gets into trouble over when it has no other occupation. With no leftover tasks to worry about, no specific future to consider, it's permitted to churn and wring out the last scoops of what it knows. Questions and opinions all swirling together in a murky disquiet of imagination.

Imagination is a troublesome thing. At least mine can be, anyway. Most days it's hard to tell the difference between thinking and imagining. No one's yet given me a hard distinction between the two which has left me to invent my own definitions. Thoughts are those things happening all the time. Spurious observations and informal notes about the world that may disappear like passing clouds. Imagination is what happens when enough thoughts form together to make something distracting. A little cloud is just that, but with enough focus and shape it can appear to be a dragon. What makes them so troublesome is when they begin to rain across my mental landscape.

They insist and persist in overtaking my attention. If I'm driving along a familiar route, the imaginings will climb down from my brain, attach themselves to the hinges of my mouth, and begin their operations. At times, it doesn't appear recognizably as me. Often as lines or notes from people I've never met but have still influenced who I've become. How much of me has sprung from my self and how much is a mishmash of my predecessors? And if my predecessors were also multifaceted—it's all too much. The endless scrolling through all the avenues of potential. Each one overseen by some successful stranger. And then there's me, introducing what I think I am. Alongside me, on the same wall of humanity, is an ever-increasing horde trying to smile their way ahead of me. It's enough to cause a kind of anti-solipsism.

Still, it would be nice to participate in the world. I'm not asking to dominate it, just to be there for it. To contribute, commentate, and connect, that's the kind of action that can fill a life. But on what? How does a person choose which slice of themselves to stick out and say "I am this! Please, take all of it."? These jobs and these titles feel too specific, too thin, to fill out decades of working time. The clerks and the administrators, the analysts and the officers, how do these people introduce themselves to strangers? Maybe you get used to the jargon and the incomprehensibility of it all, and then you smile and politely forget the least interesting but most time consuming parts of them.

Let's try one last time. If I get it right, then it's bed. If not, still bed.

Declan Murphy is emerging. His experience in the world up until now is limited, that's true, but he feels he's on the precipice of a great expansion. After working through the various standards of teenage life, Declan is ready to bring a bright attitude to any workplace. He took his time in university to study sociology with a concentration on contemporary theory and linguistics—a background he believes to be useful in empathizing with other people's needs. As an employee, he strives to work every day in the spirit of honesty and curiosity. Like the great Stan Lee before him, Declan believes in moving ever upward, ever onward, and ever in the direction of his dreams. Excelsior!

Maybe.

Chapter Two

At the beginning, it was always dark. Sloshes of unseeable waves grew louder and toppled against each other like rival siblings. A whiplash rang through the environment, hearse black in colour, and was swallowed by the waves. I stood amongst it all. Stuck in the knee-deep water, my arms reached out into the thick, unending blackness of the space. They were reaching out toward nothing, and while I tried to pull them back, they stretched farther and farther until I toppled.

I expected to hit the waves, but springing out between them, a grey floor formed. It pressed up and shot out of the water, leaving me suspended for a moment until I dropped down on it again. The surface was hard and unforgiving. When I stood up, I tested its strength. A stomp with my right foot against this floating floor. Nothing rebounded, the floor ate the sound, and my leg was numb. The structure stopped growing up and began to grow wider, each square flying out of the waves with the force of a whale. Each column rose and sprayed as the grey lightness provided more to see of its surface. It looked hopeless, like being stuck in a deep cave, and while the platforms were launching away from the water, its hissing could still be heard.

The squares began bursting farther and farther away. Like an extended bridge, their perfect pieces narrowed to a finer point until they could no longer be seen. I peered to the dark horizon and, without intent, I began to walk on uneasy legs. At first, the strides made no sound. Then they began to increase. Clicking footsteps sounded like ominous clocks ticking quicker and quicker towards this unknown goal. The faster and more direct I moved, the more the edge hurtled away. I tried looking back but everything in my body was travelling with so much momentum that to turn would have been to trip, and to trip, to fall. The waves beneath sounded far away and huddled now.

There was no space to think or imagine, only to act. I passed in and out of my head, sometimes seeing the path, sometimes seeing myself trundling on along the long stretch that resembled a comet's tail. Since there was no place for thought, there was never the idea to sit down, wait, or contemplate the situation. To ask a question like "why?" was asinine because the wonder of movement was too engrossing. Where was the end and what was there? It should have felt like destiny; but occasionally, a splash from the waves pooled on one of the grey squares. When they got wet, they became slick, and dashing across turned feet into skates.

The waves woke up and began to reach up the columns like lightning across the sky. They roared and crashed, leaving behind larger and larger puddles. My legs turned to pendulums as they tried to avoid each splash, but eventually the water became inevitable and I began to slip. Just as I lost traction with the ground, a nail of light held steady at the end of the columns. It wasn't strong and it was pale like the colour of old rope. How lovely that one fixed point looked. I stared at it as I tumbled toward the platforms, but when I crashed, it disappeared.

I had stopped on the spot of my impact. Sitting up, the desire for action that had animated my legs was gone and emerging was a new sensation. It was like a swarm of flying birds, constantly shifting and darting with no clear objective. When it felt like it was in my legs, it went up into my chest and then to my head until it pooled in my forearm, weighing it down and burning. I wrung my arm in the hopes that it would burst out. When that only added to the discomfort, I smothered it like a soldier diving on a grenade. It became hotter and heavier until I flung it off and sat up again. On the inside, against the whitest part of my skin, the veins began to rearrange.

It was like an infestation of worms as each line of life contorted itself into a new position. The pain was incredible as other parts of my body twisted and pulled away from the forearm. All the bristles of my neck punched out, preventing any sight from falling upon this possessed arm. It hurt worse than being burned with metal. If I could glance at it, perhaps I could stifle it. Or if I saw what was wrong, then I might get started towards a solution. Against the fibres of my neck, I contorted towards my now-swollen arm and saw a single word forming, letter by bloody letter.

Escape.

It was spelled out in pulsing form and when I looked, it was like I had opened a cage as the word scurried across all my body. Veins and moles and scars reshaped themselves to read ESCAPE as it felt like etching crawling across my forehead. The cruel withdrawal of the waves pulsed and chanted to the song of the word. Each spelling weighed heavier as the power of gravity increased against the grey floor. I was pinned on my side, legs separated into a triangle and arms folded over each other, sinking with the weight of freezing.

Pressed against the stone, I became invaded with its taste. It was like wet smoke, the kind that flies up and en-wraps after a fire has been dowsed. The only available resistance to the pressure and the smell was to spit. I tried to churn so that I could belch some of this weight away but nothing came up. This effort must have been causing me to move because the more I forced, the more the ground cracked. It started like an accident, one stroke of a careless pencil. But then, like a root system, the single stroke spread wide and diverged until it covered the entirety of the square. What had once felt solid and perma-nent broke unevenly like a tooth, and so I plunged.

Lurching, tumbling, drowning—there was no differ-ence. Only that I was descending without sight of where the bottom was. The waves were expected but at this pace, over this time, any water would have been mistaken for concrete. While I was in the air, I wasn't weightless. There was no freedom of movement, no altering direc-tion and soaring away—only an increasing heaviness as I spun towards a seemingly never-arriving finality. It had to end because no one falls forever; eventually, everyone crashes.

I did. Regaining myself on a softer floor that left no mark, I mused around at my surroundings. Dispatched away was the ambiguous darkness and constant heaving of an unknown sea. The floor now was dark and wooden while the looming walls were of shadowed steel, rising upwards until their tops could not be seen. Scanning in circles, there were empty benches with golden plaques affixed to their centres. They had names on them, but every time I looked away and back again, the names changed.

From the front of all the seating, a singular round and blazing light appeared. I shied away from it, throwing my arms up like an open shell, and stepped out of its line. Wherever I went, it found me again and focused its efforts. This was a light of intensity, of exposing honesty. Not the kind that warmed and reassured or pointed out disaster. This light preferred to target and to burn. Hiding was my instinct, and so I knelt behind one of the benches on a strangely soft floor. The illumination wrapped around the edges of the wood and singed the round of my shoulder. Closed and quivering, I held my bent knees.

"DECLAN MURPHY."

A voice boomed through the room from the direction of the light. It spoke with a sturdy authority that could speak loudly without shrieking. From a place deeper than the throat, it resounded again.

"DELCAN MURPHY. DECLAN MURPHY."

The voice was getting nearer, enveloping everything

in my name. It shook the light. Booming and curling around every object in the room, it was strong enough to bruise. Footsteps slid across the floor in between each drumming of my name. I should have ran, certain that I would be found, but my rebellion was quashed when my muscles seized like set cement. There had to be a way to out-think this problem, to conjure a method of escape. I looked for cracks in the floor but only saw swollen knots and the apparent cushion I was curled on.

"Oh, Declan!" the voice said with soft surprise. "I thought I might find you here."

Long fingers extended across my upper back and I was turned to face that which housed the sound of obliteration.

Standing more than twice my size, the figure bent over in observation. He wore a black cloak whose train stretched back until it joined all darkness. His hands were curled and wrinkled with each nail sharpened to an angled point. They resembled something feral, something that delighted in tearing. Continuing up the pillar of his body, one grey square sat over his throat, partially shadowed by his jutting chin. Studying me was an old face with uneven lines and bumps worn like a walnut. While the ghastly off-blue tinge should have been the most captivating, it was his eyes that swallowed my attention. He didn't seem to have any. Instead, there were only two bulbs of light shining out in softer power than the light at the front. Stale sweat stuck to my back as his eyes roamed over me in careful study. When he spoke again, he revealed his last secret: in his mouth were two independent tongues, each lashing and flicking of their own accord.

"Declan, please, you must come with me. You must see what you've abandoned."

With a power stronger than gravity, I was tethered to him as he put me down, turned, and walked away. His cloak dragged along the floor while I marched in step like a soldier, helpless as to my direction, and attached to his trajectory.

Our walk wasn't long. We had been surrounded by a new room without the crossing of a threshold. This new space was more airy, less imposing, and in tones of maroon and aubergine. It was sparsely furnished except for the same brown armoire that multiplied infinitely across the far wall. Each one carved to be a perfect replica of the others. The figure was having a look about the place as if he knew how it should be ordered and wished to maintain a certain regularity. He walked away from our shared position, nobly and upright, occasionally glancing back with his glowing eyes. I remained frozen in place without even the thought of moving.

The figure swayed towards one of the armoires and coiled his tall body overtop like a cat's tail. He crouched and hunched as his eyes shone through the now apparent slits in the front and side. They passed down with the slow inevitability of two setting moons. While I presumed his size would make him clumsy, he moved with the smooth softness of feathers. He didn't speak, but perhaps between his thoughts one of his tongues would dart out of his mouth before quickly retracting in the manner of a switchblade. After inspecting a few of the armoires, he regained his full height with satisfaction. Extending one arm towards me in quick summons, I flew through the air like a small fish on a line until I was in place under the heavy weight of his arm. I should have been able to smell him but there was nothing.

"This one," he said, widely opening the door, "is where you will belong."

With a great thrust, I was shoved inside and sat on the small seat hanging off its back wall. The glow of the figure's eyes moved down the slits until they burned at the end of my eye-line with white heat. He stopped, held, exhaled, nodded, and turned. From the lined view, I could only watch as he retook his casual stroll, hands clasped behind his back, and growing smaller towards the shadow that engulfed the room's edge. He was about to pass into the darkness but paused. He turned around and the glow from his eyes caught the curling edges of his tongues.

"This is where you belong," he said again and disappeared.

The sides of the confinement acted like an illusion. If I didn't look at them, they held sturdy in their original position. But if I wondered, if I tried to parse out their distance or material, they slid inward as if on a track. It was better not to look so I flung my gaze away from the ceiling and focused on the floor. My wardrobe had changed. Before now, what I was wearing was unimportant, something not worth detailing. Now in this glance, I was dressed like the figure, only instead of one grey square, they checkered my cloak all over. Each one pressed rigidly and with sharp corners. This garment, without strict cuts, should have been liberating and loose, but it was impossibly and immovably heavy. It sagged down my shoulders and pinned my hands to my lap. Over time, the weight of the garment lost its shock and hardened. Only if I tried to resist or shift did the full, dropping mass reemerge to refute any attempt at shucking its position. I acquiesced to the solidification, dropping my head against the wall, and hoped to be crushed. Until I heard the sound of gentle crying.

It was coming from my right side. Peeling away from the back, I turned to face it. The wall that once only had slits near its top was now speckled with a series of translucent dots, and there was someone on the other side.

"Yes, how may I help you? Do not be upset. I will be here," I said, words tumbling with the careless momentum of rocks off a mountain.

We began to speak as if underwater. Sounds sputtered back and forth in gargling, incomplete, and unintelligible forms. The content of our conversation was empty until one word would emerge clear as air. Each one bounced within my head before settling somewhere deeper. These were words like purpose, atone, honest, trust, and peace—a bulging crew of heavyweights. In between these bright words, she moved in a jagged way, animated by her personal distress. I, like a marble column, sat in sturdiness. She spoke more without my interjections and the blood of her words drained slowly from the armoire.

What had I to say in return? The audible words that I offered were no slimmer—join, wait, here, stay, and consider. Each of us only spoke when the other had finished, even if what we heard was nonsense. When this woman arrived, she lived in a posture that was bent and whittled. She was like a plant fervently clinging to the golden warmth of autumn while the forces of winter sought to surround her. During our conversation, a reblooming was occurring. Passing through the grit of the season, she warmed and rose to the heights of spring before transforming from a plant to a young person. Each phrase was like one more day of summer and she was like a young couple wishing desperately for a delay of the school year. Her reactions turned to the sincerest of physical poetry, inimitable yet wholly interpretable. Being along this growth, this change, I only wanted to continue our pursuit of conversation. I did and so did she and together a we was generated. No longer two cut individuals but a tiny collective bound stronger than all vines. It was there, live, with us and because of us.

The heat of our words died down and I did not know what to say next. Raising one of her hands to her torso, the woman touched lightly upon her heart. She closed her fist as lines like yellow knives sliced out from the space between her knuckles. Without one word, she opened and pressed her hand on the wall dividing us. Through the holes floated tiny spheres of light, rejoining in totality on my side once her palm was fully pressed. Together they made an orb. That orb floated and hummed in a way that calmed. After bumping itself against the ceiling, it settled down, passed my face, and continued into my upturned, folded hands. Its glow was comforting and whole, and it nestled into position like a newborn animal feeling safe enough to go to sleep.

The woman nodded and wiped her face, smearing a rainbow of tiny crystals across her cheeks. She thanked me and disappeared from the armoire. There was no trace, no imprint, not even a thread of perfume left tangled in the air. When I looked down to be reminded of the comforting heat from her light, there was nothing. Her vanishing was as true as she was. What was left was the upturned rose and pale of my palms. I wished for her to reappear if only so we could continue what we had made. In waiting, she did not remerge and I had to become okay with this singularity. Our time was limited and I wondered if she accepted that too.

I looked up and saw the ceiling of the armoire crawling towards me. My robes had regained their weight and when I tried to stand up it was as if my legs no longer existed. Though I shifted and twisted, the weight of my clothes pinned me down under their irresistible power. I tried to call out, but there was nothing more in me. Emptiness and silence clashed as the spine-breaking pressure of the robe increased, buckling me forward.

Now, not only the ceiling but the walls were tightening. They creeped near and I couldn't move; they pressed against me and I could not get smaller. This garment's weight was only a façade because it collapsed and held but offered no protection against the outside pressures. In one final effort, I shrugged my shoulders to let fly a cry, a plea, any kind of signal of my situation. I inhaled, expanded my chest, and…

I woke up within a thin layer of sweat, my arms pinned under my sternum.

Chapter Three

That dream again. It's been one of my regulars since at least high school. Like any recurring dream, never has it replicated perfectly. Its details and timings change in importance, sometimes switching entirely. On one night, it might have ended with a crash into the waves causing a jolt of an awakening. The kind that dries the mouth and leaves the hands clinging for any sheets. Other nights, the light from the figure or the room would be so fixed I wonder if I'd fallen asleep without turning my bedroom light off. The size of the figure shifts, the colour of the floor, the pattern of the garment—all as flexible as imagination. Upon waking, rarely does the dream leave an imprint pressed past breakfast. The realities of the day are much too distracting to hang on to dreams.

I wish I had more time to linger on them. What goes on in my sleeping hours is so fantastical, so removed from reality, that attempting to codify them is like looking at a picture of a sunset: while still beautiful and worth seeing, it never surrounds like the real thing, and the impression left is only one moment in a slow turning of blending colour. To be unbound by grammar and gravity, forces that lose their stickiness in dreams—wouldn't it be nice to just float?

This time, the dream was different. Instead of passing by like another morning train, it had fallen asleep in me and I could not shake it. In the weeks that followed, I hadn't been able to recount a single dream. The period between days was interspersed with the same dark mystery of a steep slide into sleep before being mounted by the morning. It was as if I had misplaced something, or perhaps like something had been stolen, and I now found myself beginning another day in the search for purposeful work.

In the absence of dreams, rumination remained. Chalking it up to the stress of the job hunt, my mind could not settle even when living through idle conditions. If I engaged in something distracting there was a faint echo long in the mental distance asking about what I was doing to turn my life into action. With each business day, again and again I was thanked for my consideration by this company and that manager as they expressed their sincerest enjoyment in reading my application before saying no. They had gone with an internal candidate instead, or I hadn't passed the first cut of interviews. It was demoralizing to hear every day that I wasn't wanted in such cold terms that I figured if I followed up, I would be met with a startled "I'm sorry, who are you?" from the very person whose name had rejected me. Thinking about my situation was painful and I wanted to think about something other than that damn dream.

What kept my analysis up was the ending. Normally, if it hadn't ended with a splat, the dream ended with the figure curling his fingers around my triceps and his eyes glowed brighter and brighter until they felt like an infection. Or, he would take flight and circle, peppering each lap with short phrases or words. For all of the years and fluctuating segments, never had I been put into that situation with the armoire. Nor with the woman.

It's been said that a person cannot imagine a face they've never seen. I've taken this to mean two things. First, that somewhere, logged in all of us, is a permanent memory of all the expressive lives we've encountered shuffling through subways or laughing in theatres. That each face, each life, becomes a part of our own even if we only glimpse them for a moment. The other meaning is that as vast as the human imagination is, for all its prowess to concoct landscapes of the absurd, it is filled with tiny holes out of which its authority drains. She must have come from someone, but every time I reflected on our scene, she had shifted again.

Through the superficial was the sense that our communion had meaning. That was the track upon which my memories ran with each revision. It was momentary, but it was beautiful. I wasn't sure how I solved or absolved her problem. Did it matter? What mattered was the purpose, the fulfillment of having participated in the process. Even after her departure, for all the words we exchanged, neither of us needed to reach for any fancy vocabulary to describe what had happened. It was good and that was enough.

When I woke up that next morning, it was like coming out of an ice bath. Even with the sweat and numbness in my hands, that goodness had persisted. With the images and sensations of the dream gone, I cared for that feeling like a living souvenir. As I walked around waking life, I tried to bring that feeling out wherever possible. It was beyond satisfaction, more powerful than duty, and better than joy. In that dream, it was like I had done right by someone in a way I had earned and that was important. By telling myself versions of that dream every day, multiple times, and without the interruption of new ideas, it had transformed into something tangible. It could not be ignored as it turned into something like an addictive substance, constantly poking, interrogating, and seeking to overwhelm my conscious mind until I gave in and rediscovered its feeling. I loved how it was. The three prongs of comfort, reassurance, and warmth. Wouldn't it be wonderful to pull that across the eyelid's threshold and into waking life?

Or perhaps working life?

"Declan! Dinner!"

Even from downstairs, Dad's voice filled my room. There was a settled confidence to it as if he was used to being listened to. It was a bit worn, however. He liked to say he ruined his voice singing too many old songs at too many kitchen parties in his early twenties. While that hasn't stopped him from joining in on every singalong to pop up since, it has made me wonder if I would recognize Dad's voice when he was my age. I knew what he looked like and was certain he held onto a shirt or two from that era. But without that proof of sound, he would always be incomplete.

I thumped down the stairs like a 10-year-old and saw Mum laying out the plates and cutlery. She noticed me with a smile.

"Declan," she said in French, "could you please get the other runner from the drawer?"

"What's that you're saying?" Dad interrupted from the kitchen.

"I was just asking our son if he could get the other thing from the tray."

Mum's English was normally better than that, but sometimes being asked to translate a thought unintended for translation invented difficulty. Resentfulness was not Mum's way of approaching disagreement, so when Dad's learning of her language stopped at a few dirty jokes, she let it lay. That didn't stop her from raising us three kids perfectly bilingual. Dad had to get used to living in a place he recognized and one he didn't. Though now, with Céline and Hélène firmly out of the house, the amount of French at home was draining.

My job, still, was to set the table for dinner. Nothing fancy, nothing rigid, but since I did not contribute to the preparation of tonight's dinner, this is what I had to offer. Plus the washing of the big dishes that wouldn't fit into the dishwasher. Even if I did take the plates and cutlery and the other pieces we commonly used and slotted them into where I thought they should go, Mum and I both knew they wouldn't stay that way for the cycle. Dad saw it as his personal duty to rearrange the dishes before he went up to bed. He would never admit that he had a problem with the way we put things, but Mum and I loved our private laughs whenever we heard the clinking of plates and forks from upstairs.

I set the table to the occasional interrupting flash from

the dream. Each glint of the silverware matched the hue of the figure's eyes, reaching for the drawer traced the woman reaching her hand to the wall, and the pooling of light in the spoons held gently like that orb. It was a welcome invasion.

Tonight's meal was Dad's chilli, a leftover recipe from his colder and poorer days as he called them. Mum took the time to make garlic bread from scratch. Every marriage needs a baker and cook, they agreed. One for patience and the other for improvisation. With all the food warm on the counter, Mum motioned for me to take her place. I played my part and politely refused, insisting she go first. We went back and forth in our verbal two-step until Dad cut in.

"Another Canadian Stand-Off!"

"A Canadian stand-off?" I said.

Dad mimicked two people "'You go first.' 'No, please, you go first.' 'No, really, I hate to be a bother, you can go first.'" And on, and on, and on until some ignoramus takes the thing the two bozos are deferring. How does your mother always say it, Jacquline? Everybody come and heat while it's 'ot? Well?"

She stepped in first as I inhaled the spices blending in the kitchen air. We each made our way to our regular spots at the table.

"I reckon this'll be the last chilli of the season," Dad said.

"Remind me, I'll put some aside for the freezer then as well. It's nice to give the flavours a bit of a chance to sit for even longer. I find it tastes better, anyway," Mum said, blowing over her first spoonful.

No one spoke through their first bites. I thought about how I was going to miss these kinds of meals now that the weather was turning. Dad glanced at each of us, making sure we were enjoying ourselves before embarking on the next subject of dinner conversation.

"How's the job jungle looking today, Declan?" he said. I was glad to hear his tone carried no disappointment, but it would have been nicer not to be asked at all.

"Oh, you know," I said.

"No, I don't know," he said

"I mean… it's not great out there. I'm sending out resumes pretty broadly right now and there's only so many new postings every day. I'm trying to keep it like a regular job, you know? Start sending things out at nine and then work through applications and cover letters until the end of the day. There are only so many times I can rewrite the same bits of my life and interests and so on."

"It'll come, it'll come," Mum reassured.

"Your mother's right, you know. Sometimes these things have a way of working themselves out when you're not even trying. I won't use the word faith, but you know what I mean. You'll see. Right now, it feels like you're churning and burning until one day, you'll get your notice, start your job, and all these hard times will just disappear. All that slogging through repetition—it all just goes away into nowhere. It's like now, outside. A few months ago, everything out there was covered in wet slush and the sky closed early. Now? Now, it's blossoms everywhere and the sun's putting in overtime! Trust me, after you get it, you won't even be able to recall this time of searching. And it will come, Declan, it will come. Honest."

I should have believed him. After all, he had been in HR for years and knew how those hiring managers thought. If only I had interest in his line of work. Still, I hadn't asked for his help with resume polishing or cover letter drafting. What if he saw what I did on my own and was dissatisfied? He and Mum had paid for a certain education to get started, they had been supportive and present as I grew up, and if they did that much work, what had it yielded? They often said when we were growing up that a family had no room for dishonesty or secrets. That those were suffocating forces, under which nothing lived after a while. Were they right? Or was there some extra room to hide now that I was fully grown?

I said nothing. They didn't either. For a few moments, the light clinking of cutlery covered the table. I didn't look up to see if they were waiting on me or had given up.

"So I was talking to your sister today," Dad said, introducing a new topic.

"Which one?" I replied.

"It took my entire commute."

"Ah, and how is Céline?"

"She's good, she's good. Says she's going to be featured in some kind of show at Place des Arts for the upcoming Saint John the Baptist celebration—"

"It's Saint-Jean-Baptiste," Mum corrected.

Dad winked at me while Mum let it pass with a sigh.

"As I was saying, she's staging some kind of

exhibition at Saint John the Baptist day. Sounds like it'll be a pretty big show too. Tourists coming from all over Québec and maybe other parts of the country too. If they're not working, that is. From what she told me, it'll be a right big showcase and I think she called me up just to talk through some of her nerves. Not that that child has ever needed an excuse to talk. The Good Lord as my witness, your mother and I swear she was born talking. Actually, speaking of when you kids were small, we got to talking about when each of you was babies. Seemed like each one was born with a story. Do you remember the story of your name, Declan?"

Mum's eyes lowered as her lips narrowed. She knew the story as I did and that it had become one of Dad's favourites to tell at holidays. By now, I had the main details and inflections memorized so well that I could tell it as if I was there to experience it. Dad liked to embellish and add new flourishes whenever he retold it. While our versions were different at their edges, they came from the same core.

Before our family began, Mum had told Dad that if they had children that they should bear indisputably French names to honour the history of their family in Québec. At first, it seemed like a battle worth surrendering when Mum had chosen Hélène as the first name. She pronounced it without the H while Dad placed extra emphasis on it. So followed the name of Céline which Mum always said with a short I, against Dad's dragged out double-E making it sound more like "Saline." It had been as Mum had planned until they found out they were finally having a boy. She presumed that I would have a name like Pierre, but she underestimated the cunning of a New-foundlander.

On the day of my birth, there was clearly something misplaced. Mum had been much sicker and when they got her to the hospital, it was clear a natural birth was not going to work. She would have to be sedated and operated on if I was going to have a chance at life. They assured her that this was a routine and common affair and when she woke up she would be holding her little angel. Analogies were made to having one's wisdom teeth removed, but her mind had migrated to a place of worry.

As she was being set-up, she looked at Dad and said, "Please, when the baby is born, make sure he has a French name." Whether it was the stress or the beginning doses of medication, Mum had begun to slip into a less conscious state. One in which she was functioning on her basest abilities. She must have been because she did not tell him to give me a French name with her English. No, she had forgotten to translate her wish. According to Dad, he was in transparent ignorance over what she wanted and never gave a confirmation of understanding because he didn't. Should he have known what she wanted anyway? He said his mind was elsewhere.

The surgery went by without drama and, when I was plopped into Dad's arms, Mum was still asleep. With the doctors in need of a name and Dad finally holding a son, he blurted out who I would be.

"He'll be called Declan. Yes. Declan Murphy."

Declan. The name that so many school projects told

me meant "Man of prayer" or "Full of goodness." The name of the man who, even before Patrick, had brought the ideas of Catholicism to Ireland. Upon that rock, Dad unofficially baptized me into his world. And with a dancing partner of a last name like Murphy, the references to a separate identity from my sisters and my mother had been there from the beginning.

When Mum woke up, she didn't take Dad's wily opportunism with much favour. Seeing that the papers had been signed with his choice of name, she unloaded a gatling gun of commentary about how pea-headed of a decision that was. If only it had been in English. Again, Dad was left only to infer on the fury of his wife, knowing that what he had done could not be undone, as he had already called everyone back home with the news and the name. Mum eventually got over the situation and raised me no differently from my sisters. Except when I was in serious trouble, I could hear the restraint in her voice at listing my full name. It reminded her of the time she had been lastingly outwitted.

"You kids were such a hoot when you were young," Dad said, finishing his version of the story. "Hey, speaking of babies, have either of you heard from Hélène recently?"

My mind was a moment ahead of my mouth as I started waving small circles in the air to indicate I would be ready to answer soon. Mum spoke up before I had the chance.

"Her and I were talking the other day and, by the sounds of it, she's right on schedule with what the doctors are saying."

"She's gotta be set to burst soon, isn't she?" Dad said.

"Less than a month away!" Mum said, expectantly. "I think she had her last day in the lab a couple of weeks ago and now is just waiting on the arrival of the little one.

"You know, I remember even when she was a teenager, she had said that if she didn't have a child by a certain age, she'd up and do it herself, but I never thought she'd actually go through with it! Speaking of which, you have washed the turkey baster since, right?"

Dad got a rightful shot in the arm for that one.

"Alan! Please! Have some decency."

"Have you been talking to your sister much, Declan?"

"Not much," I said, "which I guess means that everything is going fine. I mean, if something was wrong, she'd tell us. No use calling up just to say all is well."

The truth was, I hadn't been keeping up with Hélène. Or Céline. With each of one eighteen months apart from the next, it was as if we grew up on top of each other. When we were all young together, Mum retreated from her work in order to better tend to us. That was where we were filled with French, speaking nothing but during the day, and then switching to English when Dad got in. The language bonded us. Going to school in suburban Vancouver, it seemed like no one spoke French and so, passing in the hallways, we felt like we could throw secrets to each other without the risk of revelation. Our bilingualism allowed us to bicker without embarrassment and if a language can have a purpose, I believe the purpose of French-Canadian French is to be used by warring siblings. Something about its harshness and sarcasm has made it perfect for those scenes.

Since we've grown up, and they have moved on with their jobs and their lives, it has become too easy to drift. Months may go by before I've realized I haven't so much as texted Céline, but if I get caught on the phone in one of her conversation vortices, a sense of bloating arrives. With Hélène, a reason has never been clear. The three years of separation made her just old enough to feel like a superhero when we were in school. My first year of high school was her last and with her academic acumen, she was the kind of sibling that set expectations for anyone who followed with her last name. Céline at least was different enough thanks to an innate theatricality and zest for conversation that her antics could have been written off as middle-child fallout. Between those predecessors, I was never sure where I would go. I hoped I could glide past their influence.

Even with their head start of age, they seemed infinitely older than me. They had escaped moving back home. Céline had navigated a career change from banking to photography and moved to a new city. Hélène was working for UBC as a marine biologist and was now apparently ready to become a mother? Where was I? How did I compare? I knew it was wrong to measure myself against them, but having spent a lifetime as the youngest, what other instinct did I have? They had cleared the chasm of personal doubt and left me waiting for a rope.

Dinner continued. I only took in the equivalent of glances of my parents' conversation. Mum might have looked over between bites to see if I had something to say, but I turned back towards my plate. She must have noticed my avoidance, sensed that I was speaking silent words in my head. Those words, those thoughts, were like insect eggs. Little dots that made themselves apparent in the mushiest sack of my brain, waiting for an uncountable number of legs to split out.

With all the food eaten and no one needing seconds, I gathered the plates and cutlery from the table. As I was setting up to wash the rest of the dishes, Mum put the kettle on and Dad retired behind the inked edges of the newspaper. They began to talk about nothing in particular. The room was idle and in that idleness, my imagination enwrapped me without my consent. I thought what my parents might be thinking if they looked up and saw their son trying to be a man stuck in his roles from boyhood. Of my sisters and where they are. And of the dream that had once again covered some of the objects of the real world. I saw the glow in the bowls, breathed in the wetness of the grey squares, and my hands grew heavier as they swirled through the dishwater.

Why had the weight of the end been concentrated in my hands? Perhaps it was unwise to question what happened in a dream. After all, there were no symbolic charts for consistent reference I could use to look up what these things had meant. The lights could have just been lights, there only to help me see. The armoire could have just been an armoire. If there was a meaning to this dream, it could have only come from what I gave it. I had waited for it to disappear like any other meaningless memory but it seemed to have intentions of its own. This dream persisted like a lie that had once won favour and later would demand reckoning.

The whistling of steam interrupted my thoughts. Mum hurried over to the kettle. Our eyes met and she silently asked if I would like any tea. I declined. With another soundless shrug, she poured her cup and retook her seat at the counter. Dad had the newspaper splayed out and the two of them were in a jovial back and forth about an article. Blame it on my youth, but I would have thought that with a few decades behind them, they wouldn't have had much to say to each other. That they knew all the stories, all of the facts about each other. Yet there they were, engaged in the heights of conversation. Occasionally, they had brief waves of looking like teenagers still figuring each other out and becoming more fascinated.

"Would you look at that! Declan, you've got to hear about this." Dad's finger pointed to the middle of the paper.

"What is it?" I said.

"It's an announcement about a series they're going to be running about important people around town. 'Pillars of the Community,' it's called. Says they're going to be checking in each month with a different person everyone probably knows, small business owners and such, to drum up a sense of community spirit. And look who they're going to talk to first!"

"Oh look, Declan," Mum said, hovering over the open page, "they're going to be talking to Father Rogers. Do you still keep in touch with him?"

A chill went through me like the ones I had been told happened when someone stepped on my grave.

"No, I haven't. I don't think I've talked to Father Rogers since high school at least."

"It's a shame. He was such a good influence on you." Mum said.

"You see," Dad said, "this is the kind of thing the papers today should be doing. Bringing people up and making them feel like local celebrities. Then we start to feel a little tighter as a group, like we've got more common connections, and then, who knows, maybe there will be a few more waves at the grocery store and smiles on the trails. I don't know, I think it'll work."

Mum's eyes were going over the words at a regular pace and she smiled the more she read. I turned back to the dishes. For the first time in weeks, I saw new images in my head. Replacing the repetitious dream were scenes from my innumerable weekends with Father Rogers. There was the faded wallpaper, the overwhelming amount of books, and his long plain robes. I thought about how he used to challenge me, how he cared. The more I thought, the more distinct his likeness became as he sat firm in his usual wing chair. My hands dipped back into the dishwater and his image began to swirl.

His skin faded from black to blue, his nails grew longer, and when he stood, his head brushed against the ceiling. Father Rogers had become the figure and once they mingled, it felt like an explanation. Had the figure been a perverted image of a priest this whole time? He certainly carried himself with the authority of tradition and he moved with the meticulous nature of someone who had spent their life studying. More flashes from the dream came torrenting in. If he was a priest, then the armoire might not have been just that. It could have been a confessional. Yes, yes! I looked to my parents, surprised at their apparent ignorance to my steady revelations. Across my skin and up my spine there was a ripple of chilling fireworks.

I had been hiding from its meaning for years, unwilling to chase it. The figure wasn't trying to capture me, but show me how to see with light. When he put me in the confessional it was to show me what I could be and how hearty it feels to accept the role of listener to another's woe. I wanted to find that feeling in real life. If I became a priest, that was where I would find it. I believed I could comfort people, I could listen to them like they hadn't been listened to, and I could pass through them the sense of authentic grace I now knew. These coincidences must have been the hidden hands I had heard about that appeared to a person when they were on the way to their track of life. I was sure my parents and my sisters knew what this was like. The signs had been scattered, but I had the great fortune of recognizing how to order them.

Like at the end of the dream, a sensation like opening fingers bloomed in my chest, touching the whole of my internal self. I knew what I was going to do, who I would become, because I wanted to have this feeling every day and that was what a working life should provide. Looking over at my parents again, nothing for them had changed. Could they not see their son was glowing?

My shoulders turned automatically as dishwater

limped off my fingers. They could tell I had something to say, something important. So they leaned in, slightly, with goading eyebrows rising up their foreheads. The words took to the room like young birds. There was a natural confidence to them and a soaring ideal but also a tinge of inexperience.

"I'm going to join the priesthood," I confirmed.

Mum dropped her teacup and its edges shattered like lightning. Dad's ears retracted as his eyes became slivers of their former curiosity.

"A priest?" he said. "But, Declan, you're an atheist!"

Part 2
PSALM

Chapter Four

There's a part of the crucifixion story that has frustrated me. On his way up to be killed—not by any individual, but by the environment itself—it is said he fell three times. I've never known why, but that has never struck me as a believable detail. It seemed like the kind of artificial additive a writer might add in order to increase sympathy for the character. To make the reader better catch and identify with the struggle. I've never seen a real person fall three times on their way to something. A fall is final. When it has happened, it has rarely been direct. Rather, there is a stumbling, the comedic carelessness that takes over the legs until the inevitable crash. One fall was good enough to drop Adam forever, so why did Christ need the extra two?

It would have been nice to have lost my faith all at once. To have had one singular experience in which it swooped down never to recover. But faith, like any other practice, takes time to maintain and to lose. It requires reassertion in crisis and can be honed. In my life, that practice was never regular, and perhaps that is why the notion of religious belief slid off of me as it did. While mine was certainly a stumbling, there were a few days and conversations in particular that formed my response to faith. Some, I remember brightly. Others have had details added and smudged over my lifetime.

For Hélène and Céline, their lives started with one constant: Church was to be attended every Sunday. Church was an easy affair when it was only Hélène. Mum and Dad had their new and perfect bundle well-swaddled—ready to show off to other worshippers. Céline and I have been told she never stirred, never fussed, and held the most angelic tint of rose on her cheeks. She was cherub incarnate. Céline has never believed those details and, after enough wine, may refer to them as oldest-sibling propaganda.

When Céline did come along, she presented as quite a different child. Her temperament did not allow her to lay peacefully in her crib like a doll each night. No, she was born to be much more industrious and loved to giggle through the hallways each time she managed to escape her barred confinements. This change in habit and expectation of what a baby was supposed to be like ravaged our parents' ability to sleep. Not that it was Céline's fault. She was a baby and was merely born active. The more she squirmed and shrieked in the day, the more our parents needed to recover, and so their attendance in Church shifted from every week to roughly every other week. They proved the earnestness of their faith with each darkening crescent under their eyes.

When I came along, our parents were wiped. They bore the unfortunate but all-too-common reality of three children with different personalities at different stages of development. When one needed a nap, another needed to be woken up. When one was getting ready for solid food, another was still living off breast milk. To try and organize us, especially when we needed to be carried, must have been like playing Operation in an earthquake. A human life, it seems, is like a kettle boiling in reverse. It begins with a piercing squeal that requires attention, gently simmering over time until its maturation when it lies as cold as the material that houses it. No one can know which morning it was, but one Sunday, either Mum or Dad said to the other, "Let's sleep in today. The kids are settled and, besides, it's Sunday." And so began a tradition of not attending Church.

It didn't seem like long after that I was old enough to go to school. I had never met so many new people in one place. Everything was exciting and if our chatter could have been drawn it would have resembled the scribbles we were perfecting, darting from topic to topic with no clear connection and with the fervour of a shaking hand. If someone mentioned they saw a dog on their way to school that morning, everyone who heard had to pipe up and mention everything they knew about dogs. To combat these blurting distractions, our teacher added to our routine something she called Exciting News.

During Exciting News, we all piled onto the carpet and had free rein to say anything to the class that we wished. Whether it was about what we did on the weekend, how we were feeling, or something we heard on television, all voices were valid. It was during one of these sessions that a classmate broke tradition with kindergarteners because what he said was memorable. He said that last weekend at Church he got to colour in a picture of the baby Jesus with his mother Mary and that his piece was chosen by the Sunday school teacher as the best one in the class. What did he mean "Sunday School?" Nobody went to school on Sundays. Before I could complete my thought, a bold boy broke the rule of putting his hand up before speaking and called out that he went to Synagogue on Saturdays which was better because that was a day before Sunday. The two boys fought with their limited vocabularies until the teacher called an end to the exercise and sent us back to our tables for silent colouring. I tried to remember the new words I had heard.

After school, Mum came to pick us up. There was cheer in her voice as she hustled us into the van, put our seatbelts on, and rolled the door closed. As the smallest of the family, I had to sit on the slim section between the other seats known as the hump. As adults, Céline has had to take it over. We joke about how awful and cramped it is between the shoulders, but what I haven't admitted is that I liked my time in that seat. It gave me an unobstructed view out the front and into the distance.

It also gave a unique viewpoint into my mother's eyes. From that seat, all of her was condensed into one slim re-flection. After the years of wrangling kids, working when she could, and, somewhere else, a personal life of interests and desires, the light that glided from her eyes should have dimmed. Yet whenever our glances met, I saw the edges of her face wrinkle before returning to the road. Between those wrinkles were shimmers.

When we got home, my sisters tossed their bags and coats aside before racing to the television. I still needed a bit of help getting my shoes untied so I sat on the bottom step of the landing, waiting for Mum to put her things away. She grabbed Hélène and Céline's things too. Kneeling on the slate floor of the walkway, she started to untie my shoes.

"So," she asked, "did anything interesting happen at school today?"

"No, not really."

"Oh? So no one threw up all over the place?"

"No!" I shouted with joy.

"And no one ran around crying all day?"

"No!"

"Are you sure you're really in kindergarten, then? Hmmm. What about—"

"Mummy, what's a Babyjesis?"

The precise wording had slipped from memory so I improvised. I figured if I said it quick enough, Mum would be able to figure out what I wanted because, as a grown-up, she knew everything. She didn't respond right away. A cold whiteness spread across her face, taking all other colour with it.

"What? I'm sorry, can you say that again, honey?"

"What is a Babyjesis?" I tried to put more emphasis on each word, but the final, crucial one slid out like ground meat. "I heard one of the other boys talk about it today, but I don't know what it is and my teacher said that if I ever heard a word I didn't know then I was supposed to ask you about it."

Mum sighed and looked up to the ceiling. She stammered through an explanation, her hands swirling with darting glances everywhere but my face. How was she supposed to improvise her way through such a conservation at the level of a 5-year-old? If this demonstrable inability had happened ten years ago, I would have written her off as a fool. If it happened now, I would see she was trying her best. At that age, though, to see an adult struggle so much with a subject made it more alluring. My teacher had no answer and Mum could barely parse one together. I must have uncovered quite the secret. At the end of one of her twirling sentences, she dropped back.

"Maybe this can wait until your Dad gets home. Then we can all talk about it together, okay?"

With a kiss on my cheek and my shoes in her hand, she sent me off to the TV room. Hélène and Céline were ensconced in their spots. Their eyes were unblinking and their mouths chewed like machines on snacks.

"Can we watch something I wanna watch?" I asked.

"We got here first," Céline said, "and according to the rules of the couch, whoever gets to the TV first gets to pick the show. Isn't that right, Hélène?"

She had no choice but to agree since it was in her best interest. The two of them liked the same shows, *Lizzie McGuire*, *Full House*, *That's So Raven*, and while I found nothing offensive in them, it would have been nice to watch a show about a boy. I fusslessly found a spot on the single chair and submitted to the afternoon entertainment of their choosing.

After a few episodes, the house shook with the retraction of the garage door. The sounds that followed were predictable and particular. There was the slow *vroom*, the squeal of tires turning in a stationary position, and the ticks and pops of the car settling after it was turned off. A few seconds without the sound of a slam passed until the overlapping noises of the garage door closing and the house door opening. Like he was a recurring guest on a talk show, Dad's entrance was an exaggerated affair. With a long announcement of "Good evening!" stretching out all the oo's his lung could hold, he knew his kids would come running. I was sure we did it every night like a tradition. Its origins were unknown, but if we missed a night it was as if we were offending some kind of order.

Next was to greet Mum and give her a light kiss on the cheek. We would stick out our tongues or feign turning to stone at the sight of such a gross display of affection. With the family handled, his habit decreed that he was now ready to change out of his work clothes, fix himself a drink, and prepare for his role in the evening meal. It was a regular ritual, one I had already noticed. If he had been taken over during the day by an alien parasite, now intent on infecting the rest of our family, I was sure I would be able to catch it here since any slip up meant it wasn't my real father.

Normally, Dad went up to his room alone but, curiously, Mum followed him. I watched them disappear through the tiny slit left open by their bedroom door. Hélène and Céline had reclaimed the couch and, by extension, the television, which left me alone between dyads. My sisters had been so short with me earlier that I didn't want to be around them until I had to, so I climbed the staircase on all fours like a bear and took to spying on what my parents were doing. The door was almost closed as if one of them had let it go behind them without enough care to see it sealed. In the small opening, Mum was pacing in and out while Dad sat on the edge of the bed, pulling off his socks.

"Oh God, oh God, Alan. We messed up, we messed up big time," Mum said, her fingers interlocked through her tied-back hair.

Dad's face ran through a few options. It started out confused then stopped for a moment at compassion before settling into the shock of bewilderment. He didn't speak but rose from the end of their bed, intercepted Mum on the line she was pacing, and held her tight to his body. He enwrapped her shoulders completely so that it became possible to put his fingers in the backs of her armpits. Tucking his chin into her shoulder, he slowed his breathing down until hers matched his. I thought of my Dad as being so excitable, so bombastic, that to see his tenderness made me worried for a moment that he had been replaced. They held that position tight and stable like they were a wedding topper. Dad must have sensed the ripples of Mum's mind had calmed as he opened his arms and placed his hands on her shoulders. He bent his knees so that he was looking slightly up at her as if inspecting for tears.

"My belle," he said, "I mean this with all kindness. What're you on about?"

"Declan doesn't know who Jesus is!" she blurted.

Dad stepped back, out of the thin pillar of sight I

had. I could have pushed the door, but that would have given my position away and they were about to talk about me. Who, even at such a young age, would have been capable of not eavesdropping on such an opportunity? I crawled as near as I could to the other side of the door, pressed my ear near the floor, and listened to the words that escaped out the bottom.

"Say that one more time. I want to make sure you mean what I think you've just said," Dad said.

Mum began with a leftover sniffle.

"Today, after I picked the kids up from school, I was taking Declan's shoes off and… and he asked me what a baby Jesus was. He said he had heard another kid in class mention it. The way he said the name baby Jesus, like it was all one word of something like Arabic. I knew we never should have stopped going to Church, even when it was hard. Especially when it was hard. Look where it's got us—raising some kind of ignorant… atheist!"

"But," Dad stammered, "he's still a Catholic. We're all still Catholics."

Just like everyone else in the family, near and extended, I had at least been baptized into the Catholic Church. The religious aspect of our group identity was no more separable than our last name: to be a Murphy was to be a Catholic. There had never been one before that wasn't.

"I know that," Mum continued, "but we're *informed* Catholics. We were both raised with faith as a part of everyday life. It was just natural for us. Now look at what's changed. A child can grow up not knowing that they do not believe."

Dad walked back into view. He sat down on the folded quilt at the end of the bed. His face was contemplative and, if Mum looked hard enough, she could have seen his thoughts spelling themselves out across his wrinkled forehead. She took her seat next to him and started rubbing his upper back in small circles. There were my parents, working out a complex problem—not with impressive rhetoric or reference, but with a simple touch. They sat like that for minutes until Dad put his hands on his knees and stood up. First with his hips, then his shoulders. He started to walk towards the door so I tucked myself away in hiding. The door closed. With nothing left to watch, I crept down the stairs, avoiding all the spots I knew made noise.

At the stair's landing, Hélène and Céline were seated like meerkats. When I noticed them, I wasn't told why, only waved over to Céline's side and assumed the same position. Their vision remained firm on the stairs while mine flipped back and forth between what they were looking at and making sure they were still looking. Our parents' bedroom door opened and they were greeted to six small eyes and thirty clenched fingers. Before they could surmise what our conspiracy was all about, Céline made our cause known.

"Mother, Father, please. May we eat soon?"

Mum sighed into a smile as Dad flew down the stairs making sound effects like airplanes. He picked up his daughters and glided into the kitchen. I reached my arms out as long as they could go and Mum scooped me up. She blew kisses into my cheek until I squealed with delight. All of our laughs were intertwined.

Mum and Dad both grew up in homes in which dinner was a communal and convivial affair. The kitchen was the heart of their homes. When it came time to start their own family, they knew they had to pass on this convention. They handled the knives and the meat, but sought out parts of preparation that would both be of use and teach a skill for outside the home. For that night's dinner, the kids' job was to count out peas. After every hundred, we were to add them to the mixing bowl. Hélène and Céline competed silently with each other to get to the goal first. I usually lost track and then shovelled in whatever I had when they were done.

"Declan, did you really get one hundred?" Dad asked.

"Uh-huh," I said.

"Honest?"

"Yep!"

"Honest engine?"

I looked down to the counter where my pile used to be. It was so hard to keep track of them all and there were so many numbers to remember. Dad came around my side.

"It's okay, buddy, it's not about being the fastest, it's about being the truest. You can take as long as you need so long as you make sure your work is done well. Next time, can you do that?"

I nodded and he patted my back.

"So your mother was telling me you had an interesting thing happen at school today."

"Oh, yes!" Céline interrupted. "Today we did a show

and tell and Marcy brang in some dolls from her doll collections and Derek brang in a toy truck that went whirr-whirr-whirr-whirr. And Jared didn't brang anything because he wanted to show us his pet snake, but his parents said he wasn't allowed to bring snakes to school. I thought it would be so cool to see a real live snake at school so I hope he sneaks one in tomorrow when we go."

"Oh wow," Dad said, "And your Mum also mentioned that one of you heard about something called a Babyjesis? Is that right?"

I opened my eyes wide and turned my head as he said my secret word.

"A Babyjesis?" Hélène said, "what kind of Jesus is that supposed to be?"

"A kid in my class said that today! And, and, and another one said he goes to a Citygauge on the weekends," I said.

Dad chuckled. "Declan, did you know that I know who Babyjesis is?"

"You do?"

"Oh yeah, I know where we can go to learn all about him. Would you like to go this weekend?"

He turned and gave a wink to Mum. I was a bit reluctant. While I wanted to know the answer to who this mysterious creature was, I remembered the boy from class mentioning Sunday School.

"If we go, does that mean I'll have to do a lot of work like at real school?"

"No, no, I don't think it'll be quite like that. So would you like to go, Declan? In fact, why don't we all go together on Sunday?"

"Are we going back to Church?" Hélène asked.

"Only if Declan wants to," Dad said.

Everyone turned to look at me and I didn't know what to say. How did they all seem to know what we were doing already? The kitchen stood without interrupting sound for a moment. They had turned their attention to me like satellites hoping to decode some far off noise. At that age I couldn't have understood concepts like pressure, guilt, atonement, or hope. But I knew the faces of my family and across them were looks of human reaching. How could I have said no?

Even if I didn't know what we were doing, when Sunday arrived I was the first one awake. My intrigue towards the day had grown when I found out my sisters had to wear their fancy dresses—previously only modelled for grandparents and Christmas friends. I was made to wear a hand-me-down turtleneck sweater. It was a bit small and caught around my ears, leaving the top of my head exposed like popped toast, and a muffle on my mouth to cry for help. Mum came in to pull it down. I got off my bed and went over to the mirror, dropped my eyebrows, and held my lips steady.

"What are you doing, sweetie?" Mum asked.

"I'm practicing my serious face."

Mum rolled her eyes while putting in her second earring and on her way out, bumped into Dad who was struggling with his tie knot. He muttered something about a "goddamn kid, making me put on a suit on my day off." Mum's hand sailed towards the knot, quickly straightened it out, kissed him, and said thank you for going through all this trouble. Dad let his shoulders give as if disarmed from cynicism by sarcasm.

"Is everyone ready to go?" he called.

We all walked down the stairs like we had bricks on our shoes. Dad checked his pockets for his belongings and Hélène budged her way in front of her siblings, in front of her parents so that she could be the first in the car. She put her hand on the handle and pulled to no effect. She tried again and again until she whipped her head back to the door to see our grinning father holding the car key in his hand.

"Patience," is all he said as they jingled in his palm.

Driving to Church, I did my best to fit in with the atmosphere set by my elders. Hélène and Céline sat with their hands folded in their laps holding the postures of dolls made to sit on a bed. I didn't know why they had become so still only that I should probably join them. None of us spoke for the duration of the slightly long drive. Instead of going to the Church walking distance from our house, Mum and Dad had decided to go one suburb over to get reacquainted. If it was me, I would have done the same thing. To risk an out-of-step reentry into something as closed and gossipy as the Catholic Church would have been a social disaster. There, they could join the anonymous flock and fly in formation without worrying about beating their wings in time.

It must have been a hard slouch towards Bethlehem for them. Besides funerals, Mum and Dad hadn't so much as tiptoed into a Church service in years. Dad's fingers tightened around the steering wheel as he made the turn into the parking lot. Hands folded and neck twisted, Mum was looking out her window to check for oncoming traffic. I followed Mum's view out the window and glimpsed for the first time at a Catholic Church's façade. So enormous its point covered the near midday sun. I looked across the chest of this hulking fortress and saw stone, statues, and glass. My mouth was open so wide it could have swallowed my eyes.

We walked in and the Church sucked up all the sound, all the bustling from outside. I was certain we were in the biggest building in the world. If asked, I would have claimed the ceiling was a million feet high and that there were probably a million rows of benches too. There were so many benches, in fact, that I was sure my entire school could fit and we barely fit in our gym. With the awe of the place rushing through me, I hurried up the centre aisle wanting to see everything from every angle until Dad scooped me up.

"Whoa, easy there, little one. You can't go quite that far," he said.

"Dad," I pointed to a small opening beside the altar, "is that where the Babyjesis is going to come from?"

"No, not there. But a different man is going to come out and talk about him so let's find our seats and wait. Okay?"

He put me back on the floor and looked to Mum for guidance on where to sit. She swivelled around, keeping one hand on each daughter, then pointed vaguely to a spot near the back. We five shimmied over to the very outside edge of our pew, far from the view of the altar and near to the least noticeable escape. It seemed tactics and shame blended well.

I knelt on the pew to face backwards in order to see the interior from yet another vantage. This overtaking curiosity went beyond novelty. I wanted to see everything in this building, to run my fingers across all the carved edges of stone and wood. Following the natural lines of the architecture, I was led to a huge circle of stained glass. The light transformed from invisible to the brightest versions of purple, yellow, and pink. They shone so brightly that they seemed to pull light from the nearest stones, dropping them into comparative darkness until they could no longer be noticed. It was a light that had been focused, altered, and then given back to everyone in glorious tones. At first I saw only the light, but after its brilliance had stabilized, I started to look at the people through whom the light was shining. Who were they? I would've spent hours staring into their faces, imagining their stories, until the organ began to play and I snapped into position.

"Remember," Mum said in hushed French, "how many people can talk at one time?"

"One!" I said, unable to lower from my excited volume.

"Yes, that's right. So when the man at the front starts talking, what do you do?"

"I don't talk?"

"Yes, exactly," Mum said as she patted my knee.

"What are you two saying now?" Dad leaned in.

Mum looked like she was going to speak but waved her hand and motioned for us to look to the front. The priest had entered from the back. He appeared from some secret entrance and was now passing up to the altar. A hand from one of my parents lifted me to my feet as other members of the Church were already standing. This priest was a sunrise of a man. With a plump and rosy face whose salmon colouring complimented the white, purple, and gold of his robe. Out of his sleeves were worn and lined hands. Stepping to the altar with the posture of a librarian, he was obviously not a man of grandiose charisma but of patience, gentility, and kindness. He extended his hands, a motion everyone else knew meant to sit down.

"In the name of the Father, the Son, and of the Holy Spirit, amen. By the grace and the love of our Lord and Saviour Jesus Christ, may peace be with you," the priest said.

"And with your spirit," was the room's mumbled response. Mum and Dad looked at each other, silently echoing what they had just heard. They had been away longer than they thought.

Unfolding a large and shining book, the priest began his sermon. He read from the book, and then spoke without looking. Read some more, spoke some more. And on, and on, and on. For what seemed like eternity, this man spoke uninterrupted with the occasional and passing chuckle that left the crowd like dust. I could tell Mum and Dad were having a tough time paying attention as their eyes would glaze and then snap back to focus with rapid blinking and a quick check around. This sermon contained none of the Catholic Church's famous hellfire, hardly any sound, and even less fury. Perhaps this was a more effective method of instilling guilt into their followers. Not by fear or intimidation, but by being so boring that everyone left feeling like they had missed something. Hélène was sitting prim and upright while Céline had taken one of the big books from the pocket in front and was thumbing through it with the respect of a magazine.

I squirmed. The magic of the building was fading the more I was stuck in my seat. Twisting and tapping against the firm wood, I felt my patience falling through my feet. Why did this guy have to go on and on? Though I had not been in school long, I knew of one move that got the adults to stop talking and let me speak. I sat up tall, put one finger over my lips, and shot my right hand into the air. Fingers spread wide, elbow shaking.

"Declan, what are you doing?" Mum asked.

The priest was still talking so I couldn't answer, lest I break her commandment. In the muffled fracas that featured Mum trying to get my hand down, me focusing my attention forward, and Céline beginning to giggle, the priest looked over to our section.

"It would seem that one of the younger members of our gathering has a comment for us." He chuckled. "Well then, my child, what is it you would like to share?"

I stood as tall as I could on the pew, each shoe thudding into empty air. With the full power of my pre-pre-pubescent voice, I shouted, "I came all the way here to see the Babyjesis and I wanna know where he is!"

People in the Church turned to each other and

covered the room in light conversation. The quietest part of the room was sitting next to me as my family looked moments away from death by mass embarrassment. I held steadfast with my practiced serious face until I had a reply.

"Well, that is certainly a difficult request. Because you see, dear child, that's a part of the reason why we are all here today. It is because we are waiting for His return. We know that Christ's ascension to heaven is not permanent and one day He will return to take all of us to heaven. And so, until such a time arrives, we will continue to honour and worship His words and practices. Therefore, when He does return, and we are judged favourably, it will be an occasion even more glorious than any human being could ever imagine. Something beyond our most wonderful of wishes. Does that answer your question?"

There was a pause and shift in the room as all the attention turned back to me.

"So... the Babyjesis isn't here?"

"Not physically, no. But He lives in our hearts and spirits and it is through His sacrifice that we are allowed to live as we do here today. So, in a way, I suppose, He is with us all the time."

"Then can I see him?" I pressed.

"I'm afraid not," the priest continued with remarkable flatness. "But while the light and life of the Lord cannot always be seen, once He has been let into the heart of a man, His essence never leaves us. We can always feel Him, even at our most despondent."

I had nothing left to ask. The priest had ravaged my

enthusiasm and I hadn't understood most of what he said. He gave the impression that he had never spoken to a child before and presumed that a person was born fully formed with no need for intellectual scaffolding. Still, he thanked me for my inquiry and continued on with the lesson. I've never known that priest's name, but he has not been easy to forget. He was the first adult I knew of that didn't seem to care about me and responded as if I was a burden on his life and time by asking my question. It made me feel smaller than I already was.

We stayed for the rest of the service. When it was becoming evident that I was on my way to grumpiness, Dad motioned for me to curl up on the hassock and have a nap. I did just that and succeeded in participating in the tradition of Catholics falling asleep in Church undetected. When the service was over, Dad hoisted me up and briskly walked to the car. It was better to move quicker than to be stopped by an old woman of prunes and mothballs to be told how disgraceful or adorable their son was. Mum grabbed my sisters' hands and held them tight enough that they knew to be quiet.

It was on the drive home that I fully awoke and the first place I looked was the rearview mirror. There were Dad's eyes, not Mum's, and while they glanced back their real focus was ahead of them.

"So what did you think of Church, Declan?" he asked.

I took a moment before speaking and looked to my sisters for reinforcement. They were both looking out their windows, watching the world pass quickly and slowly.

"I don't know," I said. "I thought the building was really cool, but the guy at the front talked too much. And if the Babyjesis wasn't there, why didn't he just say that? I think it would have saved a lot of time."

My parents chuckled and Hélène rolled her eyes in attempted maturity. No one had anything else to say about the outing. If it was so important that we go, why wasn't there anything to talk about? I leaned back to thoughts of the building again. It was so beautiful, so mysterious, that I would have loved to go back if only to look around. The talking was boring and without the ability to read on my own, the books were useless. I was in the middle of a see-saw that wouldn't balance where the one side was an interest in the place and the other was a disinterest in what went on there. A tension started simmering as I had unknowingly split the Church into irreconcilable sides.

Chapter Five

*L*ife, Church, and school moved on as they moved together. While we never attended with a strong schedule, Church had its dashes in my early life. Mostly around Christmas and Easter, I got to know the principle characters, the parables interpreted in childish terms, and the ritual. Still, it could not be said that Church was a priority each weekend. We had soccer games, family visits, and walks through the forests of our neighbourhood. In the wrestling match of values, family was pinning faith.

Faith, however, squirmed. It found pockets of escape to remind everyone of the weight it held. On holidays, before we ate, Dad led the saying of grace in a voice that ditched his usual joking lilt and offered more reverence, more solemnity, and in a higher tone than usual. If he looked up from his hands, it was towards me as if to confirm that I was taking in how this was to be done. It wasn't only in the pageantry of belief that these ideas were reaffirmed. When we left dishes out on a towel someone would inevitably say that they were letting God dry them. Even as a child I found it odd that God, with all the work he had to do, took the time to take water off our plates while we sat down to watch television. Surely he must have been too busy governing the entire universe.

But the religious identity was only one horse of the merry-go-round of personal identity. It was older and well-worn, not like a shinier one that beamed out for all my focus. Yes, I had a family, and, yes, I had a Church—but there was one place separate from both. School. As with all primary learners, I was difficult to pick out amongst the ranks. If the teacher said to sing, I sang with everyone. When it was time to clean up, I tidied away my small desk as I had been told. How strange it is that elementary school is the last place in which everyone participates fully. When I see wayward adults, hunched and forgotten, I wonder when it happened. When did they fall away? Did they give up or were they given up on? Surely, at some elementary school somewhere lives a record of these people colouring smiling animals. They would have sat, head tilted slightly upwards, as they listened to stories drifting off in permitted imagination. Their lips crunched just like everyone else's when they worked to memorize their times tables. At some point, the grasp that held them weakened and they slid away from the protection of childhood. The only thing left for them was work, and if that didn't happen, how quickly they collapsed into the street.

Where I noticed the grip of education first began to slip was middle school. As the kids grew, some at an alarming rate, so too did their personalities. Some talked back to their teachers and soon, certain students grew a reputation for suspension. I couldn't believe that was possible because it hadn't happened to my sisters. The first year of middle school had passed without a member of my class becoming a difficult case. Perhaps this kind of thing was just another rumour. After all, I had expected to be paddled on my first day by the soon-to-be graduating class and that passed without reference. The next year, however, a boy in my seventh grade class introduced a version of reality for which I had not been prepared.

By the age of 13, Kevin had grown taller and wider than our homeroom teacher. His voice had yet to drop and his clothes were often ill-fitting and dingy. With deeply sunken eyes, he walked in and out of rooms without moving his arms and without appearing to notice anyone. In class, he had mastered the craft of sitting so inert that he not only did no work but succeeded in avoiding the teacher's patrolling gaze. He was the biggest thing in the room and yet he could become invisible. Should he have moved, it was for the purpose of annoyance. Kevin liked to go through other student's desks and take whatever was tiniest. He would load up his own desk with ammunition and when his victim had forgotten he was there, a flick would hit their head. Whether it was a bit of an eraser or paperclip, his aim was often to the places sunglasses would cover. Everyone knew about it but, if someone tried to confront him about his habit, they were met with a predictable two word reply.

"Prove it."

Some kids, the ones who had never heard of Kevin, would fall into his logical trap. Whether they both knew the truth was irrelevant. It didn't matter what had happened, it mattered what could be proven.

"Prove I stole it," Kevin would say.

"Because it's mine and belongs in my desk," his victim might retort.

"Then how can it be yours and in your desk if it was in my hand?"

"Because you took it out?"

"When?"

"When what?"

"When did I take it out?"

And on, and on, and on. Each question required a greater specificity that was meaningless. Kevin was never looking for the truth, he was looking for weakness. If the accuser could not satisfy the initial claim, then the initial claim must have been a lie. He had figured out how to snake his way around the truth, taking an aggressive form of questioning, and changing the conditions whenever it was to his advantage. He was like a boxer who won not because of his strength or reflexes, but because of his awkward style and persistence. The kind of fighter excuses were made for. It didn't matter how often he got into something with another student, the teachers rarely regulated these verbal skirmishes. They must have been either too tired or too ignorant to have acted.

A few months into the school year, during a regular shakeup to the seating plan, I was placed next to Kevin. She sat us at the desk farthest away from hers and nearest to the classroom door. Kevin often sat near this spot since it meant the least amount of disruption when he arrived late, as was his habit. At first, I was confident I could survive his annoyances. It meant I had to be vigilant to the contents of my desk and use my notebooks as a barrier between us so as to stop his melting into a wider space than he already took up. While these methods stopped the physical invasions, they did nothing to protect from the mental ones.

"What's that?" Kevin said while I was doing an assignment.

"What's what?"

"That, there, on your desk. Oh my God, bro, why are you writing on your desk?"

"I'm not writing on my desk, I'm writing on my paper like we were told."

"And where's your paper?"

"On my desk," I said with slight defeat.

"Wow, so you are writing on your desk and you just admitted it. That's bad, bro. You're a bad kid."

His persistence and matter-of-fact tone were an infuriating combination.

"I am not writing on my desk."

"Chill out, bro, seriously. Why are you getting so mad? I'm just saying what you're doing."

"I am not getting mad," I lied.

"Yeah, you are. You're getting so mad right now. Why? All I said was you were writing on your desk, which you are. Don't lie, bro. It's not good to lie. Lying is something bad kids do."

I felt like a shaken up bottle of pop and he had his hands on the cap. He didn't seem to mind if I exploded; in fact, he appeared to be anticipating it. If I blew up, he won. And if I tried to turn this situation physical then he was definitely going to win. I put my pencil down and deployed a new tactic, one I hadn't seen done by another student before.

"You know what, Kevin," I said, "I am writing on my desk because my paper is on my desk and I'm writing on my paper."

A simple, logical solution in which we were both correct. What could he have to say to that?

"So you'll agree with anything I say?"

"What? No, that's not what—"

"Bro, you just did. I've only said one thing to you and you just said that I was right. So far, you'll agree to anything I say. Why don't you ever think for yourself? Why are you always copying what I do?"

My brain had turned to fuzz. I was a good enough student, certainly better than Kevin, but I couldn't tilt the leverage of this argument in my favour. It had been a simple refutation. He should have been easy to dispel. Yet there he was, making me feel shaken and small. His joy came from my rising frustration.

"You're so unoriginal, bro," he continued, "why even come to school if you're just going to be exactly like someone else?"

The seal of my cap had twisted.

"Kevin! Just shut up!"

The room stopped and turned to us.

"Declan! Out!" The teacher fired her words out with two blasts. I threw down what I was working on and stomped out of the room. When I crossed the doorway to go stew for a while, I glanced back for a moment. There was Kevin with a devilish smirk watching me leave the class.

The outburst had a minimal effect on the rest of the school day. My teacher neither sent me to the office nor called home. I was to blame, of course, for not keeping my emotions in check and not remembering whatever rigid structure of anti-bullying measures we had most recently covered. Despite my protests and my teacher's reassurance that she would have a talk with Kevin, I walked home that day in blame. It was a blame that burned not with the single sear of a brand but with the slow and even heat of a rotisserie. I hurt all over and I wasn't sure why. As I got nearer to home, I faced one uneasy question: Should I tell my parents?

The nearer I got to home, the more I acted like I was wearing a costume of myself. I wondered if I walked the way I normally did and how my hands hung when they were casual. Hiding was a temporary solution, but one not likely to last in a house as cramped as ours. When the door opened and my husk walked in, Mum was occupied in the office.

"Who's home?" she called.

"It's me," I said.

"Oh, you're home a bit early, Declan. How was your day?"

"Good," was all I mustered in quickness. Any longer of a sentence and I might have cracked my façade. Céline liked to stick around and wait for the high school to let out so she and Hélène could walk together and talk. Without them, Mum and I would have to share the privacy of the house. I considered stepping into the office. Mum would have known something was the matter in an instant. For all the shields I could have put up, there existed no defences against Mum's powers of noticing. All it would have taken was one step from me and one swivel of her chair and she would have invited me into her arms. She could have assuaged my wordless feelings and relieved me of their burden. But I didn't go to her. I instead fled to my room without a word for the rest of the afternoon.

When her voice announced it was time to come down for dinner, a thin shock shook my head. No one had come up to check on me since I closed my door, though it was possible Dad called out something general that I was too preoccupied to hear. When I did emerge, I endured some sarcasm from Céline as she raced me down the stairs. She tore off while I hobbled with the distinct feeling of a cannonball dangling from thin wire in my torso. It was heavy and every time I lurched it banged and rubbed against my ribcage. I must have looked slightly ill.

"Declan," Dad said, hand on my back, "are you feeling okay?"

"Yeah, I think so. Why?"

"Nothing in particular."

Dinner passed with a similar amount of attempted attention. I got a couple of lob questions, remarks about school or the weekend, but each was met with bluntness. Eventually, the focus turned away and the other four kept up in the airy delight of conversation. They probably thought I was going through one of the more sullen periods of puberty. A time in which moods shortened and soured. Or maybe they didn't much notice since it wasn't unusual for me to speak the least.

After we finished, I asked if I could be excused and returned to my room. I went upstairs, Mum and Dad to the living room, and my sisters to the unfinished basement. All their noises dissipated to their corners. Lying on my bed, my thoughts unfurled about my day and my new bully. It reminded me of something we had learned about foxes in science class. When a fox hunted a nesting animal, it had a few choices. With keen smell and sight, it might dash after the prey or dig down, revealing the hidden nest before ingesting all the critters it found. However, some foxes displayed a touch more cunning. If a home had been found in the open, the fox would position itself out of sight of the entrance. Then it would tap near the edge of the opening. These taps would be light but noticeable so as to bypass the curling response of fear in the prey and appeal to its curiosity. With innocent ambition, the prey would stick itself out into the openness of the day only to be snatched and crunched.

Kevin had outfoxed me and in doing so turned me into a defenceless rabbit. In my smallness, I wished that he would turn his cheek to someone else and torment them instead. It did not matter who just so long as I passed the rest of this godawful arrangement in anonymity. His tenacity, his incorrigible logic, and his targeting proved unconquerable because whenever I thought I had the answer, he changed the question. In this solitude another idea had solidified. I was helpless, I could not go to

Mum and Dad for help. Bullies had never been dinner table conversation and so, I assumed, it must never have happened to my sisters. What if it caused Mum and Dad to worry too much and they pulled me out of school entirely? It was often the case that I was the odd one out at home and I didn't need to compound that place by also being the weakling.

I tried to distract myself with imaginings of how I could best my annoyer. The kinds of teenage daydreams which play out more like movies I had seen rather than real school days. Lines spoken by my character that were not only perfect in ending his remarks but proved me, publicly, to be the wittier, the sharper, and the better of the competing pair. Everyone in the class would applaud and this time with Kevin would close over like a scar never to bleed again. These scenarios, these dramas, provided little in lasting satisfaction. Just as easily as they were envisioned, they were replaced with a replay of what had gone on.

I sat and stirred, furied and furrowed without a sign of consolation. What I needed was someone bigger than Kevin, stronger than Kevin, and more everlasting. The oldest person I knew was Hélène but she dashed out from the options because, even though she was in high school, she was a girl. As unenlightened as teenage boys could be, they were at their dimmest when the opposite sex arrived. To bring her in would have been to bring in a dire form of weakness. No, what I had in mind was someone who could always be there as a barricade when I needed him and invisible when I didn't. Teachers had proved useless and parents untested. Besides, they were limited by their vision and time. Once they had turned away, the speed of an insult was far faster than their interception, leaving them amidst the shrieks of hearsay. If only I lived in a world of superheroes where problems could be solved with a swoop and an uppercut. Unfortunately, ideas of that kind were appearing more and more childish in a time when I ached to mature. I thought about all the possible protectors before I remembered I had one connection to something larger than any bully and more powerful than any logic. What I needed to call on was God.

How fortunate that I had been made a Catholic. Once my head crossed the water at my baptism, I was to be forever covered in allegiance to the God of the Christian faith. This God just so happened to be a personal God that could be communicated with by thinking with a bit of direction. At least, that was how I understood prayer. He never took a vacation, never lost, and always had time for every one of his followers. That was the agreement for holding dominion over us.

While I had sworn to God on playgrounds, I hadn't purposefully prayed to him. The odd times we were at Church, I was never sure what I was supposed to be praying about so when everyone keeled forward and closed their hands, I imitated and waited. The other members of the Church looked so focused that they couldn't have noticed. They were too busy surrounding themselves with belief. I got up to close my door and moved to the side of my bed. Kneeling down and raising my elbows, I closed my eyes and joined the two C's of my hands together.

At first, my prayers sounded like regular thoughts. They were common, profane—like I was trying to talk to God as if he was someone who had grown up with me. It was wrong. The Churches I had seen had been so ornate that common diction couldn't cut it. If God was going to hear me and my cause in a worthy way, I had to elevate my thinking to his level.

"Good evening, God," I began as if quilling a letter. "My name is Declan Murphy and I was hoping you would be able to aid me out of some trouble. There is another boy in my class and his name is Kevin. I am so sorry, God, that I do not know his last name, but he also goes to Clifford Sifton Middle School. He is also in my class and recently has been made to sit next to me and… and I just can't deal with him anymore. I don't know what to do. When I told him today to leave me alone, I was the one who got in trouble and I didn't even do any-thing! I think this might even be too much for Mum and Dad so I'm coming to you instead. Can you please do something about Kevin? You don't have to burn his house down or make him really sick or anything. But could you please make it so he's nicer to me tomorrow? That's all I want. If you can do that, I'll be a really good boy for the rest of the year and I'll never get in trouble from my teacher again. How does that sound?"

The prayer ended on that question mark. No great light or wind beat upon my window. No letters formed themselves in mental confirmation. I opened my eyes and surveyed the room for some measure of divine sign. There was nothing. Everything was as ordinary as always.

God must've heard me because I had prayed and I didn't ask for a sign ahead of time so that must have been why he didn't send anything. In the same way my stomach can tell me I've had enough food, my worries told me they were settled and banished. After that, it was easy to fall asleep.

The next morning met me with a trill. A pair of springtime birds had perched outside my window and sang to each other in the early sunrise. I was more than happy to start my day. I was enthused. Still sitting in the calm of post-prayer, and now with the sound of birds, I was certain God had intervened in my favour during the night. How could it be otherwise? I felt good and there was nature, gently waking me up on time. Going downstairs for breakfast, my family also remarked upon my glinting mood without sarcasm or concern. I didn't tell them about how this was all God's doing, though they may have liked to hear it. The door fell of its own weight behind me as I walked out that morning.

With a greeting for every person I saw, I passed by all the other students and went directly to class to wait for the day. Like dealt cards, I turned over the various scenarios in which God's will would be actualized. Perhaps Kevin would be just as early and apologize in front of the entire class. Or it could be that he understood how deeply his torment had hurt me and would offer up some money as a bonus. For each of the present possibilities, the ace of spades would have been the teacher announcing to the class that, in the haste of night, Kevin's family had fled the country and left no contact of how to reach them. So many offerings, so many winnings, but I had the gambler's confidence that today was a day for my prosperity.

When the bell did ring, the other students entered the room like cars exiting a busy offramp. Our teacher rushed in a few minutes behind, leaving us the time to socialize and throw things. Through the traffic of faces and backpacks, Kevin's wasn't there. I asked if anyone at my table group had heard anything and was met with various shrugs. Apparently, no one much kept up with him away from school. The second bell rang and the teacher stood with a blister in her voice, telling us to settle down and take our own seats so she could get the attendance in before the office yelled at her.

First period began and it took her the opening minutes to set up the projector. Amid her daily technological struggle, Kevin strolled in. His pace was languid as ever.

"Kevin, did you remember to check in at the office?" the teacher said.

"Yeah," he replied, not looking back.

He plopped his belongings next to me and dropped into his seat. I had a wide smile spread across my face and that appeared to confuse him.

"What are you doing?" he asked.

"Nothing in particular. I just feel like today's going to be a good day."

"Okay…"

He hadn't arrived with cash or an apology, but the morning periods passed without interference. I thought God must have chosen a more surreptitious route. He might have visited Kevin in a dream and frightened him with power beyond comprehension that, if he continued like he was, he would be going straight to Hell. After recess, we had time to work on our big term project for social studies. We had been tasked with inventing a country and had to compile everything about its geography, history, government, and culture to be presented across a wide and detailed poster. It was such a thrill to create. The work had been over a month in progress as we learned about all the variations of the world's people and how they lived and interacted with their land. I couldn't believe there was so much magnificent difference in the world, and with each group I learned about, I wanted to know how their neighbours lived, what they believed, and how they got through their lives. No assignment before had felt as important, and by this stage, I didn't want this project to end. Not with all the fascinating and undiscovered truths.

When I looked at Kevin's desk, I saw that he had barely started. His country had a name, written in a scratched handwriting across the top of the poster like a banner, and nothing else. It was only a name and had yet to be given the full life of an idea. He was looking at my poster as well, probably in awe of what I had created thus far. Even if he would have never admitted it, it felt nice to have an admirer.

"Hey, bro," he asked me, " can I borrow that glue for a second?"

"Sure thing!" I said.

He held the liquid glue in his hand for a moment and looked around. I returned to my work, placing my country's flag in exactly the spot I wanted. Kevin unscrewed the top. I went across the room to grab a ruler. With every step came potential for my country's next city or festival or song. When I came back, I couldn't see my country anymore. The entirety of the bottle of glue had been poured all over it.

"Kevin!" I screamed. "Why did you do that?"

"Do what?"

"You just ruined my project! I've been working on it for weeks and now it's all ruined!"

The class came to a standstill.

"Bro, relax, it wasn't even me, alright?"

"It had to be you! I let you borrow the glue and now there it is all over my work! Why? Why did you do this?"

"I didn't! Prove it."

It should have been simple, I should have gotten the teacher, but in my frenzied state nothing seemed clear. The splotch on the poster was seeping wider. As if it was some liquid beast that grew stronger the more it consumed. With its white, curved outline, the glue crawled its way over all the colour and contour of the poster before settling and beginning the hardening process.

The teacher was too slow again. She didn't need to call on me or recommend that I stepped out because I was already storming towards the door. Maybe she had called out in some attempt to arrest me, but the evidence was plain. As I took to the halls, I refused to cry. Despite all the liquid in my systems rising towards my eyes, nose, and throat, I willed them shut. If I had been seen crying at school then the stain those tears left would have been indelible. Rumours would have flown around like ghosts and when other kids two or three relations away from me wondered what happened what would they have heard? Probably that a little bit of glue touched my poster and I flew out. Walking through more of the school, the enmity I had for Kevin dissipated throughout the imagined student body as they twisted into crueler forms.

I found a secluded corner at the end of a row of lockers. Their burnt-orange paint pushed against the side of my cheek as I huddled down in the posture of a beggar. The rows and numbers of the lockers now appeared endless and behind each of their flimsy metal doors were unique arrangements leftover from their owners. I wished to know which ones were empty so that I could slam myself inside and treat its tight space as a cocoon. Or if I could scream into it, belching out the entirety of my frustration and inability so as to be liberated from such feelings. How had it been that only a few hours ago I was happy with eyes full of sun and skies?

While I sat exposed to the flat light of the hallway, no one called for me. No one looked for me and no one was relieved when they found me. For the rest of the period, I was never acknowledged. I might as well have been a heap of laundry with skin. No soul, no heart, nothing to notice. On that floor, I was in a state of purposeless solitude—one devoid of inherent meaning, eventual wisdom, or meditation. It was more than loneliness, it was the most hopeless feeling to ever occur to a child: abandonment.

In that isolation, one thought joined me. It arrived like a rodent in a house, skittish and unwelcome, but nevertheless present and gnawing. If God couldn't stop my bully, what could he do? Why? Why had he allowed one of his elect to be tormented by the very thing he had prayed for remedy against? The thoughts multiplied and changed from mice to harpies. Each one beginning with the same, tempestuous "why." As a word, it served as a reminder of panging curiosity, of the limits of what can be understood by seeing or knowing or feeling. What I was praying for was a divine "because." I ached for God to tell me this had happened because it was going to lead to something better than I could know right now; because Kevin would eventually receive a more powerful punishment; or because God never heard my plea in the first place. A truth was less important than a reason. At least a reason could be made into a truth. There, I would have clung to any answer.

Hands pressed together again, I tossed out more and more prayers on the chance that one would find the ever open ears of God. I was like an impatient pedestrian, constantly pressing the cross button, never knowing if my actions had any influence. God must have been there, he must have heard something. Then all was blank. My eyes shifted around as the gap between my thoughts widened, leaving only dust and space. There was nothing. No word in a voice I didn't recognize, no breakthrough, not even an out of place piece of ash near my shoes. The immutable silence dripped from my mind down my throat and pooled at the bottom of my spine with the weight and silky poison of mercury.

I was sure *I* had done something wrong.

Chapter Six

*E*ven though I had been rejected, there was enough clinging hope that kept my faith alive. This must have been my first brush with the so-called mysterious ways in which God worked. Besides, it was a selfish prayer anyway. That was probably why God let it go, because if everyone got what they craved most when they were alone then who would be living a remotely recognizable life?

That was the opinion, the defence to which I kept referring back over the next few years. I tried to keep track of how often prayers were answered, but it wasn't a ritual that made itself a habit. What did carry on from this time was a growing fascination with my social studies courses. While they had been fine and general throughout middle school, once I was in my secondary years the subject exploded. Especially once the assignments turned from the wide and the ancient to the contemporary and the disputed.

"Come to get the latest facts, eh?" Dad said over the news' introduction music.

"Just for socials class," I said. "Our teacher wants us to watch the news for a week and then we're going to have some class discussions about current events."

"Well now, that's an education I can get behind. It's important for you kids to get your bearings in this world before you've got to act in it. A bit of advice, though: don't feel like you're going to get everything they're talking about right away. Think of the news like any other kind of show, and you've started watching in the middle. It'll be unfamiliar for a while, but give it your goat and you'll see the same people and the same stories in no time. Like this idiot," Dad gestured to the screen. "What's he pestering on about now?"

That idiot, the suited figure with the same haircut he looked like he'd had since he was 10, was Prime Minister Stephen Harper. He stood at the bottom of a cloud-grey stairwell, surrounded by reporters in a typical Canadian ambush, to give his comment on the potential coalition between the opposing New Democrat and Liberal parties.

"You watch, Declan, they'll make a whole fuss out of nothing here. The two sides'll never sign on together and all this guy's got to do is a big bunch of nothing until their in-fighting tears them up. And then where will we be? Exactly where we are now, only he'll get to say his side is stronger than ever after resisting such a force. Clever bastard. A person can't put much faith in the opposition trying to cross their colours like that. No, if you're for a party, you're for them, and that's that. A leopard can't change its stripes."

"Don't you mean spots?"

"Spots, stripes—whatever's on you, that's what you are."

The Prime Minister's comment was given, not that I

heard it with Dad's intervening commentary, and the show cut back to the anchor of the national news. He wore a suit and tie that didn't distract and spoke in firm, even words that anyone learning English would have begged to hear.

"From politics we turn now to religion," the anchor said. "New research is showing that we may be on the crest of a new wave of atheism in North America and in Europe. This after several high-profile writers and scientists such as Christopher Hitchens and Richard Dawkins have released popular bestsellers questioning the existence of a higher power. Just last week, Hitchens, a contributing editor to *Vanity Fair*, teamed up with award-winning British comedian and writer Stephen Fry in a debate hosted by Hitchens' magazine. The subject of the debate: 'The Catholic Church is a Force for Good in the World.' Take a look at some highlights."

"You can't join our Church and you can't go to heaven. This is disgraceful. It's inhuman. It's obscene. And it comes from a clutch of hysterical sinister virgins who've already betrayed their charge in the children of their own Church," said a plump man in a beige suit.

"Overwhelmingly, I say to you tonight, with no apology whatever, that a world without the Catholic Church would be poorer, would be more hopeless, and would be a worse place in which to live," said a shrill-voiced woman in lily-pad green.

"The idea that the Catholic Church exists to disseminate the word of the Lord is nonsense. It is the only owner of the truth for the billions that it likes to boast about," said another man with a very crooked nose.

"Very passionate words, indeed," the anchor said, swivelling towards a different camera. "Joining me now are two individuals on different sides of the current debate. Tom Huxley, head of the Canadian Atheist Alliance, joins us here in-studio, and, via satellite from her home in Calgary, is Dr. Samantha Wilberforce. Samantha is the head of the board of trustees for the Calgary Catholic School board. A warm welcome to you both."

Both guests responded cordially and the anchor looked up from his cards, aiming his gaze at his in-studio guest.

"Tom, I'd like to start with you. As mentioned, you're the head of the Canadian Atheist Alliance which is holed up in Toronto, but I gather you've gone all over the country too. Why do you think atheism is so steadily on the rise right now?"

"Honestly, I think there are several reasons for the rise we're seeing right now. First, we have to recognize that this kind of thing, the option to not believe in any kind of god, is much older than this generation's conversation. The main difference is that now it's not quite as lethal a position to take. If we go back all the way to what is essentially that founding of our civilization—which is not Christian Europe but Ancient Greece—we'll see that when Socrates was put to death one of the principle charges brought against him was denying the existence of the gods. I want to state that plainly because we have to understand that this point of view isn't new, but being able to talk about it so openly is. So what I think has happened and is continuing to happen now is a sort of confluence in which people have always not believed, or at least have kept their doubts to themselves, and now in the wake of all the religious extremism we've seen since 9/11, people are feeling more comfortable talking about what they believe is true. That the world is wonderful enough without the need for an, shall we say, inconsistent overseer."

"Very interesting," the anchor said, now looking towards the ominous-sized head on the studio screen. "Samantha, we'll turn now to you. When you hear the position like the one Tom here just outlined, what does it mean to you? Are you noticing fewer students enrolling in your schools, by chance?"

"No, no, not at all. In fact, the number of new students enrolling in our schools is growing every year which, I think, is enough evidence to say that there's nothing to fear about a diminution of the Catholic faith, or of religion in general. But, if I may speak to the point about this issue of atheism crawling across our contemporary culture. While Tom is correct in saying that people have been guided away from religion for a long time, let's look at what has persisted: The Church itself. In spite of the, frankly, rude and shortsighted criticism of some public figures I could name, the power of our faith has held strong for millennia. Now what does that tell us? It tells us that these things are more than just stable, they're true. If books like the Bible were so easy to disprove, then they would have been tossed away years ago as some piece of historical obscurity. In fact, when you look at the stats year after year, the Bible is the best-selling book across the world. So what do I think of this new atheism? I think it is just another trend that will pass."

The anchor looked as if he was about to continue the discussion until Tom's hand extended across the desk, interrupting him.

"I'm so sorry, I'm sure you have more questions, but may I respond directly to what Samantha has just said?"

"Please, be my guest," the anchor responded.

"Thank you. To the point that the increase in enrolment numbers in Catholics schools is proof that there are equally increasing numbers of Catholics in this country isn't totally true. While it may be the case that more Catholics are choosing to send their children to religious schools, this rise just happens to coincide with a rise in Catholic school boards opening their doors to non-Catholics for the first time. Either they are expecting very slow conversions or there aren't enough Catholics to keep these places afloat. Then there is the matter of the Bible's longevity. Samantha alluded to this book's history and popularity being synonymous with its truth, but that can't be the case since we have records of older religious texts from China and India, for example, whose traditions are still practiced today. How can it be that these religions are true as well? Not to mention all of the other systems of mythology, again I'll go back to the Greeks here, that were established long before the Christians came around. Now, we don't consider the stories of Zeus and Hera to be factual accounts of Ancient Greece so then why should the Bible be any different? Not only that—"

"You know, Tom, I want to make sure we've got both

sides equally represented here so I'm going to have to cut you off there and give some airtime to Samantha. Samantha, let's return to the day-to-day influence of these matters. You're, obviously, working closely with schools, are you noticing an influence of this movement on your students?"

"Not in the slightest. At our schools, here in Alberta, when I go in and visit with the students or meet with the teachers, the work looks like it always has. And when I ask them about the Bible or God or what they believe in, they sound just like me and my classmates when I was their age. So, I know there's been quite a lot of talk in the media about this wave of non-belief, and we may cite some books that are doing reasonably well, but on the whole this is still a relatively small section of the population that, frankly, is enjoying its time in the spotlight. That's all. You know, it's like the scripture says: this too shall pass. When it does, the Catholic Church will still be here and God will still be watching out for us."

"Alright, some very interesting points made here tonight about an issue I'm sure many of our viewers will have an opinion on," the anchor said with a tone of voice that followed a similar path to a landing plane."

"If I may," Tom said, "and, once again, I'm sorry for interrupting, but I can't be the only person who takes issue with what Dr. Wilberforce just said."

Tom had stunned them. They must have thought that the segment was over. In their inaction, Tom bowled on.

"A statement like the one we just heard is exactly why our movement is so relevant right now. Think about it, if I told you my child came from school with textbooks and work that people were using over fifty years ago, you'd say it was totally out of date, obsolete even. We can't expect ourselves, with all the wondrous discoveries we've made in the past few hundred years, to carry on as we're still in the Middle East in the first century. Look, people have been made to believe a great many things that we would never claim as being factual now. People believed that the Buddha was born out of a slit on his mother's ribcage or that the reason all the plants died in winter was because Demeter was grieving. Now, if you wrote a medical exam and said it was possible for a woman to give unassisted birth out of her side or that the changing of the seasons was caused by a moody mother, you'd fail. When we end up talking about religion, we end up talking about what is true and while it may be comforting to hold these beliefs close, if someone's life was at stake, we wouldn't even consider a religious response. What we must be ready to recognize in this new century, and what people like myself are working to do, is to separate what's factual and what's just a nice story. By every measure of consistent reality that anyone can use, there is no evidence for the belief in any god, Christian or otherwise."

Tom spoke with passionate precision. It was as if these ideas had been swimming around his mind and now, when he needed them, they organized themselves into the shape of a predator.

"Well," the anchor said, taking back control, "I was going to give Tom the last word anyway, but since it seems that statement is worthy of response, Samantha, do you have anything to close on?"

Samatha sat hollow-faced. I saw in her the same reaction I felt in myself when a teacher asked me for an answer and I hadn't been paying attention.

"You know, it's like I said before, this too shall pass. And when it does, I know that the Catholic Church and God and Christ's message to all of humanity will still be here and it'll be helping people long after everyone has forgotten all of us."

"That was Tom Huxley of the Canadian Atheist Alliance and Dr. Samatha Wilberforce of the Catholic School Board. Thank you both for your time tonight."

Swivelling back towards the hard camera, the anchor closed the show with his regular sign-off. The music and the credits rolled on and I noticed that Dad hadn't said anything for the entire segment.

I looked up at my father's flat face. It was tight in its stillness in a way that wasn't emotionless but specifically favoured no emotion. His lips were retreating towards his teeth and he folded his arms so far across his chest that his fingers curled comfortably around his upper arms. We sat fixed until the opening credits of the next show popped up. Without a glance, he opened his posture only to grab the remote and turn the television off.

He placed his hands on his knees and rocked into a standing position.

"Come on, Declan. Let's go help your mother get dinner ready."

He rolled on towards the kitchen without a hint of an

opinion. This man who could get a cod to talk back to him said nothing. No gruff or grim line about the state of all things or how dare they talk like that on television these days. Throughout dinner, I kept checking on him like some kind of spy. Mentally noting the way he picked up his food, how toughly he chewed it, and read into his dinner table conversation with the intrusion of a psychoanalyst. The man went through dinner with the unchallenged face of a poker player. Never letting on that he was upset or elated, just passing through the routine with the minimum amount of participation.

Was he not swaying at all? God and the Church were never to be challenged in this home and I had been given enough examples of what God had done to his enemies. To so much as jab at God meant exposing oneself to the fiery lightning of his vengeance. When one of us had a question about something related to religion, it was to remain a private struggle. The kind of struggle that either resolves itself or is brought before the clergy. In my young years, no one had gone to the local priest to wrestle through a matter of faith. But the man on the news, he wasn't so much fighting our faith but sidestepping it entirely. To have stated openly that there was no reason to believe was a position I had never considered.

We washed up, Dad and I, and as we scrubbed shoulder-to-shoulder, I kept glancing up at him. He must have had the same words blowing through his head but did he have the same questions? Questions whose intentions might have been innocent—was the man on the news telling the truth?—but whose provocations may have been incendiary. Why choose silence now, Dad? The pile of leftover plates was diminishing. Soon we would separately retire, splitting without resolution. My lips dryly parted to say something when I was interrupted.

"Declan, would you pass me that big pot next?"

I closed my mouth again and nodded. That was all we said to each other. When the last of the dishes were done, I turned one way to go to my room and he went the other to join Mum in the living room. Hélène and Céline must have bolted downstairs.

"Thanks for dinner!" I called out from the stairs.

"You're welcome, Declan!" Mum called back. She shuffled over on the couch to make room. When I looked back, all I saw were my parents, nestling into their regular positions. Unchanged and unchallenged. Distance was not all that separated us.

I burrowed into my bedroom and opened my laptop. Despite my memory, I couldn't remember how to spell atheism, mixing up the i and the e, which prompted the condescending search engine to confirm if that was what I really meant. As the page loaded, it became clear that I did not have the foggiest idea what this cause was pursuing. The man on the news clearly had no reverence for the Church, but what was this "ism" he put in its place? Was Athe someone's last name, a founder perhaps, and instead of turning to a God or a scripture, atheists used this person's ideas to underpin their own?

The first result was a definition. Atheism: an absence of belief in the existence of deities. That sentence required more deduction so a follow-up search had to be punched in. What are deities? According to the next page, deities was only a plural of deity. Deity: the rank of essential nature of a god. Was someone trying to keep this information a secret? It took a bit more clicking around until I was able to surmise that a deity was just a dressed-up notion for God as I understood it. While it did not have to be the Christian God, it referred to any version, idea, or concept of an all-powerful being that lived outside of the bounds of humanity. With that, I went back to the original definition and pieced together that an atheist was someone who did not believe any gods existed. But that couldn't be.

Who didn't believe in God? While he couldn't be seen and, in my experience, wasn't much of a sound, the same could be said for something like the country of China. Its facticity had little to do with my perspective. Of course there was a God, how did these atheists reckon everything started? Who put the world together, gave it its first spin, and still watches over its workings? The absurdity of the position did what any measure of absurdity does: it enthralled me to try and sort out its puzzle. I put atheism back into the search bar. While it loaded, I caught sight of my face in the screen's reflection and thought about how stony Dad looked after the news. I had hoped to look more like him but the facing features mirrored more of Mum.

To my surprise, the internet of this era had a well-stocked cache of information, writings, and videos on this subject. Pages of notes and arguments were readily available to be viewed, examined, and commented upon—and they seemed quite popular. It wasn't frightening because of the content but because of the amount. How had I never heard of such a thing that appeared so popular and far from its origin? It was all so farfetched and yet was presented with enthusiastic passion.

I decided a compilation would be the best basis for an introduction. The video began with a well-dressed man standing behind a lectern. His suit was black, like his hair, and he wore a popping white shirt, like his skin. He asked his audience, which couldn't be seen, to consider a proposition. Imagine a person who hears, bouncing and echoing around his head, a voice he does not recognize. This voice is not only capable of speaking in full and intelligible sentences, but also has the power to compel the man to act. The man has no agency over what the voice will command next. Over the days and weeks, the man begins to suspect that if he disobeys the voice his life will be purposefully ruined. Not only that but he is beginning to suspect that the power that comes from this voice will crawl after him to continue its torment long after he has died. So he acts exactly as the voice instructs for the rest of his life.

The man at the lectern let his story sit for a moment. He allowed the audience to fill in its details with images of their own. Then he continued by saying if we heard someone who had recently committed a major crime describe this exact scenario, we would immediately presume this person was insane and treat them as such. We might even go so far as to suggest that they requires therapy or medication in order to cast out or otherwise quell this spilt that has arisen in their psyche. Would we not? So, the man at the lectern continued, how is that person any different than a religious person who claims to have heard God in their ear, instructing them exactly how to respond to life?

Before I could do anything but remember the argument, a new clip had begun. The new man spoke with an educated English accent and insisted upon the use of an elevated vocabulary. Speaking from the roots of his profession, the study of the world as it evolved, he considered the fossil evidence. Through reputable and replicable methods of research, he had been studying not just the origin of species but the origin of all things. His findings had not been revealed like a magician's rabbit nor had they been guessed. Instead, they were the results of decades and centuries of compiled work by other scientists who tried, and sometimes failed, to arrive at some steadfast conclusion.

Due to the work from these fields, and the breakthroughs in the use of radioactive dating methods, scientists now had the tools to accurately assess the age of the planet. When the things of the Earth that represented solid time—fossils, rocks, plants, and ice—had been taken and measured, the distance of existence reached much farther back than previously estimated. The educated man said that for hundreds of millions of years, there have been forms of like and matter that have clung to the gravity of our stony orb. They have lived, died, multiplied, or been otherwise consumed in a tippy cosmic buffet through which life itself had persevered. How then can it be possible for the dates given in the Bible to be true? With all the discoveries of science, showing numbers beyond the millions, how can the Earth only be twenty-four hundred years old? And finally, if the first claim of time and space can not only be disputed but demonstrably falsified, how can the rest of the book be taken as factual? For these questions, he received sustained applause.

In another quick cut, there was a different speaker. This one, another man, I recognized as the man in the tan suit from the news. While he was dressed differently in this clip, opting for a charcoal suit, it was his voice that was unmistakable. It announced itself with a resounding baritone and commitment to poetic expression. He did not choose to imagine, nor to lecture, but asked his audience to make a consideration. Take all they think they knew about this Christian God, about the length of his reign, about his ability to interfere in the lives of ordinary mortals, about his limitless domain, and about the standard of his behaviour. Perhaps the book had fudged the dates but no matter. Even with the evidence supplied by evolutionary biologists, that did not mean inherently that such an entity did not exist.

If it was true that the human animal has existed on this planet for at least one hundred thousand years, and if the Christians were correct that their God had created everything, then it must also mean that those years were equally surveyed. That he watched us die young, often of diseases in our teeth, that he watched us go to war with each other endlessly, that we even established other religions and other gods. This, he said, heaven watched over with the indifference of folded-arms. It had no sympathy for the endless legions of parents who were forced to bury their children year after year like a failed crop. After, again, about one hundred thousand years of this factory of misery, God decides to intervene. And how? By sending his own son to an isolated part of the Middle East to be sacrificed so that all of humanity thereafter could learn to suffer as he did. He called it a wicked thing, what this God had done, and it felt like an unsettlingly perfect word.

I didn't know enough to reject what they said. Their arguments were like the streets of a foreign country: somehow all connected, but to the new traveller, they were daunting and indecipherable. As their words navigated the grooves and bends of my brain, they refused to settle. Rather they, like outsiders, took place without acknowledging the greater whole to which they were joining. Thoughts of Catholicism and upbringing made no sign of welcome for these ideas either. They refused mixture. While the new ideas of the atheists were something to acquire, they were intriguing. To speak so brashly against the underpinning ideas of everything, that was certainly enough to captivate a teenager. So I watched another video. And then another. And then another still. Each man on screen offered their atheism with a slightly different flavour and the medium of the internet made for a perfect sampler. It wasn't until I had clicked around a bit before I saw a familiar face in the thumbnail. The man with the crooked nose from the news was there, not holding up a hand for blessing but a pair of single skeptical fingers. His name was Stephen Fry.

Stephen began his speech with reference and affability. I didn't recognize the name of the play, but he quoted as easily as remembering his address: In times like these, it becomes more than a moral duty to speak one's mind, it becomes a pleasure. He then revealed that he was approaching the day's discussion with nervousness, admitting to have been nervous all day and, indeed, was nervous right now. How could that have been? His face, voice, and hands were so steady. I had always associated nerves with frantic, jerky movements that speed up the pace of everything and manufactured sweat. Stephen's forehead was clean and yet his admission did not make him into a phoney. It only deepened his sincerity and bravery. In no more than a few sentences, he had succeeded in doing what any great writer can do, and do effortlessly: he had charmed me. By joining the most vulnerable sides of ourselves, I felt safe in hearing what he thought.

Like an expert surgeon, carefully cutting around an infection without damaging the rest of the body, Stephen first claimed that he was neither upset at or against any individual Catholic. The people who expressed their faith in a personal way were not his enemies tonight. That faith and the joy that it inspired were not within his domain of criticism. However, equally important, were his own beliefs. A counterpoint to this kind of salvation was a faith—or perhaps it was more accurate to say a trust—in the Enlightenment. There I was: the underprepared student again. I knew I had heard the term, that it had been part of the end of middle school, but its reference here conjured nothing concrete. When Stephen spoke about it, he made it sound impressive. It was as if he was pronouncing the capital letter each time he said it. But it didn't sound like a religion. There was no call to a spearheaded leader, no interpellation of ritual. Merely an organization of thought that could inform a mind as fully as any other. This Enlightenment had its values not in the wishy-washy notions of hope and belief but in empiricism, in logic, in the continuous joy of discovery through experience. It required no tithe, no ritual, only that a person continue to seek out a sense of understanding in the world based on what could be certain. The winds of the Enlightenment blew gently through my halls of faith and left whistling in their vacancy.

As Stephen continued, each sentence was as pleasing and precise at it was poetic. He spoke at convincing length to disprove the concepts of limbo and purgatory. How strange that these places were justified by keepers of the faith and yet were never once mentioned in the Bible. How many people have mentally suffered because they were told their infants, dying tragically young, were going to spend eternity floating and crying with no hope of reunification with their parents? To whom had God spoken to so that this detail may be shared and then taken with the respectful truth of the other claims of his testament? What else had God inconveniently forgotten? With meaning extending beyond the literal nature of his words, new waves broke upon the rocks of my faith. For the first time, I was considering facts I had never interrogated, far removed from their safe context of their stone-covered sanctuaries.

We Catholics had to believe in the sacrament not as a ritual but as a fact. How was it that a member of the cloth could *literally* turn wine into blood and *literally* turn bread into flesh? By this age, I had taken my first Communion and knew that there is no foodstuff as dry and sticky as those wafers. They didn't bend and stretch like flesh but splayed across the roof of the mouth like wet cardboard. But if I believed in this rite as only a metaphor, of something we participate in as a human effort, then I was offensively refusing my true faith as a Catholic. I would have been doubting, and doubting offensively, one of the key tenets of my Church.

His easy wave of speaking next brushed onto the variations present in the priesthood. If he, the jovial, known, and boyish person he was, went to meet a priest there in England, he was sure he would meet a wonderful example of a man. This priest would be informed about his faith but not rigid. With the hand-waving of a pageant queen, he might even pitch the Church to an unbeliever on the merits of the dear charm and wonder of seeing the world in Catholic terms. This priest might even smoke. (How daring!) Finally, there would be a note of humility about joining the Church and that they, as an organization, would be honoured to have someone like him as a member.

It was so easy to fill my mind with the memories of priests like this that I had known. The kinds of men that were kind to me, deeply so, and had spoken with jolly tenderness. Even if they hadn't all been that way, the others could best be remembered as aloof and nonthreatening, like a singular cloud trolling through the sky. Without knowing me, Stephen had described me. His observations were accurate without the weakness of being too precise. This was the behaviour of Catholic priests. In a quick but emphatic movement, he threw up his first finger to interrupt himself with a strong "But!"

Should one be charged with the innocent crime of being ignorant and poor, Stephen claimed, then the priest would become a verbal vessel for damnation. He would ditch all effete gestures and speak only of the choking pits of sulphur in Hell. That failing to submit to the power of the Church was to track oneself towards immeasurable torture and anguish forever. How lucky were they then that their lives had been intervened? They had been born into a world whose rules and consequences had been kept hidden from them; but now, if they only gave up their critical faculties, could they be saved from this infernal nightmare. The Church was a revealer of a truth so powerful that once spoken it required reckoning.

I had been sent into a split mental world. Yes, I recognized the first kind of priest. The gentile and soft older man whose cheeks were often tinted plum. They stood before all and wore the Church over their shoulders. But Stephen had reminded me of the underbelly of my Church. While he claimed that only the poor and ignorant felt the column of fire the poured out of the Church's mouth, it was more than them.

Having to go through with the rites of First Communion and Confirmation, I was out of place in a Sunday School class. All the other students knew each other from regular attendance but I was there like a tourist. It didn't help that the Sunday School class was so removed from the open air and grey stone of the hall. That room was brown as wood and lowly lit like it was in the hull of a ship. I was out of step with the stories and characters from the Bible and so spent most of the lessons trying to piece together what it all meant. There was a girl in the class who appeared very well read on all matters Biblical and often responded correctly to the teacher's critical questions. When we were working through the story of Noah and the Flood, she raised her hand and asked the teacher where all the water had gone. The teacher asked her to explain herself. She said that in science class she had learned that all water was part of a larger cycle, that the water in the ocean went up into the clouds before being rained down again. If there was a huge flood all over the Earth, where did the water drain to? Did it evaporate into heaven?

The teacher stood from his desk and called her up without ornament. He led her into a tiny office in the corner of the room and shut the door. From behind the thick wood, the class heard the muffled power of an adult using their voice at full power. Individual words were slammed together and produced an effect of thunder drawing nearer. The class covered themselves in silence, heads near to their papers, and fought to keep them that way when the door opened again. From the rectangular shadow, the girl emerged with her chin tucked and her wrists vibrating. She returned dutifully to her seat while the teacher followed, scanning and surveying the rest of the class. We said nothing, we did nothing—it was that noise, in such a small space, that frightened us.

These trepidations were not to be voiced during class or at any other time. Our teachers, who were not ordained, were volunteers from the community and thus represented the secret opinions that walked around our city. They were the parents, the store owners, the bankers, and the bus drivers who all passed through life unnoticed with only their small crosses, hidden beneath layers of sweaters, to identify them. They all looked calm and smiled at our parents as they took us away to our basement classroom. However, when it came to matters of the Bible, they were as strict as rulers.

It was in this drifting through my memories that I came back to Stephen's words just as he spoke on the current and longstanding history of child abuse in the Catholic Church. His accounts ran parallel to the day after Church when the girl had been berated for her insolence. Dad's parents were in town for a visit. After Church, they engaged us in questions about what we were learning and if we were ready for our Confirmations. I tried to be polite but I couldn't keep the honesty of my experience inside. In front of my parents, I asked my Grandad why were the Sunday School teachers so mean? A blackness spilled into his eyes like oil into a pool and all the muscles of his face softened. His time was a different time and, looking back, I imagined he was rolling over his own incidents with Catholic schoolteachers and was now recontextualizing them on the life of his grandson. He must have assumed something much worse than a verbal thrashing. No, what he was remembering was much more penetrating.

None of the adults spoke. By turning to silence, a discomforting truth emerged. It spoke a shameful knowledge and verified that I had seen the darkness properly. They have still never overtly said whether or not there was that kind of abuse in their tiny town in Newfoundland. But if it had occurred there, could there be an innocent place anywhere?

I tried to restrain my mental drifting and focus on the video. As if abuse wasn't enough, Stephen next commented on the Church's relationship and description of homosexuals. According to his notes, the Pope himself had publicly declared that gay people were guilty of a moral evil. Why? Simply for fulfilling their sexual destiny as they saw fit. Nothing more. They hadn't robbed a land of its greatest antiquities, hadn't chosen harm as a default method of child-rearing, hadn't told anyone that by failing to be a part of their group they were to be cursed eternally. No, the moral evil that gay people had been condemned for was due to how they loved.

Stephen described himself as being someone who was filled with love. Whose principal aim in life was to experience it and share it as openly as available. Love. Was that not the crucial message of that slim man on the cross? To love your neighbour as you love yourself? That was the highest teaching from this great teacher. Yet here was a man who had shuffled off all relations to the truth of the doctrine and could still carry on its prime message. He realized the highest teaching in my religion without believing in it and that was stunning.

How could it have been that those on the side of the Church, my Church, had not championed this noble feeling in their speeches? While I hadn't seen them, if their opponent had taken this position, it must have been left open. When I thought of my religion, the words love or kindness did not surface. Instead it was a coterie of guilt, sin, suffering, and repetition that poked through the flotsam. Channelled into an institution, the purpose of this religion should have been easy to describe. The Catholic Church was a force for good in the world because it understands, teaches, and demonstrates the principles of compassion, tenderness, and love that its founder believed in. They, being true to their ideal, had built their Church on the rock of those ideals. Instead they were flooded with scandals, breaches of integrity, and a story so saddled with inconsistencies against modern knowledge that their power proved dimmer as time passed. This was the erosion of my faith in real time.

When I started watching these videos, it was out of an innocent curiosity. It was like putting on a violent movie at a low volume and always keeping an ear out for a parent's footsteps. Now, I wasn't just thinking about matters of religion but reckoning with them. What did I actually believe? What was most honest? It had only been a short time, but a knife only needs a second to carve a permanent scar.

I did not want to watch the mountain of my belief slide into crumbling despair. It was built so marvellously, wasn't it? A firm fixture that each sentence from Stephen and the others rumbled like earthquakes, loosening the rocks towards an unstoppable disaster. And with every bit that fell, through the mourned loss of stable beauty, was a dawn whose colours had been hidden all my life. This Church, this corporation, had stood so tall it blotted out the sun and now its tip had collapsed. What was to remain of myself if I couldn't see its point anymore? I could inly hope that the extra sunlight would also bring more warmth.

In the closing of his speech, Stephen changed tactics. Instead of leaning on his innate connection with language or his performative bravado, he adopted the stance and tone of a pleading man. He reinforced the necessary pluralism of life, that we must be open to other methods of studying and discussing what is true, beautiful, and just. That there is more to life than the Catholic Church. While it would have been a fine ending, he dropped down from the expansive and theoretical to one pondering point. One that was left to drift through the imaginations of the audience with the lightness and contrast of a cardinal's feather fallen on snow.

If there was ever a person who would feel ill-at-ease or be outright inadmissible from the contemporary Catholic Church, with its massive relics and appalling wealth, it would be that Galilean carpenter. The man for whom all of this was founded. I had seen the Vatican on a school trip and when Stephen mentioned the discrepancy between the founder and the organization, a vignette appeared.

I thought of a man in tattered robes, hunched from labour, seated on the steps of the Vatican. He looked out over the central obelisk and wondered, in passing, where it had come from. There was grime on his face that had blended with his flesh and his fingernails popped white against the further browning of his hands. Looking around at the other stones that circle the square, he checked over his shoulder at the massive cathedral that stood immovable and looming. He peered into the face of each of the paying travellers with their guides and cameras. Above all of them, a cloudless sky filled only with the relentless and ever-giving heat of the sun. This was not the place to cry but he did take several breaths from the depths of himself, each one twirling out in pity. He stood from his seat, offering sincere smiles to each passer-by. They returned with looks of blankness. When he stepped down onto the Earth that stabilized them all, he took one final visual tour around the structures. Examining the craftsmanship and mentally calculating the materials that must have been necessary. And in a voice barely perceptible to the passing people, he said "They don't know what they're doing" as he left the square, usurped and unwanted.

Stephen Fry didn't tell me any of that. Rather it was his suggestion that allowed it to elaborate freely. I hadn't wanted to admit it but at that time, before the video had ended, I was going to leave my Church. Perhaps in spirit I already had. But it wasn't a celebration. The feeling of connection I was forging for Stephen and the other speakers was one I should have rejected. I felt like I was peeling myself, and from this hanging skin, a new entity emerged. While free of its old covering, it was also vulnerable and lost the protection and warmth of the old flesh. The old, stretched security laid crumpled and decaying with a face that was now only capable of grinning.

The video played on and now Stephen was answering questions. As he spoke, his voice gathered intense momentum. The question must have provoked something personal that catapulted him through his most vibrant arguments. At the summit of his sentences, he said, "And what is the point of the Catholic Church if it says 'Oh, well, we couldn't have known better because nobody else did'—then what are you for?" He boomed the final word and I closed the browser.

What was the Catholic Church for? What had faith ever done? Questions I wished I could have flushed from my mind, vomited from my memory, and disappeared into all the sludge of the world. This organization was never to be challenged, only to be followed. We said prayers at holidays because that's just what we did, we gave things up for Lent because that's just what we did. But why did we do them? Why did those things please our god? The only people I had seen provide any meaning, anything like an explanation for the whims of the world, were those who told me that religion was fictitious. That the Catholic Church showed no objective proof to what they claimed and showed no advantage to decency nor truth. Rather, they had been proven to be masters of suffering and bondage.

What more was there to see? I had been shifted, altered, like a shirt after gaining weight and there was no longer room in my old identity. Maybe I could have forced it, acted like the buttons weren't straining to be fastened over the increased girth; but, as any reflection would have shown, it was no longer meant for me.

I started to feel ill. It was as if my inner conflict twisted me up into a knot that would have won the envy of a sailor. As more time and thought passed, I couldn't believe I had overlooked the most important ramification of this newfound truth: my family. They were Catholics—all of them.

Or at least, they all said they were.

Chapter Seven

More than a week passed and I hadn't said any-thing. I was too busy snooping, inspecting my parents and my sisters for signs that they too had dashed faith away. How could I tell? It wasn't as if we acted as though there was a God informing our decisions and punishing our indiscretions. His name didn't even come up in conversation. We had no photos of the Pope around, no Bibles that I could find, and no pieces of scripture written in cursive on fridge magnets. For our ordinary purposes, we already lived like we were on our own.

Still, it wasn't an opinion I was prepared to boast about. The game was too treacherous and its rewards minimal. If I was right then we'd continue on like we always had. But if I was wrong, I couldn't have guessed what my folks would say.

"Bye, Mum! Bye, Dad!" Céline shouted, unexpectedly.

"You're going out?" Mum said.

"Yes, do you remember my friend Mary? Anyway she and a couple of her friends said that they wanted to try to run into this guy Ryan after the basketball game tonight. So I was all, why are we waiting until after the game to maybe, hopefully, potentially run into him when we can go to the game—for free—and then catch up with him and the rest of the team afterwards. It's fine, it's flawless, and I'll be back before bed."

"I believe your mother asked for the time, not how to build a watch," Dad said.

Mum stood unmoved with her arms folded.

"Yes, Father. Sorry, Mother. What I meant to say was that my presence has been requested at the local basketball game tonight for young athletes and their friends. It is going to be a school-sanctioned event and I promise to be home before nightfall so I can get a proper rest before continuing in my very important studies tomorrow. May I attend?"

Only Céline. Mum let out a pleased puff and said, "Yes, dear, go ahead. Have fun."

"Thank you! Love you! Bye!"

She let the door slam behind her and the objects nearby rattled momentarily. I heard the exchange and came down the stairs. It was just Mum and Dad in the kitchen.

"Where is everybody?" I asked.

"Céline's gone out for the evening last minute and Hélène has water polo tonight," Mum said. She looked off greyly as her words floated out.

"Oh, so it's just the three of us for dinner?"

"Looks that way. Unless your father also has somewhere else he'd rather be."

Dad picked his head up like a startled ostrich, sticking a finger in his own chest as if to say "Who? Me?"

"I heard something about your dear *père*. What did I do this time?"

"It's nothing, dear," Mum said, "I was just saying that the girls are out so it's going to be a smaller group at the table tonight."

"Don't you worry, my belle, I'm not going nowhere. Not unless you're secretly fixing to get rid of me!"

"Please don't make jokes like that. Not now."

Dad lowered his chin and raised his hands in surrender. His wisdom overtook his wit as he put his paper down and glided over to place one soft kiss on her cheek.

"It's okay," Mum said. "It's not Sunday so the rules can be a bit more flexible."

We used to eat dinner as a family every night. Everyone was not only expected to be there but also participate in the conversation. Even as children, our parents didn't shy from talking about their work or asking our opinions about our lives as we saw them. The dinner table was a sacred surface over which the rest of our lives paused. It was a gentle force that held us as a unit over which we could laugh, discuss, reminisce, and prod. Now, that force, that tether of an in-house tradition, was withering with age.

It first began with Hélène's volunteering and other extracurriculars. We were so proud that she was giving back to the community that her missing seat was a point of pride. It meant someone from our group was off in service to others. A noble reason for departing. Then Céline got a bit older and leveraged the logic towards her own personal deeds. She would need to be excused for events and entertainment, citing Hélène's departure as proof that the dinner ceremony could continue without all its members. Mum and Dad were caught in their own hypocrisy if they didn't let her go and no one wanted that argument. There was no rift, no break—only a gradual disappearance that turned a ritual into a rarity.

Without my sisters, I suddenly had my parents all to myself. They probably didn't see our situation that way. Every uneven evening must have been a reminder that they couldn't hold us as we were forever. Family dinners would go from an every night affair, to a few times a week, until the only times we were convivial together were the holidays. Habits would turn to new traditions, even if we didn't recognize them.

"Declan," Mum said, "could you set the table?"

"Sure," I said, dreamily.

She did her best to smile as I passed by. Dad showed no urgency to check on the meat. The timer would go when it was needed and then he would move. Until then, he was fine not acting. I pulled open the cutlery drawer to the familiar rummaged clinking of forks and knives. The kitchen was filled with the simple smell of lightly salted potatoes roasting in the oven while the wafts of meat on the barbecue blew in and out like waves. The two scents went together so well it was hard not to imagine one without the other. Both were hearty and made the other stronger with their combination. The timer went for the barbecue and Dad sprung up to grab the centre of our course, dashing past Mum as he went.

With all the meal's components warm and assembled, we each took our designated seats. No one knew how the seating had been established, only that it felt right, and if Dad and Hélène switched spots one night, we might not have been able to explain why it was so wrong. Normally, the sounds of competitive conversation would be tossed back and forth. My sisters would have been vying for first to talk about school, Dad may have told a story from back home, and Mum liked to bring up current affairs or a pointed "Would You Rather" scenario. This left me as the quietest part of the quintet, a stem overshadowed by four leaves of a clover. Though I tried not to think of myself in those exact terms. I enjoyed listening to their lives so, really, I was like a cozy house with its lights on underneath a fireworks show. They were the entertainment and I the great spectator.

Without my sisters, the loudest thing at the table was the silverware. My parents kept looking at each other and then to me and I scanned them back, waiting for one of them to speak first. We were as awkward as new actors, unsure as to how best to perform to a new audience.

"So, Declan, how's that current events project coming along?" Dad said.

"My current events? It's good, it's all good. It was a really quick unit so we kind of breezed through it and now we're on to other stuff. More Canadian history stuff."

I hadn't told them what I had written about atheism and what it meant to me now. Nor did I mention that my teacher had praised what I had done for its enthusiasm. There was an inchworm of guilt bending up and down through my intestines.

"I figured as much," Dad said. "I noticed my

watching partner wasn't around this last week. It's too bad, really, you missed some right good episodes of the show. All matter of proper drama and backstabbing—it's a wonder people watch anything else! It's like these political yuck-yucks who spend all their time campaigning against each other, telling me—the voter—why I shouldn't vote for their competition. That their ways for fixing things are bunk. Now, once all that's over, they're coming around saying they've smoothed everything over and it'll be better for the country if we let them work together. Fat chance, I say. All they're interested in, and maybe this would be something to tell your teacher, all they're interested in is their own selfishness. Never mind the fact that the people don't want them in charge, you can't just go around the rules to get what you want. And I didn't even vote for the idiot who got in! But it's the process that has to be respected, you understand? The way it's supposed to be done."

"You should send that into Rex Murphy. See if he'll close with it next week," Mum said.

"If only it was good enough for old Rex, but unfortunately, my head is full of words that everyone can understand."

"Oh, really?" I said. "Everyone can understand Newfoundlanders now?"

Dad took a forkful of potatoes to his mouth and chuckled as they went in. Short bursts of steam came out of his nose and as he held his stomach, he looked like a happy dragon. I laughed too, for a moment, but hoped the subject would move on from there.

"Is that what you chose to write about? This nonsense of parties trying to join forces?" Dad said.

The inchworm I felt before quickened its pace out of my stomach and up my spine. It touched its prickly feet up and down my vertebrae until it settled into the ventricles of my heart. There it swirled and flipped through the causeways of chambers, attempting with each movement to quicken the flow of blood.

"No, no, I wrote about one of the other stories from last week."

Mum and Dad leaned in, waiting to hear the rest. They didn't speak and instead left an open avenue for whatever I did write for my assignment.

"There were these people on, Dad probably remembers, and they were having this debate. About schools."

My mouth flopped around as looks of concerned anticipation spread across their faces in equal measure.

"And, yeah, I wrote about that thing we saw. It was pretty interesting and I did well on it."

I squirmed for a few moments more, appearing hesitant, bashful, and earnest. My face tilted down until I was looking at the mix of food I had made. Each colour absentmindedly smeared over the others.

"Now which one was that, Declan?" Dad said.

"You know, the one where there was the guy in-studio and the woman on the screen."

"You'll have to be a touch more specific. Are you talking about something the panel said at the end of the show? I'm telling you, those talking heads can be as boneheaded as the politicians sometimes—"

"Do you guys believe in God?"

The question fell out with the weight and noise of a dropped piano. Mum's ears pulled back as the rest of her face scrambled to catch them. Having caught Dad mid-rant, he started choking and coughing on his meal. He turned pinker than a newborn as he reached for something to drink.

"I'm sorry, b'y, can you say that again?"

"That assignment, I wrote it on those people arguing about God in schools and I was wondering if you guys still believed in that sort of stuff."

They didn't look at me but across to each other first. Each wore an unreadable expression that looked somewhere between bafflement and incredulity. It was as if they had been tied together by a line and now, after the surge of such a wave, they were looking over the crests to see if they were still connected.

"Of course we do!" Dad finally said. Mum nodded automatically but not fervently. "What could possibly make you say such a thing as that? Did that guy last week convince you of something? Declan, you know he was just trying to start a fight."

Mum's head kept even time as she reached a hand out to touch his arm. Her first two fingers spun in small circles near his elbow.

"It's just—I'm not so sure anymore." I kept my eyes downcast like a guilty puppy. "And it's not just that one guy from the news, but I've been hearing a lot of people talk about what they think of religion and, I don't know, I'm not sure I still believe like I used to."

Both of them receded into silence. They had outdone all of my predictions and now I couldn't know how they would continue. Looking into their faces, they showed depth of thought. They knew what they believed but they must never have had to articulate that belief before. It was a turbulent air—especially given that it had been launched from their own child. We sat without eating, without talking for a freezing amount of time. It took Mum's courage to be the icebreaker.

"Y'know, growing up when I did, there were a lot of people who had their problems with what was going on in the Catholic Church. There was a lot of pushback over the control they had and the influence and all that. And while, maybe, there's a part of me that would like to agree with them, would like to turn my back on all the horrible things they've done, I just can't because that's my heritage. The Church is part of my background, it's my family, it's my home. So, yes, to go back to your original question, I do believe in God. Not because the Church is perfect but because I feel at peace when I think about Him because it's nice to know that there's always someone watching out. That there's always someone who cares. I don't know, maybe your Dad has a different take on it but, for me, that's what it's about."

I was surprised at her response and, judging by Dad's face, it was the first time he had heard it too. Across his now cherry-tinged face, several feelings fought for presentation. While there might have been surprise, guilt, unpreparedness, they all mixed into the concoction of perplexity. He didn't look vengeful, nor indignant. The spirit of his eyes looked at both of us deeply as he placed his hands on the table and interlocked his fingers. He shook them like they were cold before he extended his first fingers in anticipation of his point. When he was ready, he sat back in his chair.

"It's a very big question, but one I can answer seriously. Yes, I do, I do believe in God and that He is present in all of our lives. But if that's not enough, I can also tell you why. When I was about your age, maybe a little younger, actually, I also had my doubts. Not to mention my fair share of bastard priests that, though they thought they were doing their best to keep me in line with the Lord, they were actually pushing me away from Him. I used to shake so badly walking up to Church, especially in my hands, that I insisted on walking three paces behind my parents so as not to let them catch it."

Of all the old man's stories, he had never so much as hinted at this one. The way his voice searched to place the words betrayed their inexperience in the open. They stepped out of his mouth carefully like they were getting into a hot bath.

"Anyway, life went on, and I never told anyone about what I really thought about the whole situation. If your grandparents knew that I had become a doubter or, worse, a Protestant, I'd've been out on my arse faster than the shore hits the beach. I went on through school and met your mother, of course, and while I would never say that I didn't believe outright, I couldn't say I was sure neither. It wasn't until, actually, you were born that I really got it, really understood what it felt like to be imbued with God's presence.

"You know the story already, of how you got your name and all that, and how I finally got one over on your Mum. But the part you might have missed, because you've not been in that kind of a situation yet yourself, was the fear of being there in that moment. They had put your mother under, in order to deliver you, and, after I snuck away to get the name right, she was supposed to be awake again. The doctors said she might be a bit groggy, but awake nonetheless. When I came back into the room, holding you, with all the world's excitement to show you off, she wasn't there. She was still knocked out and lay on that gurney unmoving. Some doctor took you and placed you inside one of them boxes for newborns. He told me she had had an adverse reaction to the chemicals or medicines or whatever and now they were working at bringing her back from the brink. Your sisters were home with my parents, of course, and I was now in a room with a son I couldn't hold and a wife who wasn't there.

"I don't think even your mother knows this, but I'll tell the both of you now. On that day, I was the most scared as I've ever been in my life. I sat in the whiteness of that room, alone, detached, and just scared. I was scared my wife wasn't going to wake up and now, with this new baby, it'd be up to me to raise you up all by myself. I wasn't even thinking about the girls but, well, I guess that would've been on me too."

He paused for a second and, looking up, I saw all the little flecks of rainbows that glistened across his eyes.

"A man has to have limits on himself, otherwise he'll be too quick to be run over by everything life has. In all my worry, I was just thinking, thinking, thinking—trying to figure out what I was going to do if everything awful happened. Then, like a new wind, I heard a voice in my head that wasn't my own. It wasn't big like the sea or a drum or something, but it was certainly full. I suppose it was more like a cello with its great power blended with its melody. It spoke in calming tones, told me that my wife and my son were going to pull through, and that all I needed to do was show patience and let the work of life be done. That was the word of God in my ear, my son. That was heavenly reassurance. Soon as it'd finished, your mother began to stir amongst her sheets and machines. You did too. We were going to be okay, just like I had been told."

Dad's face was washed in recollections as Mum slid her hand to his wrist.

"Your dad is right, you know. We, at this table, can see all the problems with the Church as an organization and how they go about their business. But what is important is that God shows up for us, that we know He's there because we can feel it."

She cast her eyes over to Dad in search of confirmation. He buttoned his lips and heavily moved his chin towards his neck.

But I hadn't felt it. When I needed god to show up, there was absence. He hadn't left any clues and if there was a time for him to make himself known, he had certainly had enough. These new ideas had shuttled in that void left by his negligence. I could confirm them because they didn't require any outside engagement to be true.

They were and that was all.

Mum and Dad were still looking at me like it was my turn to speak. I took a pause before I answered, wanting to be sure about what I would say next. How could I tell them that it wasn't just the arguments but the times that god had failed to show up when I needed him? Would they be able to handle what had been kept away?

"I guess what I've been wondering about is how can it be that there is such a thing as a god and still so much awful stuff in the world," I said.

"What're you saying?" Dad said.

"I mean, if the people that are supposed to be working for god can do so many bad things, and they can justify themselves by saying they were ordered to, then who is this guy? What does god really stand for? If he has a message, and it's one of peace and love, and he can talk to all of us, why not just broadcast it? And if he's so great, why can't he stop the things clearly going wrong under his watch? Why does he have to play hide and seek with us?"

The momentum of my questions was becoming unrelenting so I stopped myself. When I sat back there was an empty reply from my parents. I thought I might have felt some kind of superiority or cleverness akin to the smug smiles of my newfound heroes whenever they verbally smited their adversaries. Instead, I saw awkward discouragement. They were like boxers with dropped hands, conceding to a fightless surrender. If there had been a mirror opposite me, I would have looked like a wilting iris. Exposed, downturned, and showing a colour much less vibrant than what I was known for.

They both must've been thinking. Neither so much as raised a fork to stall their brains and chew on their forming thoughts. Dad's forehead looked much more creased than I had noticed before. Even though he was only a placemat's distance away, there was nothing I surmised about what he was thinking.

Mum broke the silence to say something just to me.

"Is this something you've been thinking about often?"

"A bit, but only more recently. I didn't know there was so much information out there and I didn't think I would have been so easily convinced."

She seemed content in that answer.

"So…" she said, now in English, "Does this mean you'll be rejecting going to Church from now on?"

"Maybe, but it's not like we have the best attendance there anyway."

Dad laughed. Not a big laugh but one that galloped him to his next point.

"I suppose we haven't been the best birds of the flock while you've been growing up. Do you think there's any chance they'll pass? Your doubts, I mean. Are you really sure you're right about them?"

"It's a strange thing to be certain about but I think I am. But I still want to be with the family and all that. I'm worried that I've stepped a different way now and you guys are way on another side while I'm over here by myself."

"Then why not just come back? Leave those things you've heard behind." Dad said.

"Because of all the things I've been taught to be, being honest is the most important. And, right now, going back on this doesn't feel honest. What do you think?"

"You know what, Declan, that's a very mature stance," Dad said. "One that, if I'm totally clear, I don't have an immediate giveback for. But I'd hate to see you throw away the God you were born to on the basis of a few night's thought. How about this: next week, on Sunday, we'll all go down to the Church and you can have a chat with Father Rogers about this little predicament you're in. I'm sure he sees this kind of thing all the time and will know exactly what to do to help you. How about it?"

Mum nodded along, her face round and open. I saw that I hadn't convinced them of my stance and accepted with a short smile. Dad seemed pleased as he dove back into his dinner, though now the food had gone tepid. They resumed the normal course of dinner conversation, going over their workdays, while I receded from the happenings. All my nerves whooshed down to my ankles, and though I was sure my skin was changing colour, either to silver or green, it wasn't mentioned and so must not have happened. I did believe Dad was serious about this trip to Father Rogers. Despite the horror stories I had been told about certain, nameless priests, the idea of going to see Father Rogers was as welcome as a warm drink. There was an inherent calm to his presence and that made him trustworthy.

That was also the first night I dreamed of the figure.

Chapter Eight

"I hear you're a heathen now."

Céline had come skipping into my room the next night and, after a twirl on her toes and a flop onto my bed, she announced herself with that statement.

"So?" I said.

"Oh, it's nothing. But actually, it's everything! Like, I cannot believe you just told Mum and Dad you're an atheist! Are you out of your mind? How did you think they were going to take your little news, eh?"

I kept scrolling through my computer as if unbothered by what she said.

"Seriously, dude? Come on. I'll bet you watched one video and now think you have the biggest brain because someone else told you Church is for idiots. Am I right or am I so right you'll never admit it?"

"You're not."

"Uh huh. Sure thing, big guy."

She tried to stay silent and pretended to be interested in the tidiness of my room. It wasn't enough that she barged in without knocking; her critical eyes were taking inventory of my space.

"So what made you tell them? Did Dad start in on

how we should all be praying in schools and you flipped? Tearing his ideas apart with facts and logic? Or did you think you could change them, turn them away from the Light?"

"It was just something I felt I needed to say."

"You *needed* to? Oh, please. Get out of your tower for a second. Are you saying it's like when you really have to pee on a road trip but you're boxed in by a bunch of luggage so much that the water bottle starts to look like a good option? Even if you call out 'Mum! Dad! Can we stop please? I don't think there's a God anymore!' Was it like that or were you more surreptitious about it? You know, I've never taken you to be much of a conniver. No offence, but if I was planning to commit a major crime, you're not on my list of possible accomplices."

I turned to face her. There was no way of satisfying everything she thought so I decided I would only answer her first question and nothing else.

"I needed to tell them because there's something inside me now that I'm not sure about, okay? So I said it out loud so I could hear how it sounded and see if I really believed it. Okay? It was about seeing if I had the courage of my convictions."

"You did not! Really? That is so hokey! That's like what people say in the movies Mum likes to watch when she's baking when the characters can't think of anything better to say. 'Courage of my convictions,' honestly. How are you going to survive as a big freethinker if you're stuck with explanations like that?"

I turned back to my desk without retort. Céline must

not have been finished because she put her hand on the back of my chair and spun it to face her again.

"Come on, I'm being serious here. Let's start fresh, okay? Hi, Declan, it's me. I've heard you had a talk with Mum and Dad about God and how you don't think you can believe anymore. What I would like to know is what compelled you to reveal yourself? And where, may I ask, did you find these grandiose ideas? Was it the internet? Television? A dusty and flimsy book, mayhaps?"

"I don't know. Forgive me for assuming that since we never talk about the stuff and we only go to Church when absolutely necessary that they might have been waiting for someone to admit it. I didn't think it'd be this big of a stink."

"It's literally the biggest stink in the world, Declan! It's the reason for words like damnation and paradise and... and.. *câlisse de tabarnak!*"

"I know!" I hated when she showed off her vocabulary. "It still seems like nobody nowadays really believes like they used to so why is it such a big thing if I drop off?"

"When I was your age—" the corners of my eyes and mouth dropped. At a whopping eighteen months older, who was she to start talking down to me as if she had spent all her life on some mountain with only a manifesto to keep company? She must have recognized my dissatisfaction as she wiped the air with her hand and started over.

"A little while ago, I had thoughts that were just as, shall we say, edgy. I thought that all the music Mum and

Dad listened to was safe crap. They wouldn't understand the eyeliner and the hair that covered their faces, and they certainly wouldn't get why the sound of quick power chords is the best thing that's ever been recorded. And would you like to know why I never put their posters on my wall or asked for their CD's for Christmas? Because I knew if they got one look at those bands or, heaven forbid, saw that little Parental Advisory sticker on the cover of an album, I'd have been locked up in some kind of chaste prison until I was 35. Get it? I know they seem nice and like they're on your side, but don't forget that they're still parents and parents frighten easily. Scaring them isn't something you want to do and hearing that your kid doesn't believe in God, it's scary to hear, Declan. Parents don't just think about things as they're happening, they're always worried about what things will lead to. Sure, today it's atheism, but who's to say that tomorrow or next week it won't be licking blood off a baby's foot as part of some underground Satan orgy."

"You know that not believing in God also means I don't believe in Satan, right? That they're both equally fictional. Besides, I know Mum and Dad and I don't think they're like that."

"You wanna bet? You wanna bet your soul on it? Because this is bigger than just some fad in music. Declan, this is literally bigger than everything in the world."

She wasn't going to be satisfied until I relented and agreed with her proposition. I was in too stubborn a mood to concede anything so I thought fast.

"Céline, you're forgetting something."

"What? No I'm not."

"Yes, you are. You're forgetting that I'm the youngest and that means I can get away with more than you've ever dreamed."

She slapped my arm and stormed off. It never failed to remind her that I always got to do things younger than her and Hélène. Go to sleepovers, stay out later on weekends, and be trusted to be home by myself. Once an activity had proven safe for the two of them, it must have been okay for me. As the sound of her footsteps disappeared, my head filled with wonder about who she thought our parents were. They weren't the type to scream and punish like that, were they? Just for what we thought?

I turned back to my computer, thinking I might watch some more atheist videos but knowing I should have been catching up on schoolwork. A knock touched my door. It was light and unobtrusive so I guessed it was Hélène.

"Hey, you got a sec?"

With the tone of a disappointed teacher and the posture of a hanging streetlight, she waited for my response.

"Sure, yeah, come in."

Hélène walked in with consideration. She sat on the very edge of the bed and brushed away the creases leftover from Céline's flop.

"Mum and Dad told us about your little conversation the other night."

"And?"

"And I wanted to talk with you about it?"

"Why? So you can tell me how much of an idiot I am?"

"Do I look like Céline?" She raised the middle of her eyebrows and tilted her head. "No, I wanted to hear your side of all this. Mum and Dad are pretty good at being truthful, but after what they told us, I wanted to see how you're doing? What are you thinking about?"

She paused and leaned forward on her elbows. Her face was free of prejudice, holding itself ready to react in any direction. Still, there was a thin layer of hope over it all, upturned and overt. The space in the room was free for my response.

"There's not much to tell. I think it's a really simple situation: I was raised to believe in god, just like everyone else, then I heard some evidence that went against that idea, and now I can't claim to believe with the same honesty. What's the big problem with being rational?"

"There's no big problem with being rational, not at all. What kind of evidence have you heard? Where did it come from?"

"I just watched some videos and did some reading online."

"Okay. And how long did it take to change your mind?"

"A night."

Hélène sat without reply and kept still. After a few seconds, she lowered her head and nodded a bit. If she wasn't going to continue talking, then I was compelled to say something. Otherwise we'd end up stuck in this weird silence.

"Look, I don't get what all the fuss is about. After all, the church is obsessed with people changing in one day.

You get baptized once, you only have one confirmation, and then there's the huge deal about the first communion. How is it so impossible for everyone in this house to believe that I had an anti-religious experience with the same power as a religious one? When someone gets baptized, people don't keep coming up to them to check if they were really dunked. Besides, once you've heard about the inaccuracies and falsehoods of the Bible, it's kind of hard to unhear. Like, what else am I to do once I've heard that there isn't actually any evidence for Jesus outside of that book? Or that the timelines don't match up to reality, or all of the contradictions, or even the fact that the church itself has no consistency with its own rules! Those are the sorts of things I know now and it's kind of hard to forget."

This frustration was the kind that arrived when something was so clear but inarticulable. The sort that could have been mitigated by the other person giving into trust and sharing in the reaction. But Hélène wasn't reacting like I was. She wasn't incensed, nor was she shocked. Taking each of my gripes without a comeback, she crossed her ankles and closed her grip on the duvet. We both avoided eye contact.

"Those are some pretty damning accusations, I must say," she said.

"But you get it, right?"

"I'm sorry, Declan, I don't think I do. And while I hear all the points you're making, it seems to me that there's more to belief than the basic facts. People don't go to Church in order to learn the exact facts of the world.

They go to get an idea of what to believe in when those facts aren't enough. Because we may know exactly how old the Earth is and can pick apart the inconsistencies of a character, but what value does any of that have when a loved one dies? Or when you're in peril? God—and religion—are there to give us something to fill our lives with and so that we never have to feel alone. I suppose that's why the facts against faith haven't worked on me: they don't help with the loneliness of everything."

"You'd rather live with something you knew was false just because it makes you feel better?"

She paused and considered her response.

"I think so. I think that's a noble sacrifice. And when people hear these stories, they do the same."

"But people don't just hear these stories, Hélène, they take them to be the basic facts of the world. How could they? A person can't live inside a whale and a snake can't actually talk. Everyone knows that. If they're wrong about those things, how can I know they're right about anything else they say is true? How can I believe that there was also a man who died, came back, and can also take on all the sufferings of everyone, everywhere?"

Hélène opened her hands and raised her palms towards me.

"It's okay, I hear you. I hear where you're coming from. But don't you think you're thinking in terms that are a bit too big? Just because you belong to an organization or a group doesn't automatically make you an accomplice in every wrongdoing they've ever performed. Besides, even if this organization has done some bad things—"

"Some wicked things," I interrupted.

"Sure. Maybe we can use that word. However we describe them, that doesn't change the stories themselves. Everyone can still learn something from them, whether they believe in them or not."

"But that only proves that these stories get their morality from us and not the other way around. We, the human beings, are the informers of these concepts and don't need a divine, totalitarian regime to dictate to us what's right and wrong. We make up the stories, we inform the morality, and we're the ones who can leave them behind when they become ridiculous. I mean, it just doesn't make any sense. If someone had a genuine religious experience, they'd be locked up in today's world because we know now that behaving in such a way is the same as being insane. Hearing voices, seeing things that aren't there—come on, Hélène! I thought you'd understand best of everyone."

I expected her to hear the inherent plea shaking across the sentences. She was such a lover of science and was considering becoming a scientist herself, why wasn't she ahead of me with these ideas? The chain that should have connected us wasn't breaking but slacking as if each word was another link ready to catch at a long distance. Hélène shifted back and forth, depressing her shoulders before standing up to leave. I hoped she wouldn't. If she couldn't put my broken knowledge back together again, then who could? As she was moving towards the door, she spun back to face me with one hand carefully placed on the doorknob.

"One last remark."

"Yes?"

"What are you going to tell Grandma and Grandad?"

I opened my mouth instinctively to reply. My lips rounded and then relaxed, dropping down as a light puff of breath exited. None of the men I had seen on screen had an answer, there was no carving from which to trace. I didn't know what I'd tell them because I hadn't considered that issue.

Hélène smiled to herself.

"If that's your best, I'd spend tonight dreaming up something as forceful as what you've been regurgitating. It'll probably crush them to hear about it."

She didn't speak with self-aggrandizement but with pity. It was as if my choice had begun to pluck the petals of the family's flower. The religion that I had inherited now felt like some kind of mental heirloom from their generation. Sets of ideas and practices to be performed on grainy film with jerky movements. Now that film had withered and holes burned through its corners. My intestines squirmed as I took to my bed, face up, like a stranded turtle.

There was now some doubt in my doubt. It had been so easy to flutter away from the Church when thinking about it in its largest terms. The most glaring evils had been shown as the natural state of the organization through history. But what about the Church of the everyday? The one common people visit, require, and commiserate. The thought had turned me into a wrung-out sponge as I let myself become clothed in uncertainty. It had looked so easy to deny my former faith, so straight-forward to ditch the institution which claimed its truth. As I looked up into my cottage-cheese ceiling, I felt like I did in the hallways of my middle school: beseeching the heavens and being met with resolute silence.

Chapter Nine

The nervous Sunday arrived and the whole family was set for Church. Expectedly, the atmosphere was tense with darting eye contact and little talk over the breakfast table. Mum and my sisters had done their hair up so tightly that each bun resembled a knot in a tree. Dad's tie was knotted unevenly and it hung down long like the tongue of an exhausted dog.

I missed the bustle and jostle of when we were kids. Getting sent back upstairs to change into newer or better fitting clothes, Dad scrambling through breakfast, and Mum kneeling down to make sure everyone's faces were clean. On those days, if we caught our reflection, we were not met with the slapdash fashion of our regular wardrobe. Oversized graphic t-shirts and layered tank tops in several colours. Church clothes were much more subdued, they looked like what our parents wore when they were young. It was strange to see my head perched atop those outfits. While they were uncomfortable and stuffy, their power was not to be resisted. Dressing like that felt like armour and it changed the way I walked.

On this morning, everyone got ready in isolation. My sisters didn't cry out for help with hair-clips. I had left all my ties knotted so there was no need to bring one to Dad draped over my open palms like a lifeless snake. We didn't model ourselves down the stairs and we didn't get sent back up for alterations. I missed the catchphrases, the ceremony of it all. If I was ready, one of my parents would say that I looked like a fine young man and that was the final boost necessary to sustain a morning in church. Hélène and Céline must have had similar lines that I never paid attention to. Compliments like that coloured the air of the place and when they weren't given, their absence made life less vivid.

None of the neighbours were out when we filed into the car. If they had been, they could have sworn we were on our way to a funeral. Perhaps we were. A funeral of who we used to be as a unit because my undermining had killed it. The car continued with an equally awkward air. Dad switched on the radio and scanned through the various upbeat stations before shutting it off entirely. It would be easier to forget if there was no music. Holding this secret tightly, we walked into the church embarrassed. It was as if we were the only people who couldn't read minds in a room full of telepaths. Every gesture, every move made by the rest of the congregation was taken politely, but with the self-consciousness of an actor forgetting how to walk normally across a stage. I figured everyone who looked at us for more than a second intuited there was some rotten between us and if we kept eye contact too long, they'd figure it out. They would know the sincerity of my faith had been dashed from my soul and I was there as an imposter.

Céline pulled out her phone.

"What are you doing with that?" Dad said.

"I'm just texting a friend, Dad."

"Put it away and you can do that after Church. You don't text in God's house. Can't believe there's even a signal in here."

She opened her mouth to fire back another stacked quip before Mum leaned out with an icy stare that said "Do *not* right now." Céline conceded and nestled back into her seat for a moment. Then she pulled one of the Bibles from the slit in the pew ahead of us and began thumbing through it. Occasionally, she tilted it in Dad's direction, pages open wide like heart surgery, with an expression on her face as if to say, "Is this better, Father?" He nodded, not seeing the sarcasm in the gesture and she mimed reading and leaned over to me.

"It's such a shame there isn't much of a description of Hell in here. Oh well, you'll just have to scream up and tell us what it's really like once you get there."

I was about to cut back, but Mum interrupted in French with the sternness of Napoleon.

"You two will not fight in here. You will both sit facing Father Rogers for the duration of the service. And you will both participate in all parts of the day. Understand?"

We knew it took more than a nudging to force out Mum's quills. Hélène looked over with a hint of disappointment that neither of us could believe. Seeing that all sides were against us, we nodded in unison to admit defeat. Céline tucked the Bible away, patted down any flyaways, and sat in rigid posture. A family in a row, looking ahead, each in a different state of internal distress, not talking. If only Norman Rockwell was there to capture it.

This was my first time in a church since shedding my belief and it became disenchanted and cold, even with the occasional, nostalgic interpretations. The stone of the walls had before seemed so out of place and foreign to the wood and concrete that dominated the city's architecture. Now it felt bleak and earthy, as far removed from the reverence of god as any object. Without the sun shining through the stained glass windows, their colours looked tired and hidden as if to have no artistic power without the addition of nature. And while they may have looked good then, wouldn't anything in that style? The fact that they were religious icons did nothing to add or subtract from their beauty.

I did like the way the pillars over the pews were joined by long arcs which spread out over the ceiling like waves. They were pleasing to look at as each line led the eye to the connections of the others, and as they got farther away, they tightened in their grouping until they appeared as one solid mass of wood. But down on the ground, the pews were even more uncomfortable than I remembered and the air in the place was surprisingly dry. I thought about how big churches used to seem, how mesmerizing they were. Now that I had seen some more of the secular world, there didn't seem to be a difference in impression between a place like this and a gallery or the halls described in fantasies about European schools. Its bigness had become its distance. I saw no god in the architecture, no spirit in the smoke, and no Christ in the congregation. The glowing face of that thorny king would have been out of place down here. All the faces that passed looked like the most ordinary of people. The same examples of tiny politeness, automatic boredom, brief obligation, or rare engagement that could just as easily have been displayed on a city bus.

My roving thoughts and observations were interrupted by the start of the service. The gentle charisma of Father Rogers was blowing across the room. His ability to command a room without demand must have been why we settled in this church as opposed to the others we had tried. That or it was the fact that, since he was Haitian, and had worked in Montréal, Mum felt he would be best suited for our family. He was exactly six feet tall, even with concentration, I couldn't imagine him as a child. With a touch of girth and a well-lined face, he was the sort of man designed for autumn clothes. When he spoke, he allowed himself to be alight with engagement, as if speaking in front of people was his most joyous task. Even against my teenage cynicism, it was hard not to pay attention to the sincerity of Father Rogers.

"Good morning, everyone, and thank you all so very much for being here with us today." Father Rogers paused and looked out with smiling eyes over the congregation. His hands were folded over each other like sleeping doves. He didn't appear to be in a rush through his duties and took the fullness of the moment to be with the people in the room before leaning forward slightly over the podium. "If I may ask your forgiveness a moment for losing my place. Before we begin with today's lesson, there is an exciting announcement that I am privileged to share with you. A few weeks ago, two of our members brought forth the most wonderful of all miracles: the miracle of a new child. As I understand it, this is the couple's first and, yesterday, they called me up to ask if I would be able to baptize their newest addition today. I asked them if the child was healthy and they said yes. I asked them if the child was home and they said yes. Then I asked them if the child was sleeping and they said they were working on it." A soft chuckle frolicked over the room. "Ah, the joys of new parenthood. So much to experience for the first time. Anyway, I suppose I had better stop myself if we are to get on with the events of the day. Larry, Fran, would you please bring the little one up here to the front?"

The room turned over hunched shoulders. After our efforts, I expected to see a charming couple with perfect hair, striding with their child in an unstained cloth. Before any of us saw them, we heard their baby. Its squawks and shrieks bounded all over the curves of the church like rubber balls. The haggard parents moved quickly up the central aisle as I glanced into their swaddle, thinking I might see a tightly bound seagull poke up through the fabric. Father Rogers did not seem concerned. He chuckled as he received the baby and stepped away from its parents towards the small pool of holy water.

He took great care to lower the crown of the baby's head across the meniscus. Even though the water was cold, Father Rogers moved slowly and calmly, supporting the weight of the child fully in his arms throughout the ritual. The parents craned their necks as their arms wrapped around each other with fingers fully intertwined. I thought about what they must really be believing at that moment. That their child, until now, had been invisibly stained, inherently soiled in such a way that required immediate cleansing. The only way in which they could begin the process of purifying their little life would be to clean it publicly and, somehow, that made them feel joy.

Yet there was nothing special about the water, not in its essence anyway. It came from a bottle and was now in a bowl and no amount of Latin over hand waving altered those facts. The water wasn't directly from god but had been here, in and on Earth since its inception. An ever-going cycle that saw it travel from the depths of the ocean, across the entirety of the sky, only to return, gushing, to all the land there was. This water, which provided life for all, had now been connected through a series of underground pipes, coiling and plunging their way through all of society so as to be summoned safely without thought. It didn't need to be enchanted because it was already amazing. An expression of the forces of life coupled with the ingenuity of human expansion.

Why did all of these people, these common, wholesome, troubled, and earnest people, feel the need to ascribe fictional meaning to this substance? Did they not see that the world was beautiful, charming, connected, vibrant, and interesting enough without the invocation of an outside being? Life was a thing to be celebrated on its own merits and did not require ceremony. I saw this ritual with the detraction of an anthropologist. After all, wasn't it odd that the Christians had to begin their lives by dunking themselves in water so that they could properly worship someone who walked above it? Did Christ know that when he took those steps, he froze everything in his wake? Ice covered a culture over all of those tricked into diving in to his sea. To continue to look up at him was to continue to waste the precious breath of life and submit to being trapped under its frigid hold. Breaking was necessary for freedom.

Father Rogers turned back, holding the child with firm grace as small beads ran clear over his head.

"Ladies and gentlemen, I'd like to introduce you all to our newest member: John William Henneberry."

A gentle release of emotion bloomed over the crowd. Music began and Father Rogers went over to the couple. They nodded their heads with eyes crinkled from happiness as Father Rogers turned to walk around the outside aisle of the church. Larry shepherded Fran back to their pew and looked out over the congregation, following Father Rogers's moves. When he and the baby stepped down from the front, I recoiled slightly in anticipation that the child would once again unhinge its jaw like a can and bellow into the stone of the ceiling. But there was no such disturbance. He had nestled comfortably near Father Rogers's heart as he was paraded around the space. Even when they walked by the organist, the child didn't stir. Sometimes, he turned his head to try and peek out at all of us. Father Rogers didn't stop him. Instead he waited for the boy to look back up at him so he could make a silly face and smile to himself.

After the song finished, Father Rogers returned the baby to his parents. He shook their hands with both of his and he returned to his podium.

"There is peace in that one, it just needs some help," he said.

With relieved faces, the new parents stared down into their swaddle as their son reached out to be held closer. They obliged, with Fran curling both her arms in and Larry draping one arm over his wife and the other across the baby. He remained silent for the rest of the service.

During the sermon, I couldn't help but be irritated by my conscience. An irritation caused by an over-critical interpretation of the story. I imagined myself powered by courage, pressing Father Rogers on how he or anyone else could verify the events of the story. On the legitimacy of the sources. On the truth. It would have been like my new idols had done when they exposed religious leaders for their inconsistencies in front of a changing public.

I hadn't considered that this was mental preparation for my incoming conversation. Like an athlete dreaming through the plays they would execute, so too was I making my expectations for how I could reveal to Father Rogers the errors of his life. Strangely, each scenario ended with him thanking me. Regardless of feelings this was not going to be a chat but a battle, a confrontation, whereby there would be a winner and a loser. Nevertheless, I physically participated in the rituals of the day even though my mind was deeply tangled in opposition. I stood when we had to stand, sat when we had to sit, read, sang, and received the proper rites of Communion in full irony. If there was a god, or if these people had any of his insights, they would've seen through my charade and proven that I was nothing but a poser. But they couldn't because they had no special power, no privilege over my life nor anyone else's.

The service ended on time. Many of the parishioners were old so they took more than a moment to regain their stances. Their feet were slow and heavy, barely letting go of the carpet while they moved. Dad took me by the arm and out of my seat.

"Now's the time. Come on, before they start serving the blue plate special," he said. feet moving swiftly in defiance.

Hurrying over before he, presumably, disappeared until next Sunday, Dad and I caught up to Father Rogers at the doors of the church. The women of the family must have been caught in the human mudslide shuffling through the central aisle, being pestered about who they were and how long they were in town.

"Father Rogers! A minute!" Dad exclaimed.

"Oh, Alan! How nice it is to see you again. And I assume this is, or used to be, little Declan?"

"Hi," I muttered, without enthusiasm.

"Hello to you too, Declan. Is it just the two of you today? I thought I saw the rest of the family back there too." Father Rogers said, looking out into the pews.

"Why they're…" Dad scanned behind him, only now noticing he hadn't been followed. He hastily waved his arm to signal our position and that they were to join us. Hélène was first to notice and so steered Mum and Céline away from a kind old woman in a long brown coat.

"Here they come, Father Rogers. The whole gang's here."

"Please, Alan, call me Lou."

"Alright, Lou," he said as awkwardly as a child calling their parent by their first name. "You remember my wife Jacquline and our daughters, of course, Helene and Celine."

"Of course! Hello again to all of you. Thank you for coming to today's service. It's so nice to see a whole family make time to spend together."

"The service, it was wonderful, Father, really," Mum said in uncharacteristic haste. "I know, I know we haven't been the most attentive family in recent years, but rest assured, we are still fully in it with the faith and the believing and everything."

"Oh, nonsense. After all, God doesn't keep an attendance sheet and neither do we. Our building is open to all whenever they are able to attend. Trust me, you're forgiven. And Hélène, Céline, how are we today?"

"Peachy, Father," Céline said.

"We're all doing well, Father. School is going great and it's always nice to be back at Church. I know I haven't had much time lately with committees and clubs," Hélène said.

"Marvellous!" Father Rogers said with a clap. "And, if my mental math is correct, you must be off to university soon, is that right?"

A brief stun went through us before Hélène snapped back into her reply.

"Yes, I'm all set for next year. I was accepted with a

full scholarship to the University of Victoria to study in their marine biology program."

"Marine biology, eh? Well, there's a subject I must confess I don't know very much about. But it is so interesting, isn't it? All that potential for new discoveries and inquiries. You'll have to be sure to write or visit when you're in town to tell me all about it. The ocean has always been a mysterious creation to me."

"That I will, Father."

All of us laughed a polite and pointless laugh, the kind so often done but so seldom recognized. We stood silent for a moment, surrounded by the leaves of fallen conversation. It was clear none of us wanted to speak up and Father Rogers had no interest in shooing us away. He must have been able to tell there was some reason for our gathering as we kept looking at each other without talking. But he didn't push us, instead he joined his hands together in front and stood with patience.

"Actually, Father, as much as we like coming here and seeing you, there's another reason for us being here like this," Dad finally said.

Father Rogers's posture loosened as his shoulders dropped back and his head titled innocently. His hands were still.

"You see, our youngest, Declan here, is undergoing a bit of a crisis of conscience, you might say. He's—"

"He's been corrupted, Father! He's saying he's an atheist! Oh please, please! Won't you help return him to the Light with the rest of us?" Céline said, dropping to her knees, hands dramatically clasped and shaking.

Dad's head twisted quickly as his eyes showed first discomfort and then disconcertment. He looked as though lightning was about to shoot out of his ears. Father Rogers, mouth closed and eyes low, gently extended the four fingers of his right hand in Céline's direction, so that she could see their underside. He might have shaken his head too. She dropped her head without irony, mumbled an apology, and slid back into position.

"Thank you for your contribution, Celine. Father, I apologize for the interruption, but what she's saying is true, in a way. It seems that Declan is… well… he's having a bit of a personal challenge, so-to-speak. He's been saying that he's not so sure that there's a God which, of course, we all know is just crazy."

A tumbling of nervous laughter followed. Father Rogers, however, appeared unmoved. He was calm and perfectly together, without so much as a twitching lip. I wondered how he could be so composed. Wasn't this the kind of news that threatened his livelihood?

"We were wondering," Dad continued, "if you have the time, of course, if you and Declan could have a little word about what he's been going through. Between the six of us here, his mother and I are a bit out of our depth on this matter and figured you might be a bit better choice since it can be difficult talking about these things with your kid."

Father Rogers waited until it was clear that Dad was done speaking. His stone face then cracked into an engulfing smile.

"Of course! I'd love to talk to Declan about his relationship with God. Would you like to meet us back here in, let's say, a half hour? Would that be alright, Declan?"

He lowered his level slightly so our eye contact was more direct. At that age, I was used to adults speaking at me, around me, or for me, but it was rare for one to speak to me. It was enough to squirm over. I nodded and grumbled, attempted to keep up a rebellious face, and Father Rogers clapped his hands in agreement.

"Then it's settled. Oh, and Alan, please don't feel you have to be back in exactly thirty minutes. I was taught to know myself and, if rambling can be considered a crime, then you can call me guilty."

"What are we going to do for a whole half-hour in these clothes?" Céline inquired, obviously not wanting to be seen at her Churchiest.

"We'll go sit down somewhere for lunch and maybe do a bit of window shopping," Mum said. "Let's leave the good Father to his work."

"Thank you, Father Rogers," Hélène said.

"Yes, thank you," Dad piled on. "We'll be back in about that time."

Dad gave me a handshake and Mum gave me a hug before they guided my sisters back to the car and headed off. I knew they were coming back but in the presence of the building and the man, the atmosphere of the situation changed. It was like a slack tide that suddenly and worryingly started receding. Father Rogers and I stepped out into the parking lot as the car drove off. We waved one last time. He smiled, I didn't.

"Would you like to go talk in my study or stay out here? It is certainly warmer inside," he said.

His study? What did he mean "his study?" Studying was an act, not a place. The chills of the season flicked at my ears and without the cover of a ceiling, a measure of privacy was lacking. But did Father Rogers really live here?

Walking around the building, Father Rogers clasped his hands behind his back and remained silent. All the while he was looking at the passing trees and listening to the songs of the birds. He had a tinge of a smile while he walked as if he was going through a memory. His gait betrayed no hurry to get where we needed to go. Being on that path seemed satisfactory enough. As his eyes roamed the sky between the trees, his breathing was relaxed.

I, conversely, was panic-stricken. The thoughts of rougher priests loomed in my head like bulky strangers. I wondered if, behind his shimmering eyes, was just that kind of person. A two-faced son of a bitch who required time alone to be as nasty and forceful as his god allowed. If each of his steps were on flat feet, with balance and control, mine were taken on jumpy tiptoes—ready for an incoming attack. The day overhead was blissful as the bright blue of the unfilled sky complemented the temperate green of the still-hanging leaves. Inside, I contrasted with sharp reds and nauseous yellows. Father Rogers benignly raised his right arm and I flinched. He didn't appear to notice, lifting it up past the top of my head and pointed to a small building behind the church.

"That's where we're going," he said.

Chapter Ten

The building he pointed to looked like a small hut made out of the same materials as the rest of the church. It was adorned with several square cross windows and a tiny chimney out of the back. This house was clearly the sibling of the church, much smaller but still noticeably related. There were no houses nearby that resembled it. The more common style was wood-based with the incidental touch of vinyl for the houses and looming combinations of concrete and glass for the ever-rising apartments. Situated between the shadows of the changing times, unassuming, but still there, was this tiny, sturdy home tucked in between the folds of rapid life.

We had been walking in tandem until we got to the steps of the place. Then Father Rogers overtook my pace so he could get to the door first.

"Don't worry about taking your shoes off when you come in, Declan. Just rub and stomp them good on the mat."

He swung the door wide and stepped aside so I could be first in. I dragged and stamped my feet before crossing the threshold. Once inside, I noticed the house smelled differently than I had thought. Given the stony exterior, I had thought the smell would have been wet, cold, and impersonal. Instead, I was inhaling the unmistakable aroma of cedar. He must have lined the floors with it because the smell covered the home like needles on branches.

"Would you like some tea while you're here? I always find that tea not only calms the soul but also keeps good time," Father Rogers said.

"That would be nice. Thank you."

"You're very welcome. And please, have a look about the place while you're waiting. I'll be in the kitchen just down there." He pointed to a room at the end of the hall.

We went in perpendicular directions. On my left was a sitting room and on my right was what I presumed was his study. It must have been since one wall was imperceivable behind all of his books. It was like there had been a burst pipe but instead of water, pages and covers had spilled out. The books were bunched up tightly against each other so haphazardly that no librarian could have looked in and left them as they were. Some were straight up and down, some were crooked horizontally, and more still were seeping out in a scattered pile across the bottom shelves and floor. I went into the room to investigate.

Each book I picked up had notes and marks in the margins. Some sentences were firmly underlined while others had lines sprouted out from their periods like hair out of a mole. These lines led to a perfectly drawn star which looked to shine on the name of another title and author, the title always in quotation marks. I looked again at the waterfall of reading and wondered if he had really read everything in this room. Himself. And they weren't even all Bibles. There were books about history and art and there were novels and plays too. Some looked delicate, frail, and yellow while the pages of others glistened white as if recently purchased. When did he have time for all of this?

I was pulled out of my sleuthing by the whistling of the kettle.

"Mercy!" Father Rogers cried and I heard his feet shuffle across the kitchen. "Say, Declan, whenever you're ready, the tea is finished."

"Thanks, Father Rogers. I'll be right in." I took another pass by the books in hopes of seeing one with a name I recognized.

The kitchen showed the plainness of his life. There were no family photos on the walls, leaving the honeycomb wallpaper unobstructed from view. It was also a tiny space without much room to stand amidst the brown cupboards and faded white appliances. Against the room's window was a wooden table with chipped green paint and chairs that rivalled in wear. Despite the spartan layout, it still felt central to the home, if nestled in the back. It was like the lungs of the house with scents cascading into each other as freely as breath. Father Rogers was fanning steam away from the kettle with a stained oven mitt when he noticed me.

"The mounted fan is broken and someone won't be in to fix it until next week. This is the best I can do to move the air around in the interim. Do you take anything in your tea? I hope you like Earl Grey."

"Maybe some milk if you have it."

He smiled as he fanned a bit more before stepping over to the fridge.

"Growing boys always need to have their milk, right? It's funny though how quickly people stop drinking it once they grow up."

He took out a little carton and poured an even amount in both of our cups before putting everything back in its place and ferrying the drinks over.

"Now, I know I had mentioned the study, but forgive me, I forgot I don't have much furniture in there any-more. I'm happy to sit here in the kitchen, but it might be more comfortable in the other room. Would you prefer to go there?"

"Sure, that's no problem."

He motioned with his head and eyes to a second doorway out of the kitchen. This was the same room op-posite the study, though from the front door I hadn't seen its connection to the kitchen. It was the most spacious area of his home. There was a coffee table, two wing chairs on either side, one ottoman which, seemingly, went with Father Rogers's chair, and a loveseat opposite the chairs. Like the study, books were crammed in here too. The amount was much more manageable, with only a few volumes turned on their backs atop those standing at attention. I wondered again if he had really read them all or if he was trying to project a sagacious image. Behind the loveseat was a window which let the light angle in sharply but gently. Father Rogers placed our cups on the now glowing table. He took up the chair with the matching ottoman and relaxed into a posture that looked un-knowingly practiced. It was clear that he fit comfortably into the room, he had the demeanour and outfit to match, and I imagined he often took up that pose to do his reading. I was still standing in the doorway, hands folded politely over my stomach.

"Please, sit anywhere you like," he said.

I took a seat on the other wing chair. Its leather up-holstery curved uncomfortably into my hips and back. The chair hadn't been sat in much and so it wasn't bro-ken in. I made some fidgets and adjustments while he sat with his interlaced fingers on his calm belly.

"Would you like me to get you an extra pillow or something? I think I have some more in the linen closet," he said.

"No, thank you, Father Rogers. I'll be alright as is."

This had to have been a tactic to off-balance me, to ensure he would be serene and I would squirm. He had the advantage. Tucked away, removed from all relations, and the stone probably sealed in all sound. Tiny gullies of sweat coursed over the crooks of my arms and legs. I had been so prepared to defend myself from this man that it was like holding an exercise in isolation: fatiguing and cramped.

Father Rogers blew over his tea. Sitting in the quiet together, I found it difficult to hold on to despising him. It was so easy to curse out the general idea of a priest with which I had been presented—all that was needed was to make them up out of only loathsome traits. Here was a real person, sitting in front of me, breathing. He was still dressed in his robe, but above that was the face of someone I had known for years, whose facial lines led to lightness. I knew this man, I was at peace with this man, but weren't we supposed to be enemies? Don't enemies hate each other totally?

He took a sip of his tea and wet his lips.

"Oh my, that's still a little too hot for my tastes. Say, have you ever heard about the importance of tea to the Japanese?"

I shook my head.

"It's in one of these books somewhere. One of these days I'll have to do a purge of sorts and clean this place up. In any case, to the Japanese, tea is not only a drink but part of a respected ritual. They say it started as a medicinal drink before it became the common beverage we're enjoying now. But, at some point in between, the drink became a sacred object and a new practice was born called Teaism. Have you ever heard of Teaism before?"

Again, I shook my head and admitted that I hadn't. I also couldn't help internally questioning what this had to do with the conversation we were supposed to be having. A conversation that was on a time limit, after all.

"It's a marvellous set of ideas!" he continued. "First founded as a kind of group that prized the—oh, how did they word it?" He tucked his chin into his chest and looked to be scanning through every page he had ever read on the insides of his eyelids.

"The… the… the beautiful among the sordid facts of everyday existence! That's it! Isn't that just a wonderful expression?

"I think so," I said, if I knew what sordid meant.

"Do you understand what it means?"

"Yeah, a bit."

"It's okay to say 'I don't know,' Declan. In fact it might be one of the most helpful phrases I know. What that sentence means is that even when there are bad and terrible things going on in the world, and there is nothing we can do about them, we may still find a hidden beauty in anything. They call it a kind of worship of the imperfect in life. Now what do you think of that?"

"It sounds pretty good, I guess. Sounds like a nice way of looking at things."

"Can you think of any examples of what this might look like in real life?"

The question mark floated over the room, casting a weak shadow. He seemed content under it, waiting for what I had to say. I didn't know what to say so I put on the appearance of someone mired in consideration. Looking everywhere but at him, I studied the objects around the room. Perhaps one of them would present itself like a great joke to an improviser. After a few loops around the room, nothing stood out. I returned to looking at his non-judgemental and patient face.

"I'm sorry, Father Rogers. I don't think I can."

"Do you mind if I share one?"

"Sure."

He adjusted himself in his chair to lean in towards our common centre.

"Now, I'm no expert on these things, but I'll tell you what I have been told. It's all a matter of memory and honesty. There's another practice in Japan called kintsugi. Is that something you're familiar with?"

Put me down for a hat-trick of head shakes.

"Kintsugi is," his face slightly followed his eyes as they drifted to the ceiling, "a form of art, but also an idea. I'm sorry if this is a little too abstract, but I'll try to make it more clear as I go. In kintsugi, the artist begins with a plate or a cup or something else usually made out of ceramic. They have this object and they craft it perfectly and in exacting detail, like a gardener of a prized rosebush. I suppose a bonsai might actually be a more appropriate analogy in this case. Anyway, they produce something that, from what I've seen, looks like it would be too beautiful to eat off of."

"But there's something wrong with it?" I interrupted.

"No, not quite. Let me ask you this: what do you think would happen if you dropped a really beautiful plate in your house?"

"I'm not sure. Maybe my parents would get upset and they'd make me clean it up."

Father Rogers smirked incredulously.

"I don't think your parents are the type to get angry over a dropped plate. But maybe they are. But let's say they don't get angry, what would you do with the plate after you cleaned it up?"

"Throw it out, I guess?"

"What would make you do a thing like that?"

"Because you've got to throw it away now."

"But why?"

"Because… because it's broken—because we can't use it anymore."

Father Rogers slapped his hand on his knee like it was a released trap. On the infinite multiple choices of a conversation, I had said exactly what he thought I would.

"Ah! So if the plate is broken, it cannot be used anymore! It's useless, garbage, right?"

"Right!"

"Not in the practice of kintsugi."

He took a sip of his tea, suspending the conversation for a moment.

"You see, the practice of kintsugi involves taking something beautiful, usually a cup or a plate, like I said, and then deliberately breaking it. Do you know why they would want to break something they worked so hard on?"

"I don't, no."

"So that it can be put back together again more beautifully than before."

"But how?"

"Instead of sweeping the pieces up and putting them in the trash, the kintsugi artist carefully collects all that has been shattered and takes it back to their work table. From there, it's like a puzzle. They study each chipped shape and figure out how they used to go together. But, of course, no amount of matching will make the cup stand again, even if all the pieces are back in place. They need something else. That something else is a kind of golden paint that functions as a type of glue that runs over all of the cracks like veins."

"Oh, I see. They do that so the thing can be like it was again."

Father Rogers lowered his face while he shook his head.

"No, my dear Declan, it's so the object can be more beautiful than it was before."

He lost me again.

"But, Father Rogers, how can a broken thing be better than a not broken thing?"

"They say that by recognizing the imperfections of the world and, even, by making them the focus of an object, we can appreciate a new version of beauty that didn't exist before. Instead of presenting something that appears to have come from nowhere, manufactured by hidden hands, you might say: it's the breaking and restoring of a thing that is *the* human act."

At the end of his statement, he sat back in his chair. I tried to say something back, but he lifted one finger to signal silence. We sat there wordless for a noticeable amount of time. All throughout, my head buzzed with questions and links about what he had said. About broken things and humanity. About restoration and, what did he call them? The sorry aspects of life? Father Rogers took another long sip of tea before slowly and deliberately placing it back on the sunlit table. It seemed brighter now..

"Can I say something now, Father?"

"Please do."

"That's a cool idea, but I don't see how it relates to what I'm supposed to be here for. Didn't you hear my Dad? I've become an atheist and they don't know what to do about it."

Another pause, another brief look of glee.

"I heard the words of your father and, I'm sorry to tell you, but your case isn't very original."

"I'm sorry?"

"Oh, lots of kids your age are acting like they are fed up with the Church. It's not every week, but almost that often where I get a letter or a call from a deeply concerned parent about the state their child is in. They go on about their worries, how they believe their child is on the path to Hell, and so forth. To tell you the truth, it's not the sort of thing I expected I would be doing with my work, but they reach out with such sincerity that I can't take them as anything but worthy of my efforts. In having these conversations, I like to begin with the same question. Declan, why do you think you're here?"

"As in, on this planet?" I said, aching to be clever.

"No, not that big," he chuckled, "just here in this room today."

"I know I'm here because, it's like you said, my parents don't really know what's going on and they need help dealing with me. Because I said I don't believe in god and stuff."

"That sounds like most of the others. If I may, let me ask you this: did your parents force you to come here today?"

"Not exactly. It was my Dad's idea, but I sort of agreed to it."

"Ah. So why did you make that agreement?"

I took this as an indication to think about what I was supposed to say. Did I have a reason or was I just being obedient?

"I think I'm here because I don't know if I *believe* in god anymore."

"I see. And what brought you to that position?"

I recounted the story of discovering the opinions of atheists on the internet. How, in the days that followed those initial clips, I hadn't watched much of anything else because it was so captivating and there was so much to see. Then I told him about my parents' distraught reactions and the arguments I'd had with my sisters. While I agreed with what I thought, telling the story to a stranger, leaving out pieces of context, made the process seem rotten.

He asked me what I believed in and I responded with remarkable plagiarism. I recounted all the crimes of the Church I had memorized, discarded their metaphysical claims, and railed against the meaning of what the existence of a god would mean for humanity. How horrible it would be to live under a god that constantly needed to be praised when the best he could do to return our favour was work in mysterious ways. There was nothing to wager because there was nothing to lose. Besides, if I believed in god simply to appease him, wouldn't he see through that? Or was he so vain that he would be pleased with such a submission? If this god truly existed then he must be an utter maniac.

That was my amalgamation of a position. While I had heard those ideas expressed with cold ferocity, I couldn't help notice tabs flicking out in my throat. These tabs bumped into the words as they left, causing them to waver slightly, and impeded the smooth flow of their exit.

"You know what, Declan, I must say that you've come here better prepared than most. I believe you. But do you also hear something in your voice that's keeping you from full conviction?"

"I don't want to, but I do. And I think I know what it is."

"Oh? Would you like to tell me about it?"

"I think it's my family, Father. Everyone else in my house still believes in this stuff—even my sisters—and it's hard being the only one who doesn't. It's like we all got milk from the same carton, but only mine has gone sour."

"Hmmm. And you'd rather not drink anymore than face the taste?"

"I don't want to worry them about what might be in their glass. There's no amount of hoping that can change the flavour back to what it was and, now that I've tasted it, I don't want to drink it anymore. I'm trying to be honest, but what if that honesty is hurting people?"

My eyes were becoming wet, but I refused to let the liquid spill out. Doing so would have been an act of surrender.

"Declan, I don't think you're worrying your parents."

"Then why do they need me to talk to you? Why can't they figure this out on their own?"

Father Rogers took a considered pause before replying. I took another sip of tea.

"I know a thing or two about your father and, for all his virtues, I know he's not too handy with new technologies, right?"

"I guess so."

"So when he runs into a problem with his phone, he probably needs to take it in to see a specialist or at least someone who works at the store that he bought it from, right?"

"Yeah."

"Then I think the worst thing that's going on here is that he's recognizing something that he and your mother can't solve. So they've taken you to the person whose job it is to help. That's all it is. Call it spiritual difficulties."

A bit of laughter puttered out from both of us. I hadn't checked the time, but I also didn't want to. Never had I spoken to an adult where it felt like they were trying to reach me on my terms. It was maturing.

"What do you think I should do about this?" I asked.

"First of all, my dear boy, there are no 'shoulds' in this world. It's much too complex for that. I do, however, have a suggestion. Sometimes, when I meet a young priest, they talk to me like you do. They've come to opposite conclusions, of course, but they have that same passion for the subject, but it's an immature passion. What I think we might try is work to make you a real atheist."

I was shocked and nearly spit out my tea.

"Now, let me explain a bit of what I mean. What I don't want to happen is you, how does Hitch say it? Take your faith *à la carte*—"

"You know Christopher Hitchens?"

"I do! He's been a superb writer for decades! I especially liked his little book of letters to his students. Come to think of it, you might like that one very much too. I'm sorry for digressing. Where was I?"

"Something about taking faith *à la carte*?"

"Ah! Yes, you mustn't approach faith or anti-faith

that way. Anyone can take the best ideas of the best minds, commit them to memory, and then spit them out. What it really means to know something is to feel it. It's like the difference between *savoir* and *connaître*. Anyone can *savoir* something, but it takes a bit more to *connaître* it. How do we get to this kind of knowing? Not by going through the greatest hits, but by studying deeply all aspects of the thing we want to know. If you're really sure that this is how you see the world, then I want to see your eyes and nose deep in the foundational books of your new fascination. Here, give me a moment."

Father Rogers got up from his chair and left me in the cozy room. The sounds of rummaging knocked about in the house. There was sliding and dropping, I wondered where he was digging and how he knew where anything was. As he searched, I politely sipped my tea and did not check the time. We must have gone over anyway.

When Father Rogers came back into the room, his whole belly was covered by the books he had cradled in his arms.

"Here you are, young man! A personal loan from the library of Rogers!"

The stack before me was forbidding. Some of the books were new and mass-produced while others looked like copies he had owned all his life.

"Are you giving these to me?" I asked.

"Not physically but intellectually. That's the beautiful thing about ideas, Declan. There may only be one book, but we both read it then we multiply it. Go ahead, look over the spines. See if there are any you recognize."

I mumbled the titles as I read.

"God is not great. The god delusion. Letters to a young contrarian. A portrait of the artist as a young man. The ethics. The meditations. In praise of folly. Unpopular essays. The power of myth. Tao te ching. The genealogy of morals. Fear and trembling. The book of disquiet. Leaves of grass."

"I'll bet you recognize a few names from this pile, eh?"

"'A few' is pushing it, Father Rogers. But why do you have all these? I mean, if you—"

"If I am a Catholic? Don't worry, I know exactly what you mean. You see, I'm not concerned about learning something I may not like. It concerns me even less if I don't agree with it. What does concern me are people who only take up one book, one resource, and call themselves informed. It is curiosity, Declan, that makes life exciting."

I spotted a chance to challenge him.

"But isn't that just what Christians are lacking? No offence but, isn't that what they do with the Bible?"

"The ones who pass by it, yes. And they're the ones whose faith is often flimsiest and so they feel the need to defend it against different ideas. That is not how I see things. I believe that faith is strengthened by learning more broadly because it is the tests that reveal what is true."

"So then how do you do it?"

"How do I do what?"

"How do you read things that go against what you believe and still do what you do every day?"

I had forced Father Rogers into consideration. It didn't feel snarky to have done so, rather it was profound. To challenge him to think was to put a new idea into his mind. It was a good feeling to give.

"I think there are two perspectives that have helped with my understanding," he said. "The first is that I believe God is everywhere and has appeared to all people, but not everyone has seen Him in the same way. It's like He's somewhere behind us and it's our job while we're alive to find a mirror to angle back so we can see as much of Him as we can. That is first, and whenever I read about people talking about their gods and how their lives have been informed, I believe them in the same way you can hold up a die and I can see one number and you can see another. But, and this is the more specific point, the God in which I believe is the God of the Bible, and I believe in Him because of personal experience. I believe He has helped me stay on the right path in life and do good for others. And through Him, I have understood the most important principle of His Church which I also believe is the most important principle in life. Do you know what that is?"

"Faith? Power?"

"Forgiveness, Declan. Forgiveness. I had a professor a long time ago, back on the east coast, and he told me something very important. He said, 'Lou, there's one thing that evil cannot stand and that is forgiveness.' I've thought about that statement for a long time. In fact, I still think about it now."

He had stumped me again. No internet atheist had

ever rebuked such a charge. So I was underprepared to both respond to it and understand it. I did wonder, in the part of my brain that itched, if a non-believer could extoll such a virtue,

"Have you found out what it means?" I asked.

"It means, Declan, that when someone has made you very angry, the worst thing you can do is continue to be angry yourself. If you can let go of that thought and tell the other person that you are free from what they have done to you then, if they are truly good, they will also let go of the harm they did to you."

"And if they don't?"

"If they don't, if they insist that you stay angry, or that they stay angry too, then they have missed the most important teaching in the world. This Church teaches redemption, but I believe there is a stronger force at play when it is done right: reunion. Through the act of forgiveness, we can come together more easily. Anger may be the most destructive force in our world because it survives to keep people apart. That is why I do what I do. It is so that through my work I can be responsible for the reunification of all people."

"All people?"

"Well, all of the people I may meet."

I was surprisingly touched by what he said. Dashed from my mind were the various amazing arguments and clever comebacks that had filled me. Though I couldn't help but notice he did not mention god in these, his closing remarks. It was so wonderful to think about bringing people together, could it be possible without a religion too? The faucet of my faith ran without holy water, but now it was beginning to sputter again. It dripped with the substance of unity and without the authority of a church.

"Thank you, Father, for everything today. I'll be sure to return the books after I've read them."

He put a hand on my shoulder before I could step away.

"Oh, no, you're not going to take these home with you."

I froze.

"My apologies if I was unclear. You're not to take these books home because if you read them on your own time, I'm sure you'll go right through them. One after another after another, breezing over paragraphs that require a bit more time. Have you ever heard of Claude Débussy?"

"No."

"Ah, Claude Débussy was a wonderful French composer who said something about music that I love. He said that music is the space between the notes. Isn't that great?"

"Sure," I said, without knowing what he meant.

"I find that reading is best approached in a similar way. Leave some space between your sessions so that you will not only be more interested in reading what's next but also so you can have the time to hear the music between the notes."

"But how will I do that?"

"How about this: while your family is at Church on Sundays, you tell them you have special permission to come back here by yourself. I rarely lock the door so don't worry about a key. While I'm teaching out there, I want you to learn in here. And, afterwards, if you have any questions, I'll come right back to guide you. How does that sound?"

"That sounds like a very interesting education. Thank you, Father."

"So much politeness, your parents have done well. Now, I'm sure we've been at this much longer than your Dad anticipated so let's make some apologies and tell them our master plan."

And so we walked the same walk back to the car. Céline spotted us first and rolled down the window so she could bemoan how long and torturous it had been to wait for my return. She mentioned something about practice for the Second Coming. Mum and Dad got out of the car and Father Rogers informed them about our little deal. They were certainly surprised but relaxed once they were assured that Father knew best and, overall, this would be a good thing for me. I was reminded to thank him and shake his hand. He shook mine with the same force and grace with which he shook my parents' hands. Patting the roof of the car after we were all buckled in, he reiterated how much he was looking forward to our first session. We drove off and I watched him stand there until we had safely turned into the street.

Chapter Eleven

Our system of study began the next Sunday. Each week I reported to Father Rogers's house, often passing him in the opposite direction along the path. Mum and Dad started going back to church with more frequency but had to miss the occasional service due to personal conflicts. I still insisted on being driven and dropped off. It had become like a sports practice and I looked forward not only to the reading but to the discussion when Father Rogers got back. He never mentioned the days when Mum and Dad weren't there even though he must have noticed. Not that there was much time for outside talk anyway. While I was alone, I had stumbled into so many impressive but impenetrable passages that I bailed questions at Father Rogers from the moment he sat down. It was so exciting to see him excited, especially when his memory bolted and went into the stacks, burrowing to find the quotation he had forgotten he remembered. The original stack had reformed and transformed into a never-ending ladder of reading. I was happy, then, to just read and talk. It was about a subject rarely broached in school and with the personal attendance that school couldn't provide.

On top of the original stack, he had me read the elementary religious texts of the world. While I had a familiar gist of the Christian ones, he put forth those from Japan, India, Greece, West Africa, Central America, and the Indigenous cultures of Canada. Each one had such a different conception of what a god was supposed to be. Some lived in another place, others walked in and out of the world at will, while more inhabited the very objects that populated everything.

With so much variety, who could claim to be right? Reading these ideas in flat succession equated them to one another. None leapt out of the open pages and ensnared me in their jaws. They certainly differed and challenged notions of wishy-washy teachers that claimed all religions were trying to communicate the same message. And it was in their difference that showed their incompleteness. The Greeks were so dramatic with their gods and the Japanese so benign. Life wasn't little enough to only be one. While I had not been made to believe in god, the anger I carried towards him dissolved into fascination.

It was a fascination that was not as buoyant in the secular considerations. These were the names of titles that I had recognized as being so casually tossed out by the people I had come to admire. I wasn't sure if it was my youth or my inexperience but when it came time to read them for myself, I was lost amongst their argumentative contortions. It was like standing at the base of a mountain on a cloudy day. Looking up, I was sure there was a point, but it was so heavily fogged that its outline led nowhere. They lacked imaginative excitement and potent imagery to help their reader. The myths, by contrast, thrived with them.

I would clumsily ask Father Rogers about various ideas and he would explain in his simplest English or French. Sometimes he looked so defeated. He would curl his arms and tense his hands before letting out all their resistance as they dropped to his hips, light anguish exhaled. I wanted to understand but what I lacked was the maturity to have seen the world as these writers had seen it. We had hoped that these sessions, these ideas, would form like whiskey. Beginning with simple, scattered ingredients, we would mash them together into nothing of clear worth. Over the course of time, they would sit with each other, naturally interact, and ferment until ready to be shared properly. An underdeveloped opinion would carry all the bite and stinginess of an underdeveloped whiskey. By virtue of their long combination, the ideas would improve as they swathed amongst each other until they turned honey-amber and glowed. We did not doubt the long-term necessity of this project, and knew that discipline and repetition would be its core ingredients. But week to week, there were afternoons in which our drink tasted of imbalance.

There had to be a thinker that could settle all sides of this conundrum. Someone who could reconcile the awe of religious stories with the rigour of philosophical thought. It was a book I had skipped over because it was short, presuming it had less to say. I read it in a couple of hours. When I finished, I returned to the beginning the next week. At first, I found it repulsive. It held and presented an idea that proved why faith was so putrid and impossible. But that was the easy reading. It was only by reviewing it again that I was able to hold two ideas in mind at once. My opinion and his.

The author's name poked up like spikes on a graveyard fence. Kierkegaard. This dead Dane had scoured his mental wasteland and returned with terrifying knowledge. What if Abraham was the model for ethical behaviour? He was so shattered by this thought that he couldn't render the story into one authoritative version. Recasting it four times, changing the details slightly with each retelling, he pleaded through his pages to explain the essence of what happened on that mountain. Like so many of the Bible's stories, it was sparser than its memory, leaving Kierkegaard with the perfect amount of room to worry.

Abraham had been told directly, but secretly, by God what he had to do: take his son, Isaac, the child he had waited decades for, and sacrifice him away from all to prove his faith. Did he snatch his son first thing the next day or did he pause to kiss his wife? When he arrived at the mountain, did he hesitate? Did he beg? Or did he act with swiftness? God waited with cruel patience until there could be no doubt in Abraham's actions. Abraham, knife clenched, swung while sweating towards the neck of his only son. Then God was kind and replaced Isaac with a lamb. The father and the son descended the mountain, each full of the memories of that morning. What happened to them then? Did Isaac ever forgive his father? Did Abraham ever see the colour in the world again? What became of the two faiths once the day had fallen?

For the next one hundred pages, Kierkegaard was weary. He was so convinced of his truth that writing it down was the only safe place for its life. This was not an opinion to be shared casually in a tavern. No, his view was to be locked away, published under a false name, and left for reckoning. What if Abraham was not only righteous in his action but was the model for the minimum of faith?

On first read, I hated what he implied. He was trying, mightily, to prove to everyone who could read that this man, this monster, was the greatest example of the greatest virtue available to humanity. That the common ethics, known so well to all people they could not be spoken, were not the best we had access to. There was another superior way of living which, conveniently, could not be uttered.

On the day of the sacrifice, Abraham did not speak. He knew, and he knew in such a way that it could be recorded later, but to those in his life, he did not reveal. Not to his wife and to his son. By being called on personally, he was imbued with an idea beyond understanding and instead of attempting to share, he resigned. During the trek, Isaac noticed there was no lamb with them. He asked his father where it was. Abraham said their Lord would give them one. He lied because he had been given no such information. If he had, where would the faith have been?

Reading about this exchange, I was furious. I wanted Abraham to speak to his son—to tell him everything he knew. Even if he failed, by attempting to share his revelation, would he have added or subtracted to his faith? It was this kind of action, this deranged belief, that pushed me farther from this religion. I took it personally, placed myself in Isaac's position and my father in Abraham's. My father was a man who believed with his entire body yet I had no doubt that he would deny his god if it meant I lived. I was certain I had defeated Kierkegaard with this familial fact, torn down a great mind by the bricks of his own making. Until, near the end, he revealed a detail I hadn't expected.

After all of his defences, all of his logic, Kierkegaard admitted that he could not understand Abraham, only admire him. Was this more of his absurdity? Another paradox whereby he singled himself above his readers? No, it wasn't a consolation. It read like a man who had worked feverishly through a problem only to arrive at a solution he was too inept to understand. Abraham had broken through the common plague of problems that anyone faced if they seriously considered the effects of human interaction. He didn't need to explain himself to anybody, he didn't need to worry. Abraham could simply act and, if he was wrong, he would be altered with a lesser consequence.

Over the course of his frothing argument, the second time, I pitied him. Here was this isolated man, so tortured by the particularities of his life and disagreeing with everything socially. In such a time when the order of the world was so against him, he pleaded that there had to have been another way. That the highest and most noble way of being was to prove that as a single individual, one could shoot out from the muck of suffering. The one who could bypass the universal because there was something secret and superior waiting for the person with the power of circumvent. By being the great paradox, Abraham flew over all judgement. He could not be harmed by ethics or critique because he had passed into a realm beyond its boundaries. It sounded more like that was what Kierkegaard wanted to be.

Running through the book were tones of a man in immense pain, unable to comprehend why. From the opening line, syllables and commas unfurled without restraint. It was as if he had been pinning down a terrifying question about what was most horrific to him: there might not be anything below his emptiness. Whatever pain has been brought to him has been done without sense and without intention. What would he then have to do confronted with such unfathomable yet random power that was powerless to keep despair away? He seemed to be a man who could not stomach a world that had been made with such inexplicable sadness. With such a talent for language, long and well-decorated sentences, had he overlooked the one word that could have saved him? Not faith, not hope, not even love. Commiseration.

Even amongst the masters of language, he found no consolation. Those writers whose brilliance had been left behind, still warm after centuries, left the world without comment on the secret he found within himself. How tragic that he had run out of people. He must have had to turn to god because he didn't feel there was a person alive that could understand him. If only he had known someone that made the suffering stomachable. Instead of seeking to soar away from everyone else, what if he dove into humanity? There had to have been enough people around that some of them, at least one of them, could have been there to touch him.

Free from the disasters and disappointments of his own life. How odd, then, that the man who argued that by giving something up, you receive its greatest gifts never considered faith as the thing to be given up so that it could be transcended. He so desperately ached to be outside of the social whirlpool, superior to the enwrapping crowds of commonality. Faith was his way out. If he could adhere to an idea that no one else understood and admire a paradox, he would be free from the limitations of being human. I thought about how he despaired and belittled the people of whom he was one.

If only he hadn't been so original. If only he lived in a better time in which more people read, pondered, sulked, and fretted—then he could have expressed the bottom of his ideas. The world moved too fast and too slow for a man like him. Caught in that bind, he had clung to faith as the last vestige of sanity. It held the secrets no one had spoiled in an amorphous shape that could swaddle as easily as it could strike. He admired Abraham not because of his faith in god but because of his connection to him.

Though not overtly, Kierkegaard had issued a challenge. It was to find stability, beauty, contentment, meaning, and conviction in the world without resorting to god. He contended that the person who leapt through life without god would reveal their weakness upon landing. It was god that oriented the faithful to land sternly and were rewarded for having leapt. While having a helping hand may stabilize from the beginning, what can faith do against practice and observation? If faith was lost, and the person wobbled, could they regain their composure and learn to leap without faith? No books showed me how. Kierkegaard instead challenged anyone who dared to read him with a proposition much more anxiety-inducing than a perfectly laid out statement: the chance at truth with no clear way to be made false.

It took months before the stack had stopped regenerating faster than I could read. By engaging in the habit I had become more competent and predictable as a reader. When the Sunday arrived when it appeared I would finish the last book chosen by Father Rogers, he pointed to a note he had left on the desk. It read: the next one is up to you. As if all the Kierkegaard hadn't made me weary enough of choice. He sealed me in his cobbled sanctuary and, as expected, I finished the final book with time remaining.

I stretched myself long over my usual chair in the sitting room. How nice it was to have finished all those books and, with the time to spare, perhaps I would take the rest of the day's session as a rest. But I was reminded of something Father Rogers had told me when the stack was at its most endless. In response to a brief lament about the process, he offered his opinion in three French words. *Le travail continue*—the work continues. I had recognized the phrase as being pencilled into the ends of so many chapters and books that I took it to be a bit of a mantra for the man. When asked what he meant by it, Father Rogers explained that he had picked it up from another university professor. This one was ruthless and unrelenting in terms of assignments and standards. Hers was a class feared because it was tough and because it was mandatory. At the bottom of her remarks, which were always accompanied with a tangle of scribbles, under-lines, and corrections, she would leave a valediction about the state of the work. No matter how well Father Rogers did or did not do, she signed each paper the same: *le tra-vail continue*. No matter how well he had learned, no mat-ter how much he had demonstrated himself, she was warding off the beast of complacency. The project was ongoing and we only had the rest of our lives to finish as much as we could.

I walked into the study and looked again at the note. The next one is *up* to you. Father Rogers hadn't added that flourish but after so much stiff material, I thought it was deserving of its cheek. Instead of reaching into the wall at the height of my heart I lengthened the entire right side of my body, standing only on the balls of my feet, and grabbed three books from the highest shelf. All three were large and heavy. They nearly dropped out of my grip as they left the shelf. When they were laid out on the table, each offered up foreign names in various sizes. The first with its cover coated in long, blended strokes depicting springtime landscapes said Van Gogh. Its letters were curly and childish and nestled in amongst the colours of windblown air. The next showed curious, chubby angels, looking up at the looming name Raphael.

I thought of cartoons. Both books seemed innocent, optimistic, and I would have reached for the first had there not also been the inherent mystery of the third.

I couldn't tell if the word on the cover was a name, a movement, or a monster. Its letters stretched full-length across the bottom of the cover in bloody maroon. Above the white-wrapped letters was a painting of a boy holding a severed head. Behind him was an unnatural darkness which crept over his shoulder and around his face. He looked concerned, sorrowful. The head dangled by a few hairs while the strings of blood fell so darkly they became lost in the background. I ran my fingers over the bottom of the cover as if in braille and pronounced the name.

"Caravaggio."

The kitchen table was cleared so I took the book there and opened it widely. Its pages spread with confidence across two place settings. The paper was dense and lacquered and it made a delightful swoosh and scrape whenever a page was turned or touched.

What stained me about these paintings were their colours. Each was steeped in the shades of plums, dirt, and salamanders. Yet no matter how dark the base scheme was, a brightness had flown across the painting to cast its subjects in one brilliant shine. A line of light that carried the viewer out of the darkness and onto the bodies and faces of the figures. This light was direct and curved to illuminate precisely what he wanted us to see. Anguish, hope, contemplation, and pain stretched over the faces as clearly as film. What a shock it was to read that these were religious paintings. The halos were barely perceptible.

The notion of religiosity did not turn me away from what I saw. It was an inconsequential fact against the images that radiated like candles. The book said that each model represented had not come from Caravaggio's mind, the elite of Italy, nor from recastings of other Christian artists. He used drunkards, thieves, mistresses, and himself to play the parts of the people in the paintings. It was his insistence that the most pious would not have looked any superior to the rest of humanity and so they did not need to be dreamt of to fit his retellings. He had taken in the most jagged lives of his era and shown them with the careful expression of an artist.

The beauty I was inspecting lay in the sympathy of the people's faces. Hesitation on the face of Saint Matthew as he is called to join with Jesus; Judith's confusion when she slayed Holofernes as if she didn't expect the neck to spray so much; the look of solace on Jesus's face amongst Judas's kiss and the guard's seizure. When I peered into these paintings what peered back was not divine but wholly human. For each turn of the page, my imagination bounded through the scenes. It made its happy leaps through thoughts as it made stories without words for the people I was seeing. Each of them had their own life, connections, venalities, and advantages that were being expressed in religious paintings without the divine presence. Even when Jesus himself was pictured, there was no halo, no levitation, but a mixture amongst the humanity of his time. I kept turning through the pictures, sliding around through eras, as the religious and non-religious paintings began to mix.

The emotional lives that could no longer be concealed behind thin flesh. There was torment, woe, longing, and inquiry—that was all the meaning necessary. Through the visages of common people, placed upon gods and saints, Caravaggio had exceeded the sublime and showed the human. The silent images first entered through my eyes before climbing down and settling into my stomach. I loved feeling pregnant with this terrible beauty.

I may not have been able to articulate it but this book, these scenes, were confirming my new beliefs better than any argument or treatise ever could. When Father Rogers returned, he called for me but I didn't answer, my head was too immersed amongst my new coterie. He crossed the corner of the kitchen and saw me, standing over the book with an automatic expression of intense focus and ingestion.

"What have you got there?"

I peeled myself from the pages and he rounded the room and stood over my shoulder.

"Ah, Caravaggio. You know, I've often found his work to be rather daunting. Do you like what you've seen?"

"I do. I think they're amazing."

It was around that time I stopped going to see Father Rogers. Life had picked up and celebrations for my high school graduation had to be recovered from. Then summer rose, the last summer of school before shipping off to university and attempting to become an adult. Like my parents, other things had gotten in the way of church.

A few weeks before I was set to go, I arrived on his

doorstop unannounced. He was surprised and I rambled through a thank you. He ducked behind his door and came back with a small piece of paper. On it was his mailing address which he tapped twice as he handed it to me.

"Declan, you are about to go through the greatest times of your life. Oh, if only I could go back to university again! You know I'm not very good with technology, so if you ever find yourself with a few spare moments, if you'll have any, you can always write to me. That's my mailing address and, believe me, I don't intend on moving any time soon."

I reached through the door to hug him and stumbled through one more goodbye, promising him I would write. He patted my shoulders and looked with distinguished pride. It was when I stood just out of reach of the door that I noticed something.

"It's kind of funny," I said.

"What is?" he said.

"You on one side of the door, me on the other but we're still able to hold on to each other. I guess that's what we've been doing this whole time, eh?"

He didn't try to one-up me, didn't reference anyone, he bowed his head and clapped his hands together.

"Be well, Declan. And Godspeed!"

I didn't mind the sentiment.

So why did I stop writing? It was never my intention to let this rope of a relation fray and untie itself, but it did. Enthusiastic, frequent letters eventually dwindled. The end of the week had come and if I realized I had forgotten to write I figured it was better if I didn't. Next week would come and I could try again, then try to get it perfect. The less I participated in our scrawled ritual, the less I thought about it. What had planned to be a letter a week turned to a letter a month which turned to a letter every few months which became something sent hastily at Christmas. By my final year, even that much was too much. I had moved again to a different residence with a different address. Had he tried to send me anything? I never asked so I've never known.

When we were in the same place it had been so easy to chat. He would comment on how gradually I was changing and I could hold a book open to ask for clarity. It was shameful how easily my excuses arrived. I couldn't write to him because I was studying for midterms; I didn't have time because I went to Québec for the weekend; his handwriting slowly lost its elegance and became scrawled. Those letters were hard to read and thus harder to respond to.

We had been two rivers running parallel and, at times, allowed the same wildlife to travel through us. Was it the distance or the silence that caused our streams to bend? Leaning to the side, as if wondering what was over the horizon, we diverted. Oxbowing away, our paths allowed land to interrupt our connection and grow the trees that separated our sight and sound. We left no mark, no trail showing how close we used to be. Did they still feed into the same western ocean or had one snaked too far north? Frozen and inert. What sun and stone could ever reunify the two?

Part 3

PURSUANCE

Chapter Twelve

"A priest?" Dad said. "But, Declan, you're an atheist!"

"Where is this coming from? I'm so confused," Mum said, completely distracted from the broken teacup at her feet, its liquid tepidly creeping under her arches.

Both of them trembled in their seats, awash in a reaction much more specific than fear. They looked quickly around the room, as if following a scurrying creature, until they raised their gaze from the floor, locked on to me, and scanned like I was an invader. Who had replaced the son they thought they knew? It couldn't have been Declan Murphy who didn't wish but certified that he was going to pursue a life in the Church. That was not who they knew. I thought it was worth repeating.

"I've been thinking about career opportunities and I think the priesthood might be my best fit."

"Now just hang on a minute," Dad said. "Let's all of us get our heads screwed on right. Declan, is this some kind of joke? Something kids are saying to their parents now to see how they'll react for the internet?"

"No joke," I said calmly, "more like an instinct. Let's be real for a second, okay? This job hunt hasn't been going well at all. I've been trying to stay positive about it but, really, I haven't gotten a single callback from any of the recruiters I've talked to, and the other night, I had this strong dream."

"Recruiting's usually slower in the summer, that's all. You just have to wait them out," Dad said.

"A dream? You mean you had a dream about becoming a priest?" Mum said.

"It's not so easy to explain."

"Was it a new dream?" She continued.

"No, I've been having versions of it for years. It usually starts with nothing and I'm weightless. Then everything gets way bigger than me, shooting up in all directions, until this huge, cloaked figure appears. He's got eyes that… when they look at you, and you look at them, they burn. Sometimes I get tossed around or have to run forever, but this time it was different. I was made to sit in some kind of confessional and I had to hear someone, a woman's, confession. It just filled me up so well to be able to help her and I've just never felt like that before. And I didn't even think it was related to the Church or anything until you mentioned the bit about Father Rogers," I motioned my open palm to Dad. "I know, I know, it sounds like it can't work, but I think I can do it."

"Declan," Dad said with an expressive exhale, "this is your life… it's not some kind of… I don't even know where to start with this. So you're telling us that you've decided to become a priest, a profession that requires the person to believe in God, based on… on what? Some kind of dream? Something you made up to yourself? Wha… how… are you sure you've thought this through? Why the priesthood?"

My chin twisted into my chest at Dad's question. There was no set plan yet, the idea was still too new. But it was definitely alive now, breathing in the room, and wasn't that enough to start me towards a goal? If I could perfectly explain what I had seen, I was sure they would understand.

"I mean, doesn't it seem like a nice kind of profession? You get a little house, you get to talk to people at their nicest, people come to you for advice, you get to have a title that's recognizable worldwide, there's no hard labour—"

"By Joseph, Declan! You've gots to believe in the thing you're preaching! I know you think this stuff is all fluff, but to the people you're working with, this is everything. A priest isn't up there to be some kind of recording that can spit back the words of the book. He's got to represent what he believes in. And you—look, it's taken your mother and I a long time to come to terms with your… ways of believing. I'm still sure you'll come back around to it once you've had a real crisis, but this doesn't sound like it. It sounds like you're trying to bake a pie without the filling. Sure, the crust is nice and supportive, but there's nothing of substance there. It's hollow, you understand?"

Mum was still and silent. I had seen her stand like that before when Dad was riled up. He could spew his words with the incessancy of an incoming tide. Sometimes it was best for him to go out according to his own cycle rather than try to dam him in. This stance, however, was not without attention. Her eyes darted back and forth as if watching a verbal tennis match. Could she understand Dad's accent when he was upset and spoke without consideration? Had she stored all the sounds that only his kin knew? I glanced in her direction this time with an expression of assistance. She remained as she was, in a mental crouch, unsure of whom needed pouncing.

"Excuse me for not thinking this would be so controversial," I said. "I mean, the Catholic Church is basically a business now anyway so why can't I work there? Will they make me sign a contract sniffing after atheist tendencies like we're still in the Cold War? It's got employees like any other workplace and takes in way more money. If I was going to work for some mega-corporation that was causing actual harm or damage to the world, I'm sure you'd be thrilled. You'd tell your friends that I just hired on to a company whose sole task is to produce more plastic until it blotted out the sun! Goddamn—"

"Don't blaspheme in my house!" Dad said.

"Aren't you glad I have something I want to do and, as a bonus, it's related to your beloved Church? I've been doubting things my whole life and searching for a job has only compounded those feelings. It's been a steady set of rejections and ghostings. I keep having to reassess who I am and what I may be worth to someone, and it needs to stop. For once, I just want to be sure of something. To close this part of me that's always questioning, always wondering. So, yes, I do want to work in the priesthood because it feels like something solid. And maybe I might even be able to do a bit of good for others."

Dad held his hands up next to his temples. He stood, turning away from the table. His hands dropped down the edge of his face until they reached the hinges of his jaw. They pressed in tiny circles around the bone.

"It's not that we're not glad that you've found something. If it turns out that, somehow, you've landed on your calling, then you know you have your mother's and my support." He looked over his shoulder as she closed her eyes and nodded. "But, Declan, are you sure you're sure? Is this really how you want to go on? Spending your whole life working for something you don't believe in?"

"Do *you* really believe in your work?"

Mum took in a short breath and with it all the moving air from the room. None of us moved and the house made no noise. I stifled any uprising of regret as I waited for his next verbal tide. He never needed to explain himself to me and I didn't feel like I owed him any more reason for my choices. It was as if I was trying to be more of a man than he was. With this assertion was a cry for independence.

Dad's shoulders rounded as he processed what was just said. His face fluttered through shock, audacity, and sternness. His boy, his only boy, rebelling against his faith and his authority within his home, criticizing the heart of his life. His posture shifted like a black bear about to rise on its hind legs. Redness passed over his eyes and seeped into his face. Mum reached out an arm as he shirked both of us on the way to the front door. His shoulder thumped into my chest like a hammer into paper. We watched him throw on his coat and how his hands shook, fumbling for the car keys. He was about to leave when he pivoted back so he could see only me. With a scrunched face, still trying to land on one emotion, he raised a crooked finger to my throat. I was totally arrested.

"You listen here, I may not be happy every time I go to work and I may be even more depressed some days when I come back. But I do it all and would do it again so that I could provide for your mother, your sisters, and even you. If you see a job as just something to fill your time then… then I've done my work because my work has been about survival in ways you'll never understand. You never had to go collect coal that had fallen off the train so that you wouldn't have to go to bed cold to the ribs. I did and I swore while I shivered that no one under my name would ever be that cold again. That's what I believe in, Declan. I believe that warmth isn't a given and if you don't believe me, you just try going out there and surviving without our help. Maybe then you won't be so dreamy."

He passed through the door, out of the house, and into the car. I walked in a daze over to the window. As he backed out of the driveway, he didn't look once to the window to see if I was there. He looked so flustered, so determined. In part of my heart, I hoped he was going to the church and not the bar.

I stayed staring at the lamplight on the sidewalk. No one walked through it and no cars rolled across the orange carpet spread over the street. It was dark enough now that my ghostly reflection hung in the intermediate darkness. That was when Mum appeared. As if stepping out of the night, she approached me, arms folded, and a face like melting ice—sharp but getting softer. She stood like that long enough for me to see the grey of her eyes in the window. They were not like that in reality but out there, in the lonely cool of the evening, it was enough to convince someone otherwise.

"Don't worry about him. When he comes back, he and I will talk, okay?"

It was my turn for silence.

"He will come back, Declan. You know that."

She turned and softly strode to the table, pulling out a chair at the end. Without speech or motion, she sat with the expectation that she would be joined, eventually. She opened and closed her hands as if checking a pocket-watch before looking left and right. It was enough to make me relent in my staring so I hurried over to take my usual spot at the table. There we were, like we had sat at a thousand dinners before, my Mum next to me, the baby, just in case I needed help cutting my food. A stirring and nameless emotion spun itself between my stomach and throat. I swallowed as if trying to digest it. She didn't mind the waiting and didn't rush me to explain myself. Her hand reached out and landed on my upper back, right between the shoulder blades, and started circling. When words did come, they came in her language.

"Mum, do you remember when I told you and Dad that I didn't believe in god? The first time, anyway."

"Oh, yes, I remember it well."

"I remember it too. There was one part of that I don't think Dad or I understood. Didn't you say you wished you could get away from it all? The church and the beliefs and everything, but you just couldn't? What's keeping you tied to the place?"

Taking her hand off my back and placing it on the table, she took a pause the length of a cigarette drag. She sighed before she turned back to me.

"When I was growing up, there was a lot of change going on in Québec. Did they ever teach you about the Quiet Revolution?"

"Mum, I went to school in B.C., even my French teachers didn't speak French."

"What else can you expect from this part of the country? Anyway, around the time that I was born, it seemed like everything was changing at home. Before then, the Catholic Church ran everything, and I mean everything. They ran the schools, the hospitals, even the politicians seemed as if they were set up by the Vatican. I remember we went up to see the National Assembly on a school trip and right there, above the speaker's chair, was a crucified Christ. He had been nailed to our culture from the inside."

"How did they get the nails out?"

"Normally, when people are angry with an oppressive government telling them what to do and how they can live, the people rise up in the streets and demand justice, right?"

"Sure, at least that's how it always seems."

"Never discount the Québecois for our ability to go

against the mainstream. If there's one thing we are as a people, it's stubborn. And when you're stubborn, you can only take other people's crap for so long. We were living in a religious state and, since we don't like to be predictable either, we turned the institutions around from within.

"It started with electing politicians that were reformers. These people were so obsessed with Québec that they put the needs of the place ahead of the needs of the Church. We were to realize that we were to become the Masters of Our Own House, as the slogan went, and with that, a wave of independence rolled over everyone. With that independence came a new excitement for secularism so they got the Church out of the schools and the hospitals and they turned as many of the private companies into government projects. Where they succeeded was in giving the people of Québec something more important than the facts of politics."

"What could be more important than facts?"

"A vision, a symbol, something to believe in beyond the words and the people who spoke them. It's what also started the movement for separation from Canada because, once you take down a beast as big and hairy as the Catholic Church, something like Canada doesn't seem so threatening."

"Just as long as they could stay on the Canadian dollar, right?"

Mum smirked at the common criticism.

"Yes, something like that."

"If that's all going on for the textbooks to record,

what's happening in the lives of everyday people? Did you notice things changing that dramatically?"

"Life went on with new faces on old organizations. More and more people I knew went to schools with teachers instead of nuns. We were still Canadians, by law, but it was more of a regular thing to hear people asserting themselves as distinct, as Québecois rather than Canadien. It was like we were trying to become our own adults, but we were stuck in our parents' house."

I shrunk at the comparison.

"Back then, it seemed like everyone was excited to grow up. There was such a swing for personal liberation all over the world. Women were going to work, men were wearing their hair long, it was like everything was changing. First we only saw about these things in magazines, the rare times they would get delivered. Reading about the ideas and the fashion was like being sent letters from the future, but it wasn't a future everyone was ready for."

"Oh?"

"You know that I've liked to think of myself as a feminist and particularly of the kind I read about growing up. A forward-thinking woman, one who could do more than one thing. Anyway, this kind of idea wasn't for everyone. Especially my parents. You see, while your grandmaman was raising us, Grandpapa was at work. What else could she do but turn on the radio or take us to the city where it seemed like everyone else had moved somewhere else? Grandpapa had no ideas about these changes, of course, because he was either working or talking in the bar and those conversations have never changed.

"Your grandmaman, like so many women of her generation, didn't finish high school because she was the eldest and had to help with the family and the farm. Now here she was, a new mother herself, with both her parents gone, and siblings that were too young to know anything. She heard words of revolution that, for the first time in her life, were in her favour. Naturally, she was all in for it, and just like the Church had no idea about the changes coming their way, Grandpapa couldn't understand what had gotten into Grandmaman."

"Did they fight?"

"Not often and rarely while we were awake. But when they did, it was always about that. Grandmaman would cry out that marriage was just another form of slavery and men had no right to make women their servants and on and on and on. Grandpapa, having heard nothing of the sort, had no intellectual defence, so he just yelled back or stormed out. It was like they weren't ever talking to each other. One made an assertion, the other would respond with a misunderstanding, and they would fight over that."

I thought of my own father.

"Did he ever hit her?"

Mum looked at the table, then to the wall, then to me.

"No, I don't believe he did. I don't think he could."

I had never heard about this version of my grandparents before and it manifested in a unique form of being upset. When I was in my later years at university, I took an art history course as a free elective and we did a section on Van Gogh. Like everyone else, I was enamoured with his vision of things; and fortunately, the professor was a vigilant guide. For the final essay of the course, I wrote a paper on the famous sunflowers. It was about the history of non-human subjects in European art and how Van Gogh commanded yellow to break from the lineage of other still life painters. No other painter had ever shocked me with a single colour before. Taking some quotations from his letters, I was meticulous in pouring over his references to the colours of the world, as if his eyes were blazing yellow instead of china blue. When I got the paper back, I had a good grade, but I was stopped by a comment my professor had written in the margins. It said: "You are so amazed by the initial beauty of the piece that you've overlooked what was there the whole time—the flowers in this painting are dying." When I heard about Grandmaman and Grandpapa fighting, I thought about that painting.

Mum could see there was some distress forming in me. Perhaps her mother was right to tell her that there are some things a child is never meant to hear. She put her hand on mine and looked at me reassuringly.

"I'm sure it never happened. And just because two people break apart from each other for a short time doesn't mean they can't come back together. Right?"

I nodded but wanted a subject change. Something to refocus our conversation.

"But what about Church? Did Grandmaman stop going to that too?"

"No, she didn't. And she rarely brought up her private thoughts in public anyway. We have to remember that all of these changes, all of these shifts, were taking place in the cities. The government passing these measures was up in Québec City and the new centre of it all was in Montréal. We were out in the townships where life moves a little slower, where the emotions and the tendencies take longer to change. So while people in town were agreeing with the new platforms and ideas, life itself was slow to change. Maybe we didn't feel as threatened by the Church because it was so banal. Also, so much of this change was to set ourselves apart from an invasion of English. We didn't have to worry much because, where we were, there weren't any. You know this. Some of my relatives still, even after I married your father, don't speak anything even related to English, and couldn't survive in Ontario if they needed to."

"Remember when we went back to Ottawa that one time and, at the dep in Hull, there was that cashier that couldn't speak any English?"

"Oh, yes! Your dad was so frustrated! I remember we got out of the store and he opened his hands towards the bridge and said 'How can they not speak English? Ontario is right there!' Oh, those were good days with you kids."

We laughed until we forgot why. Was it that bright a memory or did it seem that way under present darkness? After a mutual exhalation, I looked up at her. She was dabbing near her eyes in the deep lines she had earned. It was comforting to see. With the air out of us, we sat as if lost for a moment. The echo of earlier in the night had withered, but it still rumbled with every passing car.

"Did those changes ever stop Grandmaman from going to church?"

"Oh, no, not at all. Like I said, things were a little slower to change where we were. In those days everybody went to Church, and I mean everybody. It was the one thing amongst all that novelty that the whole town agreed on. Sure, they could throw the Church out of public life, but that didn't mean people stopped believing. In fact, it probably concentrated people's efforts. It was certainly even more formal than it is now."

"That can't be."

"But it was! Every little girl in that place wore their most special dress with saddle shoes. You knew someone was trying to show off if they showed up with a little sailor hat as well instead of a clip for their hair. And the gloves—you should have seen them. Every grown-up woman wearing white gloves, with some of them going right up to the elbow. I used to pester Grandmaman so much to let me wear hers, but they were always too big. By the time I was old enough to wear them, they weren't the sort of thing people wore. Even self-described ladies had locked them away in some box in their closet. A remnant that will probably never return to style."

"What about the boys?"

"The men all dressed like your father but what was cute was that their sons did as well. They wore the tiniest little suits and combed their hair over. Really, they all looked like they were ready to interview at Sterling Cooper Draper Pryce and they couldn't have been more than 10."

"That's ridiculous."

"Maybe so but those were the days and that was just what people did back then. I know now when we look back at how dressed up everyone used to get it's just so silly, but I've always liked it. It felt like there were some invisible rules about being out of your house and when everyone was participating, you felt like you belonged to something. Whenever Grandmaman and Grandpapa put on their Church clothes, or any outdoor clothes, really, you knew they were going to get along. People didn't get mad in public like they do now and, you can call me superficial, but I think it was more than just etiquette. It was purpose. That's the sort of thing that brings people together and that's what I loved about going to Church.

"There were some people that lived a town or two over but would make the trip if they got on well with the priest at a different Church. So it was fun to have people that didn't see you every day. They were the ones that always said the nicest things to the kids. We'd get there a bit early to chat and catch up. Oh, and afterwards!"

"Yes?"

"As nice as Church could be—and I'm not saying it was always fun—sometimes you fell asleep. But afterwards, it put everyone in such a good mood that we didn't want the day to end. Grandpapa might take us out for ice cream or we'd go over to the Lévèsque's. I don't think you remember M. Lévèsque, but if we went over to his house, and stayed through dinner, he'd sing for us. It was so unexpected because he looked like a regular guy, but when he sang it was like he could fly. After Church, all the regular things in life seemed shinier. It was the tradition of it that made it worth it."

"That's why you still believe? Not because of the grace of god or the truth of the word, but because of your memories?"

"The memories and the effects. The Church I grew up with had the power to transform people into the versions I liked best. I believe in people coming together and being happy and, for me, I can't separate that from my early life in the Church. Listen, I know how horrible they've been—whether it's been about the altar boys or anything else—but if I turned away now, it feels like I'm turning away from my whole life. On all the family and memories that made that place so special. If I have to believe in God to do so, I'm happy with it. In the grand plan of everything, our town in Québec won't mean much. No one from there will become famous or rich and, from the outside, it looks like a place where nothing happens. The things we do when we're at our smallest may seem like bits of nothing but… but it's all those little bits of nothing that give you a lifetime."

She was talking about the undramatic, the inconsequential, the way a person stuttered or insisted. These were the seemingly trivial details of living that filled in all the lines of life. If I wasn't internally sobbing before, I was now. How could I have been so arrogant? To her, this place wasn't about long history, theology, or truth. It was about experiences and relationships—about real, lived life that surrounded them. She had received her communion not from god but from other people. Did Dad believe the same?

Mum's eyes were tearing and so were mine, even if I kept my eyelids high like levees. Who could explain why? This wasn't an answer for the rationalists and, besides, who could rationalize all their memories remembered in a new order?

"Oh, Mum, I just don't know what I'm supposed to do about anything." My tone was rising. "I don't know who I'm supposed to be, how I'm supposed to act, in what way I'm supposed to get it, and, just, any of it. I just don't know!"

I dropped my forehead to the space between my arms like a child. Mum wasn't distant nor authoritative, just there, waiting. She placed her hand on my back again and ran it softly between my shoulders.

"I wish I knew exactly what to say. I wish I had all the answers you could ever need. There are some things that can't be explained by someone else. But I can tell you that you're loved and you have our support. All of us, not just your dad and me, but your sisters as well. Families do that for each other."

I looked up through glossy eyes. Mum straightened herself up, and after a moment, I matched her. We each dabbed our sleeves around our faces and shared a liberating, if uncomfortable, giggle. I trusted her to be able to fix this. That was how it was growing up. She was like a non-stop emergency responder, rushing in without hesitation or difficulty to dowse the blazes of childhood distress. Seated before me now wasn't that same kind of hero. She wasn't invincible, she wasn't omniscient, she was an adult, and being an adult didn't mean she had conquered everything.

With fingers dancing on the table in equal count, we both kept our words hidden. Mum's mouth pursed and scrunched under her nose, sometimes glancing up with the jerkiness of a bird. I looked over whenever she moved. Her shoulders raised and she looked at me, opening her mouth and then sealing it without explanation.

"What were you going to say?" I asked.

"It was nothing, nothing serious anyway."

"Mum, you should know how important a little bit of nothing can be. And right now we're sitting with less than nothing. So come on, it might be an improvement."

"Okay, here's my thought. What if tomorrow morning, before your Dad gets up and no one else is around, you take a walk and just think about what it is you really want to be. I know it can sometimes be hard to think and be still, so maybe a bit of quiet movement will get things going. We don't have to tell anyone where you've gone and, I don't know, you might feel better when you get back. How does that sound?"

"I mean, I don't think it'll worsen anything. And we don't have to tell anyone?"

"Not unless you want to. This is your life and life is about decisions. And don't worry about your dad, really. I'll talk to him. I'm sure he's just shocked is all."

She stood up from the table and gave me a kiss on the top of my head. With two pats on the shoulder, she walked by me and into the kitchen to finish cleaning up the dishes from dinner. I stayed in the chair while I listened to the sink water splash and the baking sheets crash. Once the sound had gone away, I got up from my seat, went into the kitchen, and hugged my Mum.

"Thank you," I said.

She responded in English.

"You're welcome, Declan, you're so welcome."

Chapter Thirteen

When I woke up, the sun was still a suggestion. Its beige curve poked out like a timid neighbour, its radiance low and unobtrusive to the sky. Comfortably covered in navy with the occasional speckled guest, the moon was still the host of the sky. It was full and confident up there, appearing to be the source of mystical light that covered all surfaces like snow. Of course, it was just the shadow, the mirror of the real thing. The moon was a substitute whose brightness was insufficient against the true heart of the cosmos.

Had dad come home last night? I tiptoed out of my room and heard the crawling wisps of his snores. He was like that bear again, breathing heavy and strong, from inside the dark cave of his bedroom. Being ever-so-careful on the stairs, I descended through the guts of the house. I kept my hands close and my feet light, insisting I touched as few objects as possible. It was an attempt to be invisible, as if leaving a trace spread a contagious and dirty sin. The edge of the door and its frame kissed closed as I turned the lock so slowly it didn't click. Then there was nothing.

I stood for a moment, still touching the door, and let

the sounds of the morning float by. Distant engines, the thin cries of summer birds, and nothing else. No bugs, no people, and no sirens. The lack of noise provided space to be filled with thoughts. Guilt, purpose, redemption, and expectation all stalked through my mind with the quiet weight of jungle cats. I looked up to the bedroom window of the house, listened for the sounds of my parents, and let go of the doorknob. They would remain inside while I headed off without guile or conviction.

Just around from where we lived was a gravel path canopied in salmonberry trees. When I walked under its branches, it hung like a cover preserving the times I had come here as a child. Through its leaves, the sunlight blotched the ground in untraceable shapes, providing the warmth of the summer with the damage. Céline, Hélène, and I used to lose ourselves in the trails and trees after elementary school, darting in and amongst the trunks, playing games of fantastical pretend. Each step through this enchanted forest was like walking through the birth of my imagination. Scenes played out like phantom films as the empty woods provided ample space for projections of the past. We had fun then when everything seemed limitless.

As I walked along the trail that day, between the memories, the atmosphere was much more sombre. There was no sun yet to wash the ground of the unknown and to turn the forest into the colours it required. The green leaves and brown branches melded into different shades of cobalt. It was also much quieter since the dogwalkers of town were still asleep along with the rest of the wildlife. An infrequent buzzing from a careless insect proved that I was not totally alone here. Beyond those, I was the loudest thing on that trail with each crunch on the infinite gravel. I looked up through the curves and lines of the trees to glimpse the indigo sky. The stars were retreating like small fish from a passing whale. Soon, the sun would be up and I wanted to be at the inlet when it did.

The curve of the water waited, as usual, at the bottom of the trail. Again I saw the pale phantoms of childhood dashing into the small pool to cool off. Neither too deep nor too murky, we used to take to the inlet like seals, gliding with surprising ease along its surface. Reeds and long leaves of grass poked out near the drop off, a welcome warning about depth and distance. It was so nice to sit there in the middle of it all. Between the fringes of the greenery sat one of the many northern mountains that watched over our lives. Those peaks which looked remarkable in snow, intriguing in mist, gentle in rainbows, and warm in sun. What else had such a lasting and flexible beauty?

I've looked at those mountains all my life, yet I still don't understand how they make me feel. Those lumpy, imperfect mounds out of which the sky seemed to hatch. They, covered in trees, stood firm in their interruption of the horizon. By hiding away the edge of the Earth, they formed anticipation for each sunrise. They provided warning and time for anyone that wanted to watch the aurora spew its colours. It was miraculous that the rising sun still beguiled. After a few hundred generations, anyone could sit and stare into the east and be struck by the momentary mixture of dawn unrolling like a king's cape. Even today, under the pinkless sky, the mountains belonged to the sublime.

Walking out of my memories and into the day, I stepped around the edges of the last enclosing bushes and trees. They closed in my wake and covered the trail I had come down by. Being there was like being away once the leaves huddled up. No longer belonging to the concrete of the suburb. With the plants behind, the mountain's outline was receding into light as the low orange haze crept its way over the horizon. The greens of the leaves became brighter and the water was speckled and purple as it reflected perfectly the sheltering sky. Everything, except for the mountains and the grass, was in that water. I had to join it. As quietly as I had walked out of the house, I took my steps closer to the edge of the land. The morning's glow was as welcoming as a homecoming.

I stepped carefully over the fine rocks and took off my shoes, holding them in my left hand. The water was perfect without the disturbance of a ripple. It had beckoned me; but now that I was so near, it felt like an intrusion to cross it. Nature had balanced in this place and my presence, my human presence, would have been enough to offset it by taking the flat lines that had settled in the night and disturbing them. I stopped a few feet from shore. Near enough to notice the temperature from the passing dark as it glided off the surface. The rocks turned to sand around my toes, and by remaining still, the Earth slowly engulfed my weight. Both feet sank down, fastened to the sand, surrounded by rocks and calm. The sun would come and it too would bury everything open enough to be unobscured.

They glided graceful and low across the orange-tinted water. Three great blue herons, heads tucked and wings at their sides, flew in a tight triangular formation. No sound, no imprint. As they neared the border of liquid and land, they split apart in the way tree branches do. The two that flanked the original formation took to their posts on the outside edges of the curved shoreline while the third placed itself between them, in direct line with me. Even in the decreasing dimness, it was clear this one was the oldest and most weathered. With a few lingering scratch marks on its wing and a battle-worn beak, this was an animal that would not be conquered easily.

All focus went to the farthest birds. Slender shadows that fussed over their mutual task. They seemed agitated. When they moved through the water, they thrashed it, sending mutual ripples tripping over each other. Their wings swatted along the bumpy surface before stabbing it like a broken sewing machine. After a few attempts, they flew back and forth in a crisscross change of position. When they passed, they squawked as if perturbed, either by the other or the situation. Over and again they unsuccessfully plunged, only to retract with a vigorous shake and nothing else. Their heads dropped back and curled their bodies into sketches of treble clefs. If it was a meal they were after, their hunger had ruined their skill.

The nearest heron seemed not to have moved at all. Its head made no sweeps of the aquatic terrain and its eyes were not following a fish as if in a predictable maze.

At times, it tucked its bill into its neck like it was stretching out an old stiffness before resuming its pace. Each step taken skillfully, mysteriously, and without impact on the situation outside of itself. The twigs on which it stood bent out of the water, leaving the feet to remain constantly beneath the pool of its reflective stance. No feathers shuffled, no wings adjusted. The bird was so still the wind could have blown right through it.

The previously darkened mountain which stood out in contrast to the lightness in the early morning sky now had a comfortable and recognizable hue of deep green. It was the colour it was best meant to be and fit in with the kaleidoscopic harmony of the rising sun. Still, against this background, within the curved mouth of the inlet, the herons had not made a catch. A mutual frustration bonded me to the two distant ones but, upon refocusing on the nearest, an uninvited but altogether welcome patience settled. It took its careful strides with its neck craned away from the water, beak pointing up towards the drooping leaves of the overhanging trees. I was sure that if I moved my position, I could see it silhouetted with the newly sun-soaked mountains over its back. But I didn't want to move; I couldn't. What if they flew away?

The nearest heron turned back as if on a tightrope hidden beneath the surface. It had taken effort to notice how it was not walking back and forth at random but in a repeating line. Had one been drawn in the sand below or was the bird so light it hadn't disturbed anything? These steps lacked the nervousness or anxiety to be called pacing. The movements were too deliberate, too practiced, and lacked all external expectation. It passed again and again with the banal relentlessness of an incoming tide. Until it stopped.

With no drawback, no hint that this animal was about to strike, it did. Like a silent whip, it cracked its spine from coil to straight and pointed through the water. Breaking through the image reflected on its surface, its head disappeared for a moment, only to reappear as quickly as it dropped out with an addition to its outline. The beak, which had just been a perfect triangle, now awkwardly bulged in the middle as a small fish flapped from between teeth. In one quick, synchronized movement, it flipped the fish into the air, opened its jaws, and swallowed it whole. Then, with refinement, the heron deeply dipped its beak into the water like a pen into an inkwell. It shook off the excess and resumed its relaxed pace on the sand. The other herons, still restless and unfocused, remained ignorant to the success of their third. They called out with the echo of empty bellies to each other and to the sky. The third heron made no such pleas. It cast its eyes down and took up its pace again parallel to the shore.

What a wonder. This bird showed as little celebration as hesitation. It returned to its firm pace while the sun started on its same fixed trajectory. Morning had crossed with the same quietude as the heron. Every day began with a bright smear before the pinpoint of light hung with invisible attachment. The whole of the land was humming as it rose to life.

A chill crawled up my legs. Until then, I had forgotten they were there. It was when I looked down and saw the sea exhaling itself against my shins that I noticed how deep I was. The sand had sunken and covered not only my feet but up my ankles as well. They were fixed in thick wet mud with the strength of a marble base. Between my base limbs, a tiny stream formed with water passing in and out, forward and back, to a slightly different speed than everything else.

How long had I been standing there? Time had been bypassed in the morning calm. In one waking snap, my body regained its feeling. Fingers ceased to float and returned to dangling. The wind knocked at my hips and I had to tense and loosen some muscles to keep balance. All things I had been doing without thinking and now, when I tried to concentrate, it seemed I was worse at them. In this time of readjustment, my eyes had lost focus. They were looking into that so-called middle distance in which nothing tangible existed. An illusion that appeared to be full and could never be seen if looked for. In regaining concentration, the water laid once again as a unified sheet of reflection. The herons had flown away.

I looked softly, keenly, deeply across the vista, but the three birds were nowhere. Not sheltered under branches, not reinstalled in some other area of the inlet, they had just gone and they left without any evidence that they were ever there. The inlet reflected everything and recorded nothing. With no one else around to shed the solitude of the moment, the we made of me and the herons turned back into an I. The dreadful, towering, isolated I that stood without attachment. Looking towards the sky, thin wisps of clouds resembling feathers dragged out between the mountains and the sun. My imagination took over as it wondered if the herons had been there at all or if they served as projections of a selfish mind.

The water was nearing my knees now. I could worry about the possible realities of birds all I wanted, but if I didn't move soon then my shorts might stain in the saltwater. It was a weak excuse. Unsticking my feet from the collapsed trenches and carefully avoiding the rocks and shells now sheltered by the tide, I routed my course for home. Nothing beckoned me to leave. It was an instinct that told me I was done there. The leaves bristled goodbye when I fanned through them.

Sunlight dropped down like ropes between the trees over the trail. It was an adjustment coming from the vast amphitheatre of the inlet. Before I fully saw, I heard. The quick crunching pats of joggers, bells ringing from dog collars, and tweets of morning birds. I had again been stopped as the first crew of morning runners passed me. Each nodded or puffed out a good morning as they breezed by. Once I began walking and in turn made passes of my own, I felt the same obligation. Greeting everyone I saw and being greeted in return was a great social embrace. There was a shimmering quality to each of these passersby. In their faces, I saw everything. Who was rushed, who was content, who was dreaming, and who was determined. Each brief moment of jointure was like an *amuse-cerveau* that preluded a grander meal of connection.

I knew, intellectually, that they had inner lives. New combinations of feelings and ideas that melded together with their blood and breath separate from others. Of course, they were similar but not exact, and that was what made them enticing. Could they stop? Would they be interested? It's been said that everyone's favourite word is their own name. Is everyone's favourite collection of words their own feelings? If only there was infinite time and infinite tables over which each of us could sit with one another and chat about who we were, what we've been expected to be, and if we were happy. That sounded like paradise.

Throughout the spreads of people and nature, I walked transfixed. It was filling to take in all my senses allowed, and in combination they fortified. In the space of my awestruck mind, I remembered why I had come here. It was about work, but it was more about god. As a component, god hadn't entered at all. The world was full enough. Looking around at everything alive, they seemed to be living and interacting without the need for a force outside of nature. The plants, the birds, and the deer found sustenance and purpose in the world around them. Could a person as well? Surely the sky and the mountains and the sun and the herons had no use for god because they had no method of thanking him. If all the rest of the world was godless, why make an exception for people?

It was the people, the lives, and the interactions that moved me. The church made people calm, and when they were so, they spoke about themselves gracefully. It could connect me to them, it would let them let me into their lives. Over the course of time, I could counsel them. Mum's words about the social unity of the church rippled through and covered all divine misguiding. I remembered my Kierkegaard, the paradox that speared his life, and how it was only through an illogical, irrational, or seemingly impossible action that his truth could come. Only when standing on the brink with no way to know the outcome did he believe one could arrive at enlightenment. Perhaps this was my paradox.

Chapter Fourteen

I got home and there were no cars in the driveway. The street, like so many other suburban streets on a summer morning, was empty except for the covering sound of lawnmowers. I opened the front door with caution and let out an unarmed "Hello?" Neither an echo nor a shadow stepped out in return. They had gone, stuck to their commitments outside the home, and left behind the peaceful freedom of an empty house.

It was breakfast time. I dropped the English muffin into the toaster and locked it to its heat. An even balance of yogurt and granola went into a small bowl and was set in my place with the spoon sticking out. In front of the toaster went a side plate and beside that, the tub of peanut butter with a knife placed at an angle over the flipped lid of the jar. It was a comforting routine.

With the predictability of order came a mindlessness. Since I didn't have to think about what I would do next or how long it would take, my thoughts were free to roam anywhere. They visited last night's outburst only to quicken when they tried to replicate exactly how loud Dad had been; they jumped from mental movies of our childhood walks to photographs of Mum's days in the Eastern

Townships. Her photographs seemed more everlasting, grander than what we had lived through. The people in them looked firmer as if they had all been born exactly as they were with no awkward scars of maturation. From people, my thoughts circled back to nature.

The toaster popped, taking me away from my wanderings. While one side of the English muffin was smothered, I put the other side back in to keep it warm. The knife bent over every rift and peak as the peanut butter trickled into waiting pools. Levels rose until the entire circle was so well-covered that it appeared flat. I pushed the cancel button and did the same thing to the other side. Returning everything to its proper place in the cupboard, I spun from the counter to the table, ready to resume my considerations.

Each bite brought a different possibility. I could still say I wasn't sure. Bite. I could claim I was. Bite. I could do my best to explain exactly what I had seen and hope that my parents would understand as I did. Bite. It was all a risk. I put the English muffin down and sat back to think longer. What did I know for sure? There was no god and there was no need for one. But then why go into the church? The line "I want to" sprang to mind. Did I have to want it? Would liking be enough?

To like and to want, these were words fundamental to a life. I could want the goodies and bonuses of an oil tycoon, but would I like that work? Would it make me happy? Inversely, I liked movies. Would I want to make them the object of my life's orbit? If I chased only the wants of my life, I would be living in delusion. The wants would never run out and might grow like hunger. Then again, the likes might serve better as hobbies. Joyful distractions without the burden of necessity or expectation. They were the things that framed a life, complemented the subjects so as to make the whole experience sturdier and more pleasing. At some point, between these poles, didn't I just have to pick something? Did my forefathers stress themselves this much over the work that made their lives?

Before I saw the tail of that thought, the phone rang. The house phone rarely rang in the morning. I got up from the table and went to its base. Glancing at the caller display, the numbers five-one-four were on display.

"Allo?" I said with cheek.

"You're going to be a priest now?" Céline said.

"Who told you?"

"I have my ways. I can be just as mysterious as God, you know."

"Isn't that blasphemy?"

"Look who's talking. Anyway, no, that's not how I knew. I called here earlier this morning—or was it afternoon? It might have been afternoon here but not quite late enough for it to have been afternoon there. I'm never sure if the difference between B.C. and here is three or four hours and, frankly, it's not something I need in my everyday life. It can pass just fine without my knowing. What were you asking? Oh, yes. I had called earlier and Mum picked up the phone. We start chatting about work and my show at the end of the month. You should really see it. I'll send pictures, but I find pictures of pictures can be a bit glossy and you never get the scale right. So then I start asking about Dad and you and she says you're out at the moment. I thought 'What? He doesn't have a job so where could he be so early?' That's not how I said it, obviously, but she laughs and tells me you, her, and Dad had this big chat last night about your career and, let me tell you, I was as shocked as they were. I mean, my baby brother? Wearing the garments of the clergy? I couldn't believe it, so I figured I'd call back and hear it from the horse himself. So, are they telling truths? Or are they living in their own interpretations again?"

"They're telling the truth. That's really what I think I'm going to do. How are you, by the way?"

"I'm just marvellous! I started my day by taking a walk down Earnscliffe. Do you remember where that is? It's been so long since you've been to Montréal, but it's kind of in the Snowdon part of the city, near Monkland Village and Côte-des-Neiges. I just moved into the area and I like going out to explore. Did Mum tell you I moved again?"

"Nope."

"Another reason for a visit! I'm right around Parc Mackenzie King. Isn't that kind of funny? That someone who is half French and half English ends up living near a French park named after an English guy? I told the realtor as much and he didn't seem interested, but he was only wearing brown and beige so I guessed he was no fun."

"Oh yeah?"

"Oh my God, he was awful. In the way that there was no way he could have known how boring he was because to be that interested in even himself would have meant he had to have been interesting. I did spy a wedding ring on his finger though, which means some dame got tricked into spending the rest of her life with him. It's so weird when you see people with wedding rings out alone. It means they're connected to someone else all the time and want everyone to know it. But enough about him, isn't it weird that they can't call it Mackenzie King Park? The government's done its best to translate all the names of the places into French so, like, Starbucks is Café Starbucks and McDonald's is Chez-McDonald; although, and this is really interesting, Simons gets to be Simons because it's a family name that already ends in an 's' so even though it sounds like it could be Simon's with the apostrophe it's not—it's Simons—and it's a Québec company, I think they opened the first one in Québec City, actually, so they get to get around the language laws. If you're interested, Mordecai Richler wrote a bunch of pieces, I think, about these laws and they're all great. I can send them to you if you want."

I was remembering why I rarely called my sister.

"I was walking down Earnscliffe and I passed by this duplex. It was so gorgeous, Declan, much prettier than the regular brown brick boxes that seem to grow out here. I get it, the winters are harsh and everything gets dark, but can't we zhuzh it up like they do in Newfoundland? Where each house has a bit of personality? I mean, I love the twisty stairs as much as the next local, but what kind of city wants to be known for that? Oh, look at us, we can go up from down—it's pathetic is what it is. Anyway, this duplex was stunning first because it was confidently white with rectangles outlined in black. They were probably brick, but they didn't look like it. What mattered is they looked chic, y'know? Like something a Parisian would paint into a background. Not like the rest of this city, which always looks like it's falling apart in real time. Honestly, the place is covered in snow for, like, half a year, and then they tear it all up in the summer just to go on a two week 'construction holiday' right in the middle! I'm like 'Hello? Aren't you supposed to be working now? You know, before all the snow comes back?'

"Anyway, I'm walking by this duplex and this woman comes out like a character in a play. I mean, she was stunning. She wore her mid-length blonde hair in a tight ponytail, she had white, horn-rimmed sunglasses, bright, bright pink lipstick, and a champagne coloured dress with glittery sequins all along the shoulders and chest. Her frame was also exactly like a flute glass so it couldn't have been more perfect of a combo. Oh! And her shoes were these tasteful little heels with the straps that go over the top of the foot and around the ankle—I know you don't know what they're called, but if you ever get a girlfriend, buy her some and she'll be with you forever. Seriously, this woman looked like she'd walked out of the pages of *Vogue* or maybe *Chatelaine* when it still meant something to people."

"Uh-huh."

"She was walking down towards me on the sidewalk and I'm just stunned, right, and, luckily, I have my camera on me. I had planned on doing some urban shots, playing around with natural lighting and the shapes and city and things like that. But, like I always say, I never take pictures of other people's art. So no murals, no sculptures, nothing. It's too cheap, and it's not my art anyway, y'know? Where was I?"

"The well-dressed woman was walking toward you." By this point, I had gone upstairs to my room. I put the phone on speaker and threw it to the end of my bed while I lay stomach-side up, forearm draped over my forehead. If I said enough monosyllables, she'd eventually tire out. Eventually.

"Right, right, right! Just as I said, this stunning, thin, pointed woman comes down the little staircase with curly ends. I actually almost bumped into her. She starts excusing herself and I say 'No, no, no, no, no, no, don't apologize. My name is Céline and I'm a local photographer on my way to take pictures of the city but, I mean, if you wouldn't mind, could I take some photos of you too?' She didn't hesitate for a second, but she had a condition. 'Only if my house can be in the photos too.' Can you believe it?"

"No, I really can't."

"You should because that's exactly how it happened. She goes back and even though she dressed for a cover shoot, she somehow looks comfortable in her garden. I can't believe it. It's so rare to find someone who looks good with both gold and dirt, yet I had found such a person. As I'm getting the camera all set up, fiddling with the settings to account for the big white background, she stands patiently as if I'm no inconvenience. We start talking because I find clients always give me the best poses between sentences. They either have something to think about or react to. Anyway, I ask her about the house and her life and she says it belonged to her mother. She said to always leave the house as if she was going to meet the love of her life. And do you know who her mother was?"

"I don't."

"Take a guess."

"Céline, of all the women who live or lived in Montréal, I really don't think I know."

"Spoil sport. Her mother was Mme. Landry!"

"Who?"

"You don't remember? Mme. Landry? She was Mum's second grade teacher way back in the Townships. That's the teacher who showed Mum the trick for tying shoelaces with the two bunny ears that I know you still use. Right?"

How did she remember Mum's teacher and how I tied my shoes?

"I guess you're right."

"Of course I am. It's such a small world out here, so much more connected I find than Vancouver. People have actually been here for a while. In Vancouver, everyone either just got there or is passing through. I'm surprised people are there long enough to die—I thought that was what the island was for. In Montréal, even in the city, which is also an island, by the way, when you leave your house, you still see people you know. I told Mum all this when I called this morning and she said if she remembered anything she'd write back to me."

"Write to you?"

"That's right. I'm calling you from home. I got rid of my cell phone."

"Céline, you need to have a cell phone."

"Why? I didn't need all the beeping and buzzing, it was so perturbing. I didn't need it for a camera either since I rarely leave home without mine now. If people want to get in touch with me, there's a perfectly good mailbox downstairs, or they can wait until I get home. You should try writing letters to people. It's fun! You really get to think about what you have to say, how you feel. Not like the unrehearsed blathering that everyone else does in conversation. And so unoriginally too."

"But what if something happens while you're out?"

"Oh, come off it. Things happened for eons before cell phones, everything was fine. People were born, died, travelled, and got lost, and there's no way that the invention of the cell phone has positively affected those happenings. If anything, they've made life more boring since they've taken all the 'Who knows?' out of decision making. Which route to take home? No one says who knows anymore because they insist on being on the fastest route all the time. Unless Google has installed a scenic option in the last few months? No, I remember all my friends' phone numbers and all those apps are just tracking us anyway, so why carry those little square spies around? Nope. No, no, no sir-e-bob. I'm going to pretend I'm living in the good old days. Or, like Julie says, in the good young days."

"Julie? Julie who?"

"Julie! My new friend? Julie Landry? The one I've been talking about for the last however long. You remember, the woman in the white house with the great dress. That Julie! Hello? Are you listening?"

"I don't think you told me her name."

"Didn't I? Are you sure you've been listening?"

The painful thing is that I was listening. To all of it. Because there was no escape from her incoming verbal tide.

"Maybe I missed it. Sorry."

"It's all okay, little brother! I know you've got a whole whack of stuff on your mind anyway. Like becoming a priest, right? How did that come about? Because, from what I remember, you're a pretty hardline atheist that don't need no God and don't care who knows it. It just seems like a rather odd choice. What made you do it, huh? Are you a secret atheist double-agent? Have you started doing any of the work yet?"

"No, no, I haven't started doing the work yet."

"Well, maybe you should before you make it the focus of your whole life, y'know. I remember when I started working in finance, whoa, let me tell you, I wish I had done more practical work before I signed up. I mean, I liked doing all the math and stuff but the slog of the work and the slugs that I worked with, yuck. Maybe if I had done an internship or something when I was at school, then I could've seen the work for what it was: deftly boring. Oh my God, Declan, you have no idea. There were some days that I arrived at my desk, on time and well-made, and I would not have even stood up from there until the end of the day. No movement, no vibrancy, just numbers and work, numbers and work. And, don't get me wrong, I love a good and balanced sheet, but I just couldn't believe that this was going to be my life—that it *was* my life while I was in it. It was so horrible. I remember pacing around my apartment thinking about rebellion and shiny things, and then I got an idea. The next day, I would wear mismatched shoes to the office. Partly just for the fun of it and just to see if anyone would notice, and do you know what happened?"

I couldn't fill the time before she did it for me.

"No one noticed! Not a person, if you could even call people that did that kind of work people, anyway. I was so crushed that when I got home, I cried for two hours non-stop. I couldn't believe it. How was it that nobody, *nobody*, could see the mismatches of colours right in front of them? It was unbelievable and that's when I knew I had to get out of there, y'know? I'm not even sure they noticed I left. Honestly, I could have flashed the office on my way out and no one would have peeked out of the sea of grey. That's what that place was: a sea of grey with nothing wild to chase. And now look at me!"

"And now look at you."

"I'm in a city I adore where I get to spend all my effort focusing on beautiful things that everyone else passes by. Then I get to make it huge in front of their faces so they realize what's around. You know, I did a series not so long ago where I stopped various people in various professions and took pictures of their shoes just to kind of get back at all those people from that job that never noticed mine. It was so interesting to see how no two stains were the same and how much I could tell about a person by the shoes they wore and how they kept them. And yet, who notices them? People spend all day walking around looking down and no one's noticing anything. It's not natural, I say, y'know? But I don't know sometimes, sometimes I feel like everyone is just taking their steps to get the next thing because of the last thing they got, y'know? Like they have to keep going for the promotion because they just got the house and, oh my God, I need this bonus because I just got my kid braces and on and on and on. Do you think anyone just stops anymore? I mean, do you think they ever just go out into the world and forget all the connections they've made to themselves for, I don't know, five minutes? It's so crazy to be on two feet right now. You're often drifting through some kind of dreamland. Don't you think it's true?"

"I suppose."

"Hey! I just had a thought! I was talking to my friend Sara the other day. You remember Sara, right?"

It was becoming impossible to keep up with Céline's life on the other side of the country.

"Can't say I do."

"Sara St-Pierre? Really? I can't believe that, you must know her but can't think of her right now so you think she doesn't exist. She does, and she's been my best friend ever since I moved here. You'd love her. She used to work on a cruise ship so she's been all around the world, knows something like six languages—all of which she's found uses for here—and now she works in some prep school for the rich Anglos in Westmount. Anyway, I remember her saying once that to become a teacher she had to do a… *stage?* Do you know the English word? Whatever, it's also what chefs and stuff do before they're ready. She said she went into schools for almost a year and volunteered in the classrooms to see if she actually liked the work of being a teacher. Could you not do the same thing with the Church? Why don't you go down to Father Rogers this afternoon and tell him your plan!"

That wasn't such a bad idea. Obviously, I couldn't accept it outright. If I did, I was sure I would hear about it at every holiday get-together. She'd take the room and remind them how she was the one that set her little brother straight in his career. With her turrets of words, I'd never be able to amend the story and a new myth of my life would be spoken without my input. I wondered how she, of all three of us, became the perfect pairing of French-Canadian sensibilities and Newfoundland stories.

"I mean, that's certainly an idea. I know I haven't seen Father Rogers in a while, and maybe he'd remember me and want to help me out."

"Of course he'll remember you! That man knows the name of every baby he's ever baptized, trust me. I'm sure he'll not only be beamingly glad to see you but also will love your proposition and probably let you start working, or at least, volunteering, today! Ah! I'm so excited for you and excited that you're making moves in your life!"

"Yeah. Thanks." If I was making moves, why did it feel like I was attached to a rolling boulder?

"It's nothing! Anyway, I gotta get going pretty soon here because there's a festival down at the Old Port and I'm sure all of Montréal's wildest characters will be in attendance. Talk to you soon and give Mum and Dad a great big hug from me! *Bisous!*"

"Cheers, Céline."

She smacked her lips into the receiver and hung up. My phone locked on its own while I remained horizontal on the bed. I didn't want to check how much time that took but I'm sure the sun had passed all the eastern windows by now. As I tried, actively, to drain the inconsequential stories from my ears and resume my own thinking, there was one line too big to drop out. I should go see Father Rogers. No, not should. It would be a good idea to go see him. Céline had a good idea.

Dammit.

Chapter Fifteen

A faint honk of a locking car served as a warning. One of my parents was home and by the sound, I couldn't tell who. I knew who I wanted it to be, but I also knew what was inevitable. An echo of Dad snoring resurfaced in my memory. I ambled down the stairs and stopped at the bottom. Mum was going through her bag like a thief looking for money.

"Did you lose something?" I said.

She huffed. "Just a file from work, something I wanted to finish after dinner. I thought I put it away in here before I left, but I guess I forgot. The joys of paperwork. What's up? You look like you want to say something."

"Oh, nothing. I just—"

"You were checking to see if I was your Dad?"

"Maybe."

She cast a look that cut through the understatement.

"He came home after midnight last night. I didn't find out where he went, but he was still quite upset when he came upstairs. He kept going on about mistakes."

"Mistakes?"

"It wasn't very clear. Whatever he was feeling, he couldn't get it out. Declan, your father takes these kinds

of things very seriously—both work and faith. To trivial-
ize them both was frightening, and I'm not saying that's
what you intended to do or even did, but that's how he's
taken it. There are some things that can't be said without
warning."

"I guess that was one of them."

"Your dad's back is strong and his memory is long. I
won't tell you what you should do because I know you
don't like to think that way. Just, please, be careful with
these things. For all his strength, his passions make him
fragile."

We hovered around the kitchen for the next little
while. The television was on low in the background.
When the garage door opened, it was like an earthquake.
The car took on the sounds of a subterranean beast that
had recently pierced the land. Again, the house shook as
the door to the garage swung open and closed with
control.

Neither of us said anything.

"Hello? Jacqueline? Anybody home?"

My mouth felt stitched shut so I looked over to Mum.

"Hi, dear! We're in the kitchen."

Dad came around the corner with a pip in his step.
He kissed Mum on the cheek and then dropped his whole
weight into his hand as he patted my shoulder.

"Evenin' Declan, I missed you this morning."

"Oh? Yeah?"

He passed by me on the way to the cupboard to grab
a short glass. Then he went directly to the freezer to fill it
with crushed ice. Whistling an unknown tune, he grabbed

a bottle of rum from the cabinet and a carton of orange juice from the fridge for his daily grog.

"So, how was work today?" I asked.

"Nothing too special—they say that a man's work is his life and, if that's true, I'm going to have the longest life on this planet. I tell you, some days I just talk and talk and talk all day, so much that I drive home without the radio on. Not that I mind sometimes because it's nice to have some real thinking time. In fact, I had some new ideas about working today.

"You know, as I see it, we're telling our young people all wrong when it comes to working. I'm sure it's more than just that but, in working especially, we're setting them up badly. What we're telling them is that they need to be happy with their job and that happiness and passion is the most important part of a working life."

"But?" I sensed he was leading to some greater thought.

"But," he said as he stirred his drink with his finger, popped it in his mouth, and wiped it on the inside of his other hand, "I don't think that's the right way. Passion is too quick to pass by. It's a thin emotion, and the life of a working man is long. There's just no way that a person can really be passionate all that time. So while it's a nice idea, who can honestly sustain that kind of thing? And, to the other one, happiness, I mean, is so difficult, and no one's ever been sure how to get it exactly. They've been thinking about that one for ages and where are we still, I say. I mean, think of all the people selling books and seminars on the secrets and keys to happiness and where are we now? We're somewhere near to nowhere! Instead, I've got a different kind of theory and I wanted to see if it'll help you." He leaned over the counter and made sure I was watching him.

"I think a man—or a woman, because they can work all they want to too, I suppose—should strive for satisfaction in their work and that's it."

"Satisfaction?" I said.

"Yes, satisfaction and nothing else. A person can't be in a great mood all the time. That's impossible. But if you can find a piece of work where, just about every day, you can feel like you did something that someone else couldn't do for themselves, or you really accomplished some kind of task or what-have-you, then that's an honest day's work. And if you put all those days of work together where, most of the time, you were able to succeed at being satisfied, then maybe you'll have a fine kind of career. Life's too short to waste yourself on something that doesn't reward you. Of course there's other things to life than working, but if it's something you've gotta do with your time, then you may well be feeling like you did something good for your fellow man. Now how's about that?"

He took a sip of his drink in the intervening space and I hadn't moved. While his words were cheery, and he spoke with interest, I doubted the sincerity of his speech. It was as if he said it not because he believed it but because he was trying to make me believe something.

"That's some kind of theory, Dad." I said.

"Thanks! Thought it up all by myself." He walked around the counter so there was nothing more between us. "I know you've been going through some hard times recently and I thought this would help steer you straight. Your mother and I had a long conversation late last night and, well," he looked over to the kitchen door. Mum had sidled into the threshold, arms folded and leaning some of her shoulder's weight against the frame.

"You know we worry sometimes," she said.

"I know, I know," I said.

"No," Dad said, his drink hitting the counter, "no 'I knows' because when you say that you're looking for a way out of what we're telling you. Now, last night, you made quite the statement that we, frankly, weren't prepared to hear from you. It was a shock, is all. And though I may have overreacted a touch, it's only because I still want you to be honest, to us and to yourself."

Didn't he have any leftover faith to put in me? If he could live his life sure of something that couldn't be measured, how could he not translate that to his son?

"Can we not argue about this anymore?" I said. "Especially since Céline called this morning and had some not bad advice for this problem."

"Oh?" Mum said, perking up. "What did she say?"

"She said to take the practical route. Instead of staying in my head and thinking about what this might be like, it would probably be a better idea to get some experience. With that, I'm going to go down to see Father Rogers to ask if I can volunteer. Treat it like a *stage*."

Both of them rested in equal silence. They weren't looking at me, nor each other, but to the infinite invisible space now hovering over the counter. I couldn't leave, but

I couldn't join them in their moment. The pause caused a receding that took me back to the original dream. I still remembered the linking and how it felt. It was like fresh bread in my heart.

Dad pointed the corners of lips down before speaking. "I suppose you'd want to know if you've got a stomach for the ocean before setting out to become a fisherman."

Mum nodded. "That sounds like a very sensible idea. I'm sure he'd love to have you."

"Are you going to call him?" Dad said.

"I'm not sure he has a business phone, and besides, we've not been phone people. And I'm not much in the mood for a letter."

My parents looked to the air around them and turned up empty hands.

"Guess there's not much more to say if you're sure about that," Dad said.

"Yes, Dad. I am sure."

With no alternative propositioned, the conversation flowed naturally into common topics. Mum and Dad talked about their day, the traffic, and colleagues. I participated with all the remaining focus I had, but there was still a sliver of attention that split over what I had seen that morning and what I might go through tomorrow morning, producing another amorphous reaction. Whatever it was, it circled anxiety like a shark.

The next morning, I woke up later than anticipated. Mum and Dad had already left for work, leaving me with a quiet house. The breakfast routine began as usual.

Toaster started, granola drowning in yogurt. When the English muffin popped out and I covered its surface, I suddenly wasn't hungry anymore. A tightening knot had appeared somewhere between my heart and my stomach. The more I tried to ignore it, the more it asserted itself. Bobbing up and down as if attached to my Adam's apple, I angled myself over the sink. For a brief moment, it felt like vomit. A dry burn coaxed the back of my throat. I coughed and spat into the sink. Nothing came up. Unsurprising because nothing was there. My forehead wasn't clammy or hot. The longer I stood there, leaning slightly, the more space there was for anything to escape.

I held myself like that until the tightness passed. Then I did my best to eat breakfast but found that, after one side of the English muffin, I was stuffed. The rest of the meal went into the garbage—although the granola could have been saved if covered. Taking a bottle of ginger ale, I went back upstairs and slumped on my bed. Normally, sickness was fatiguing. Hours could be spent staring at the ceiling and I wouldn't notice because the weight and sensitivity of the experience was too overpowering to do anything else. Now that I was down, questions bolted around my head like whipped huskies. What if god was real and this was the beginning of a long punishment? Would he be so poetic as to exact twisting revenge by twisting my intestines? Why did he always have to be so ambiguous?

My rational brain took over and soothed those thoughts away. Surely a being as jealous and powerful as god wouldn't be so subtle. He'd want me to know exactly why I was suffering. Since I didn't, it must have been for me to figure out. It took about a half an hour and most of a bottle of Canada Dry before sitting up didn't feel like a crunch. I lurched towards my closet, desperate for composure. On the other side of my closet door were wings of childish clothes. If it had been a regular day, shorts would have been the correct answer. Then I remembered my trip to the Vatican and how we were sent back to our rooms if we came down with our knees exposed. Father Rogers probably wouldn't mind, but he might.

With a pair of chinos and a button-up short sleeve shirt, I went to the mirror. The outfit was sensible if a bit conservative—definitely the sort of thing a compulsive Catholic would wear. What remained unresolved about the ensemble was whether or not to tuck the shirt in. When it was in it looked like I was wearing my Dad's clothes. A look that was further troubled by my face. It was too smooth, too light—the kind of face that made no home for shadows. If I took it out, I looked too young. Like a stretched out 12 year old with the added deficiency of wrinkles cracked across the bottom of the shirt. In or out? The bunches of fabric told me the answer and demanded to be hidden. I obliged and tucked the shirt in.

The way to the Church was marked by black power lines, grey concrete, and the fading façades of storefronts. Surely the shopkeepers did their best to keep tidy, but against the relentless rains of autumn, winter, and spring it would be impossible to keep their signs from fraying. We had always driven to the church, but it wasn't that far of a walk. Perhaps Mum and Dad were nervous about crossing the streets with three young kids when our legs were too short to be punctual and the cars too quick to be predictable. It was only a bit farther in the opposite direction than going to the inlet. While the distances were comparable, the journeys were not. The walk to the inlet was exciting because of what awaited us. We could get dirty and scream if we wanted. Church required a bit more composure. Even if it was a nice enough day to walk, it probably would have made us too sweaty.

It was a pleasant day out. A white line of continuous cloud surrounded the bottom of the open sky. The blue became smoothly darker the more it arced overhead. Everything was held in and where it was meant to be. I had walked far enough out of the neighbourhood to be covered in the sounds of intersections. Cars crested in volume as they passed while the buses and trucks exhaled short puffs whenever they stopped. A siren pierced the air and it stuck out like an auditory tree root. I patted my pockets for headphones only to feel the flat shapes of a phone and a wallet. They must still have been on my dresser, forgotten while I was focused on my shirt.

I couldn't remember the last time I had gone walking without them. Like everyone else, once the technology existed to block out that part of the world, I partook. Without the option, without a real-time soundtrack to stroll to, it was odd to hear the volume of the city. When cars sped by they were so loud it was difficult to hear anything else. They cloaked conversation as easily as buildings blocked the sun. How loud were our headphones that we could cover these sounds? Or could we concentrate that much on what we wanted to hear?

Thinking provided surprising company. When I looked up and noticed I was a few blocks away, a tugging resurfaced. It was the knot and the line again, bobbing like a lure. At first it was easy to ignore. A few coughs and swallows paired well with thoughts of denial. But like the moon, it kept circling and growing fuller.

I found some privacy behind a tree about a block from the Church. Steadying myself with one outstretched hand, I bent forward at the waist making due care to spread my shoes as wide as I could. I was going to throw up, I was sure of it. As the line made me gag and the knot tightened and twisted, there was nothing coming up. An exaggerated cough created driblets of spits to be discarded like trash. Waiting was frustrating. In the absence of an obvious sensation, I decided to intervene. I readied my first two fingers and jabbed them down my throat. This was an old college manoeuvre—one often performed on the altar of the porcelain god, while the floor rocked and spun in an unforgiving manner.

My whole torso heaved and contracted. More spit pooled around my lips, but the best that came out was a deep belch. The back of my throat tingled like a rubbed wound. I had to catch my breath and stood up slightly, one hand still anchored to the tree. Looking around to see if anyone had noticed, I saw no one. A car hadn't slowed to check on me and there wasn't a pedestrian in sight. It was probably going to be nothing and the more I ignored it, the more it had to go away. There were still remnants of the knot and the line, but they were looser.

The top of the Church blocked the sun. It stood

sharp and confident to a point that seemed unnatural. Trees didn't come to a point that focused, nor did mountains. I stood in the shadow of the building to pause and reconsider it. Buildings like these reached so high they made me uneasy. What if the wind came in too strong and knocked them over or what if the earth quaked and they fell in on themselves? They seemed too huge to be sturdy as everything I associated with being firm and safe was low to the ground and solid. The church was mostly empty inside and while that made it hollow, it also allowed space for wonder.

Even in a building so enormous, where every part leaned towards opulence, it was the tiniest spaces that held the most detail. Stepping a little closer, the arches over the door of the church revealed themselves not to be paintings or blank arcs but rows of people. Each one carved out from the same slab. Their faces looked in all directions. Some gaped towards the sky, others looked down in consolation. Blank, stony eyes bulged without direction. Maybe that was how they kept watch on everything. If no one knew their sightline, they wouldn't know when they were being watched. Effective surveillance, but also distant since their covered eyes hid what it was they believed. Did they doubt? Did they hate? Without blinking they left all interpretation to their viewer.

The old pathway around back was dingier than I remembered. Covered in the glow of midday summer, pine needles were strewn over its concrete. I brushed some away with my feet. After a few steps, I noticed I was walking like Father Rogers. Hands clasped behind my back and unhurried in my gait. He never seemed to be rushed and, when we were on this short strip of nature, he seemed to take all his needed time to consider each of the things that lived and were placed around us. It was like he was most interested in regarding and respecting all aspects of the world while he was in it. Sometimes, an inadvertent smile crept across his face as he looked at the trees and rocks and I would ask him what was making him so happy. He would reply with a cheery exhale and say, "Oh, I'm just happy to be."

From the stone footpath that led to the door, I could see through the translucent and yellowing curtains that there was a light on in the place. It was faint, but it was there. His home still looked like the same cozy construction, a place in which no evil could live. Not because it wouldn't be welcome, but because it would be accommodated so well that it couldn't be evil anymore.

On the door was a small, bronze knocker. It hit with a squeak every time it swung into place. While the house was well-armoured in its materials, the space was far enough away from the road that I heard a chair push across the floor and the creaks of floorboards. There was nowhere to go as the sliding grew louder. Soon, I would have to explain myself, to articulate the contradiction that I thought housed my future. The line crept up the back of my tongue with the knot pulled down deeper into my stomach. Opposite directions and opposite sensations flooded through my being. I wasn't sure if I was going to be sick, if I was going to pass out, if I—

"Declan? Declan Murphy?"

Father Rogers was leaning through the small opening left by the door with a look of welcome surprise on his face.

"I'm so glad to see you!" he said. "Please, come in, come in. I was just doing some reading. May I offer you some tea?"

"Yes, Father. Thank you. Tea would be perfect."

He smiled as widely as he could and opened the door in welcome.

Part 4

RESOLUTION

Chapter Sixteen

"*O*h, and don't bother taking off your shoes. You can rub them on the carpet and that'll be fine."

He turned his back and took his paces down the dimly lit hallway. The place was set as it always was with the only differences coming from withering. Wallpaper drooped in corners, dust clung to the tops of high frames, and the curtains fluttered with effort. This place had been a sanctuary of sorts and its decay was natural but equally sad. It was in accordance with the order of things for objects to dull as they aged, but it was also possible to overlay them with memories of how they were. Was that delusion or nostalgia?

Staying near the doorway, I watched Father Rogers move. He looked much less steady on his feet. His knees knocked with nearly every step and his shoulder curved forward as if an uneven weight was perched on them. It must have been heavy since he hardly picked his feet up between steps. Every few feet, one of his hands would reach out towards a wall as if to catch himself preemptively in case of a wobble. He had always been old, in the way grandparents are always old, but looking over him now, it seemed like old age was pulling him down. Not harshly but with a gentle degradation. His plumper bits hung heavier, his neck barely moved, and he left a trail of hard breath in his wake.

When he stepped out of sight and into the kitchen, I followed after. Stopping for a moment at the opening of the study, it looked like the same shabby, disorganized mess I remembered. He had once told me that, in Dublin, at the Trinity College Library, there were so many rare and old books that there was no proper organizational system and, for reasons of security, no one librarian knew where they all were. That's how he envisaged the organization of his books: mostly at random, but he knew where to find them. It was such a treat to fight through the stacks, ask him about some title he had mentioned, and watch his hand move perfectly through the air and pick it out of the rubble of paper.

In the sitting room, the small window let in its small light that covered the coffee table like a cloth. I was certain that not only was the furniture all the same, nothing about the arrangement had changed. What makes the place different there was what made it different anywhere else in his home: the thickness of its fading. It probably had left perfect rings on the ground from being so still. Shadows of dust which held true to the undisturbed colours of the past.

"You know something, Father," I called out.

"Yes? What's that, Declan?"

"I remember the way your place looked, but I didn't count on my memory being so exact. It doesn't look like anything is a centimetre out of place from what's in my head."

A chuckle leapt out through the air.

"Yes, yes, you're probably right. I'm not capable of moving the furniture by myself anymore and, without any children of my own, I don't get too many visitors anyway. But, you know, that's life."

His voice dropped when he spoke about visitors. I couldn't think of anything to say. The kettle whistled like a bird and I heard its mouth open, exhaling the steam previously trapped inside. Cups and saucers slid over each other.

"Do you take anything in your tea?" Father Rogers said.

"A bit of milk, if you have it. Please," I said as I entered the kitchen.

He opened the fridge door and it crashed into the nearest wall. A strip of plastic had been put there as a barrier but not accurately as it only caught half the door's edge. I placed my hand on top to hold it firm while Father Rogers poked around for what he needed.

"Which one's mine?" I asked, looking over at the cups.

He glanced over his shoulder, raised his eyebrows and then let them soften.

"Don't worry about that. I can get them," he said.

"Father Rogers, you've been serving people long enough. Please, let me do the final preparations while you go sit down."

His lips sprung into a smile.

"Okay, but just this once," he said with a saucy wag of his finger. "And if you could, put three sugars in mine.

I know I'm not supposed to have them, but I figure if I choose the number of the Trinity, then God can't get too upset with me."

I did as I was told while he shuffled out of the room. Three sugar cubes dropped sweetly into the tea. The water was hot enough that they dissolved on contact, breaking from their form and mingling with the drink. I poured in my milk and watched the liquid explosion. It looked like a cloud that grew out from the centre, rolling and spreading until it enveloped the whole of the drink. The milk too became inseparable from the tea, but what it added and what the sugar added were totally different.

Carefully taking up the saucers with spoons balanced near the cups, I walked into the sitting room. Father Rogers was in his usual chair with the top of his head peeking out over the top. I must have popped into his periphery because he jumped a bit when I passed.

"My apologies, Declan. I didn't hear you come in," he said.

"It's alright, Father," I said, placing the tea on the table.

He thanked me and brought the cup to his lips. While I was walking around the table to my chair, light passed across him. The lines held deeper shadows than what I remembered, running over his face like a well-worn chair. Each crevice and wrinkle was deep enough to run a dime through. Thankfully, the deepest of these emotional legacies were around the corners of his eyes and near the bottom of the wings of his nose. They became deeper as he smiled at me after finishing his sip and tilted his head in approval.

"Very well done. Thank you, Declan."

"Not a problem, Father. It's been a while since I've been in here."

"It has indeed. I don't think we've talked since you finished your studies. You majored in… sociology, correct?"

"Yes, that's true. University was good to me. I met some great friends that I'm lucky to still talk to on occasion. I took some fantastic trips and I think I even learned a few things from my classes."

He smiled at that last remark in a way that suggested it wasn't only for appeasement.

"I remember my days in university too. Plenty of late nights and dances. Of course it was all a bit more formal back then. Would you believe that I wore a jacket and tie to my lectures? It's true, every boy was dressed smart. And while there weren't as many women in universities as there are now, they arrived to campus done-up as if they were going to be on the cover of the newspaper. It's so funny how times and fashion have changed. When I see young people now on the little bits of television I watch in the evenings, it seems like everyone is so much more casual than when I was young. Have you noticed something similar?"

"I think that's accurate. We certainly wear sweatpants whenever we can and I don't think I saw anyone wear a tie to class ever."

"Part of me thinks that's for the best. Those things can start to weigh down on a man after a while. Does your father wear a necktie?"

"My dad? Never. Or maybe he does sometimes and I just don't notice. He certainly wears collared shirts to work, but he's not above showing up in jeans. Not like when he goes to church—then he's always in a suit."

"Yes, I do remember that about him. How is he, by the way? And your mother?"

"They're both doing fine. Mum is still working at the same place, but she's moved up into a more managerial role recently. She says she likes the work but there is certainly more of it now. And Dad, Dad is still where he was when I was in high school. Come to think of it, this might be the longest he's ever been at one job. He says it's his last job, but we don't know what he'll do with himself if he retires."

"I'm sure he'll find something. Some men realize how much their work has given them after they've left it. How it filled their days and so forth. When they get out, they either take on a hobby no one imagined or they go back to what they did in a more casual way. What matters is that they have purpose to their day because purpose is what keeps us out of the ground. But that is wonderful news about your mother. She is so kind and intelligent— in two languages, no less—that it's no surprise to hear of her success. Please, share with her my best."

"I will."

"And your sisters. How are Hélène and Céline?"

"They've both got on very well for themselves. Hélène got a full ride to university and to grad school, obviously, and now she's back working at UBC in their marine biology research department. Although she's not in the lab as much anymore with her baby being due so soon."

"Oh?" Father Rogers said gently. "Did she get married?"

"No, no, she didn't get married. She doesn't even have a boyfriend. It's been this thing with her that, whether she had a man or not, she wanted to be pregnant by the time she was 25. Mum and Dad tried convincing her otherwise, but once the process began there wasn't much they could do. I think they've come around a bit and now they're excited to be grandparents."

"I see. It's certainly a surprise, but a joyful one. To be so focused on career and family, that takes great ability."

"That's one way to put it. At least she's in town, so when she needs help she can call on Mum and Dad for childcare so that's nice."

"Has Céline left the lower mainland?"

"She has. A few years ago she moved back east to work on Wall Street in some kind of accounting job. But she found the work miserable so she packed up, went to Montréal, and now makes her life as a freelance photographer. Her stuff is doing very well and now she feels as if her soul is being taken care of. At least, I think that's how she feels. I can say I only take in about half of her phone calls."

"How splendid. It is such a good thing to hear about a family that has come together and been so successful in so many different pursuits. This must be an exciting time for you too. You've finished your studies and now you're ready to step out and join the world. Have you found where your place lies in the world?"

The knot and the line tugged again. My tongue went dry like a metal slide in summer.

"Actually, Father, that's kind of why I'm here today."

He tilted his head. "Has something happened?"

"It's not that easy to explain so I'll try to be direct and then work my way back, if that makes sense. Father Rogers, I'm here to talk to you about the possibility of doing some work here. The thing is, I haven't been able to find myself very well since graduating university. It's like, when I was there and growing up, the world seemed so endless. Like there was so much to see and understand. Now I've got to try and pick one thing. Recently, I had this dream. Actually, I've had it since I was a teenager, but this time it was different. I won't bore you with it but, not long after, the subject of the church came up and this dream that, previously, had been so much nonsense and noise suddenly straightened itself out. I saw it as a kind of coded message that I could have a life, or at least a career, doing something good for other people. But what it is doesn't really make sense."

"I see. Take your time, Declan. Try to keep from rushing."

I took another sip of my tea while my tongue settled in its place.

"Father Rogers, I think my place is in the priesthood."

He folded his hands over his stomach and curved himself back into the chair. His chin tucked, he took a few consolatory breaths with his eyes low to the floor. I took another sip of my tea and let my eyesight float around the room so as to not seem like I was interrogating him. One side of his mouth curled up as one strong exhale came out of his nose.

"Declan, please forgive my memory. I'm afraid it's started to let things slip of its own accord. Do you, by chance, play music?"

"I don't, no."

"When I was a child, it seemed like everyone could play the piano. In fact, in many houses, while televisions were still on the rise, it was common for families to have pianos in the sitting room for people to gather around. Even at dinner parties, it would be assumed that at least one guest could sit at the piano and sing and entertain everyone who was in attendance. Naturally, with that kind of expectation, when I was a boy, my parents put me in piano lessons. Now you must also understand that, while the traditions of piano lessons rely on classical music and names that everyone's heard of, when I was young there was this new thing, though I suppose it's quite an old thing now, called jazz. Oh, I loved Duke Ellington when I was young—and Bill Evans too! When they sat at the bench it was like they were kneeling on the altar of beauty. Now, in a lot of this jazz that was coming up on the radio, there was a change to the sound of the music itself. I don't just mean the structure of the music, how fast or how slow, but the compositions themselves. Have you ever heard the words consonance and dissonance before?"

"I think so," I said, feeling like I was a child again. Father Rogers smiled his warm smile.

"It's okay, Declan, you don't need to pretend here. In

fact, sometimes, it's more courageous to say when you don't understand because that's what opens you up to what you didn't know."

"Okay, then I don't know. I have never heard those words before."

He clapped his hands with the energy of a younger man. "Excellent! Because they're quite easy to understand even without a piano here. When I say that something in music is consonant, it means that the two notes sound very nice together. I'll show you. Can you sing a note for me, please? Any note at all."

"Father, I'm not really a singer—"

"Oh, don't you worry about it. Let me find you where you are."

The sound that came out resembled a car gaining speed. It wobbled out into the room in a rickety pitch, and so Father Rogers asked me to repeat myself until I hit upon a consistent tone. On the third time, he sang out a note that made what I produced stronger, more defined, and like real music. I almost lost my tone in what I heard. Out of his rounded mouth came a noise of deep and stable power that surrounded my sound in a gentle way. My note was like our tea, bubbling and ill-formed, and he was like the cup, holding it in and allowing it to rest. It was resounding and comforting.

"That was the fifth interval of the major scale," he said. "One of the most powerful tones in music. It anchors itself to the tone and makes it stronger. That is what consonant sounds do: they make the notes sound like more than what they are, but without interfering with their identity. Do you agree?"

I nodded.

"Could you sing that note again, please?" he said.

It took a few tries to replicate but when I did, Father Rogers opened his mouth. He sang something that sounded like it was badly competing against what I was singing. Like it was trying to force itself ahead of what I sang in an inconsiderate manner.

"That didn't sound so nice," I said.

"Maybe not. That one is called a minor second and, in general, we call that kind of tone a dissonant tone. The first one was consonant, it went well with the original sound, and that one was dissonant, it didn't go well with the original sound. Right?"

"Right. They sounded like they were both trying to be first in a line-up that was two people long."

"That is very true, very true. Do you think they ever make music?"

"What do you mean?"

"If you ever heard those notes again in a song, do you think people would like it?"

"I can't imagine a scenario in which that would be the case, no."

He tucked and shook his head. "Then you must hate the theme from *Jaws*."

"Father, I'm not sure I follow you."

"That's quite alright. In the theme from *Jaws*, the two notes that make up the core of that piece of music—the duh-nuh, duh-nuh, that gets faster as the shark gets nearer—that is exactly what we just sang. But, of course, it's not an awful sound, not at all. What it is is off-putting and ominous, you see? So when it's sung in a home like this it's not appropriate to our situation. But attach it to a man-eating shark and it's more than appropriate, it's perfect."

"That's… certainly something I never noticed."

"Don't feel ashamed, even those with a serious background in music miss these things on casual listening. With a little bit of study, we can discover a rich deposit for our emotions. But only if we have the means of self-expression. Let's bring ourselves back to our original subject and that may help. For a long time, the music we knew and listened to was very concerned with being consonant all the time—making the sounds that people generally like. When jazz came along, they began to embrace dissonance. But they couldn't just play off-notes together, no, because people had too much experience hearing other things. So they had to hide them at first, you see? They invented different contexts and situations that would make them more pleasing to listen to. In that case, the problem was never the notes themselves, but how they related to all the other notes in the piece. Now do you see?"

"I have to be honest, Father, and maybe it's my lack of musical experience, but I really don't."

Ever patient and kind, he took another sip from his tea to allow the silence to give us both time to think. Placing it down on the saucer again, he looked up to the ceiling and then to the floor. He didn't seem frustrated, nor overbearing with quips. His focus was not on showing off how much he knew but on how much I understood. It made me want to be a more attentive student.

"It's alright, Declan, maybe I'm not the best music teacher. But what I meant to say was that, in music, when there are only a few notes being played, it can be easy to hear which ones don't belong as well with the others. Now, this is not because the notes are bad or worthless, but because they don't have enough support from the other notes around them. That's what we call harmony in music, the support of notes from other notes. In my studies of music, when I learned about harmony, do you know what it made me think of?"

I really wanted to get this one right.

"Did it make you think of the church?"

"Not quite. It made me think of people in general. That some people can do great things on their own or with only one person around them, like in a marriage. But other times, and for other people, they need the help of many others to sound as great as they can. The problem with, perhaps our whole society, is when we don't offer that support to the dissonant people. When we say that they don't belong, or that they'll ruin this wonderful composition we're all working on. Well, I don't believe that. Instead, I believe that when we are faced with someone who is going through dissonant times, we must help them find their harmony."

He silenced me. I sat back with my whole spine on the chair as I replayed his words in my ears. With unnoticeable ease, the knot and the line had drifted away into nothing. Somehow, I was relaxed in the most internal parts of myself and, frankly, nearly felt like crying. I was sure I could have cried in front of him and remained comfortable, but I didn't want to alter the conversation we were having, nor its tone.

"Wow," I said, "that's really something to think about."

"And I'm glad you're taking time to think about it."

"What do you think we can do about my problem, here?"

"I take it, then, you haven't given up on your lack of belief?"

I shook my head but held my eye contact.

"What would you like to do about it? I'm sure it's all you've been able to think about for the last little while," he said.

"It's not my idea, but I was wondering—if I wouldn't be too much of a problem—maybe I could do some volunteering around here? To see if there's a place for someone like me and to make sure I understand what the work is all about. Would that be okay?"

Father Rogers clapped his hands as his mouth opened and his cheeks lifted.

"I think that would be a marvellous idea! And, truth be told, I think I have been needing some help around here but have been too stubborn to admit it to myself."

"The joys of the aging man."

He seemed to like that line.

And so it was established. I was to come down in the day, three days a week, and Father Rogers would have me tidy up, greet newcomers, and then, after those tasks were through, he would show me how he filled his days. When we finished our tea, I cleaned up the glasses and made a quick remark about starting early. He walked me to the door with a pat on the back and a handshake to pass along for my parents.

"You're doing a brave thing, Declan, and I am so pleased to be able to share it with you."

Walking out of his house, I felt like I was in the rays of a new sunrise. I listened with effort to the birds overhead, trying to hear what new harmonies they were singing.

Chapter Seventeen

Mum and Dad reacted with restrained enthusiasm to the retelling of my conversation with Father Rogers.

"He's really okay with you dropping in like that?" Dad said.

"He is," I said.

"And you're really sure this is what you want to try?"

"I think so."

They kept looking to each other while I talked as if to confirm reactions, and when I had finished, it was a few minutes before anyone said anything else. Instead, the sounds of running water and knives on cutting boards filled the room. When it felt like we were verbally avoiding each other, Dad broke through.

"If the Lord can work in mysterious ways, I'm sure his employees are just fine to follow," he said. I shrugged and that was the last we spoke about the subject all night.

The next morning, I woke up just after my parents, dodging the expected cracks and jabs from Dad about finally being up with the workers. We didn't talk much, leaving space for the small collective of sounds that nestled in the morning. A faint radio, smooth traffic, the coffee machine, a cereal box turned on its side, the tap, the dishwasher, the keys, and the door, and the light chirps of seasonal birds. Mum was the first one ready. With a kiss for Dad and touch on my shoulder, she was on her way.

"Good luck on your first day, I can't wait to hear all about it," she said.

The door fell closed behind her. I gathered up my plate and bowl and dropped them in the dishwasher.

"Declan," Dad said, "on your way out, could you grab a piece of white fish from the freezer? We'll have that for dinner tonight as a sort of celebration."

"Celebration?"

"You're finally working! I may even get you a candle."

I thought about quipping back with a line about the difference between working and volunteering. But in a long enough battle, the Newfoundlander always wins on wit.

Dad left with a wave and the house rumbled with the garage door. Then it was still. Once that stillness had settled, I went upstairs and got dressed for the day. Without knowing what precisely I would be doing, I put on an outfit that looked professional but was also unsentimental. The shirt I chose had a collar, though not the kind worn by priests. Again, I tucked my shirt in without assuredness. I was nearly ready to leave when I caught sight of my headphones. They were curled on my dresser like a limp twin snakes, calling out to me to be my distraction. The walk could be survived without them and so I left them in their nest amongst other knickknacks.

Along my walk, I became preoccupied with questions about what I would do. Each one was a portal that took me away from the world that was and dropped me into a world artificially envisioned. In those worlds, anything was possible; and because anything was possible, nothing was certain. The truth was in one of the worlds whether I could imagine it or not.

As if suddenly waking, I found myself in the church parking lot. It was empty. Around the building and across the concrete, people walked. Nearly all were plugged into something with no hint of what it could be on their faces. Buses passed with the same piles of humanity and wildlife darted on and off of power lines. Within this setting of fleeting movement, the church remained. It was the one unalterable building that towered up from the ground like a remnant of place since passed. With angles and curves, it declared itself in the environment as stable and powerful. It was certainly imposing—even if the buildings around it were taller.

From the morning shadow of the Church, I turned from the noise of the street toward the door. When it closed behind me, it was like an encasement. It cut out all the light and sound from outside, creating a perfect separation from the world. There, inside the cold and airy hall, the sun was between two windows as light filtered in unevenly. It rebounded off the floor and shot up to the ceiling where it was caught and filled as if in a cup. I stood in the last remaining shadow under the lowered roof of the entryway. When I crossed over, I exhaled the city's air and inhaled the stone, wood, and light of the church.

It was as silent as a butterfly's landing. The space existed in such tranquility that I worried about sneezing or knocking something over for fear that the reverberations would rattle on forever as an eternal accident. The church was big again in a way it hadn't been since childhood. Without the crowds, the air hung wide; and without the organ, the gap of the space was distant. My hands ran over the scratched wood of the pews. Deep, jagged cuts worn in from rings catching the edge or books inaccurately placed. They must have been like that for a long time, longer than I had been without faith. The hands that left the marks had been searching for something and, absent of intent, had left something else behind.

Bibles lined the backs of the pews in an irregular pattern of red, green, and aubergine binding. Their pages were well-travelled and the ones not coated in red had all faded to the colour of dying wheat. On them too were grooves of experience. Tiny tears on the fringes of the pages. Spines loose and fraying. In some, there were splotch stains over passages commonly read at funerals. These books and these pews were clinging to their forms, refusing to fall into entropy by being treated carefully and with grace. They could have been replaced, but then what would the new ones mean to those who attended week after week? The importance, the meaning, came from the evidence that these things had been used and they will continue to be used until they crumbled.

"Declan! Good morning!" Father Rogers cheerfully exclaimed. He had appeared from a side door, one I didn't know about until he walked through. He chuckled while shaking his head as he spoke.

"I'm so sorry, I suppose I never told you where to find

me. But I figured I would find you in here and, look at that, here you are! Right on time and very well put-together. How are you? Did you have a pleasant walk? Or were you able to be dropped off?"

"It's quite alright, Father. I'm doing very well today and I did walk over here. It was a nice way to start a day. Although, I must say, being in the Church like this with no one else around has really been something special. Not necessarily holy, of course, but still special."

He leaned in towards me. "It's my favourite time too. Gives me time to think about what I do." He tapped his temple with his first finger.

"What do you often think about?"

"Lots of things. Last time we spoke, it was either you or I that brought up our studies in university. Recently, I've been hearing more and more young people ask what it is they are paying for when they go. It's a very good question and I've found an answer that satisfies me though I don't know what it would do for anyone else. May I share it with you?"

"Please do."

"I believe it is of the utmost importance for people to have time to think about what they believe in. When a young person goes off to university they are not just paying for books but have bought a few sections of time each week in which they are responsible for nothing other than thinking about things that matter to them. I'm sure you've found that, in our society today, people are being interrupted all the time. They have to think about their jobs, their families, their responsibilities; and somewhere in that, they lose the time to think about how they are. We don't really respect time for things like that unless they have been paid for. If you are in a university class, you can tell people you can't come to the phone or to a meeting. But once a person is out of the age of studying, they aren't given the same allowance for reflection anymore, and I think that is a terrible loss. So when I have this time, and it's usually in the morning, when the building is free of people, I like it because it allows me to have the freedom to think. We are so lucky to live in a place in which we have that freedom, but we must remember to use it. You can call it introversion if you like, but I am happy enough to call it rest. Like our bodies need to lay down after hard physical work, we must find the time to let our minds lay down from all the activity of the day."

A smile broke through his words. It wasn't a smile of superiority, the kind that gloats after being clever. This one broke like dawn, and in its radiance, I took comfort in what he meant.

"Is that all you'd like me to do today? Just walk around and contemplate?"

"No, not quite. Though there may be some time reserved for that. It's been a while since someone has done a once-over of the place. Swept the floors, polished, that sort of thing. Unfortunately, dust loves to grow in here and, especially in recent years, I've found it's taken to outworking what I can do."

"I'm sure that'll happen to all of us."

"And I'm hoping it won't happen to you for a long time yet. Anyway, I'll show you where I keep the brooms and the rags and let you get to it as you see fit."

We walked together to a room tucked around the corner from the entrance foyer. It was a dingy closet with an exposed concrete floor. A shelf stood unsupported against the side wall and on it were various cleaning supplies draped like clothes on a line.

"Don't feel like you have to get the whole place done today," he said as he was about to leave. "I'm going to be in the back room just behind the altar if you need me. Thank you, Declan, for being here."

With a happy face and pat on my shoulder, Father Rogers was off to yet another room I didn't know existed. The number of secret doors and rooms made the church feel more like a castle.

"One last thing," Father Rogers called out.

"Yes?"

"Don't forget to contemplate!"

He closed the door behind him and I followed to start my work from the altar. Getting there, I turned and faced the wooden congregation like a real priest would. The long row between the pews intersected into a perpendicular line near the front. While the altar was adorned, the floor continued in its path for a few metres more behind it. Being in the church when it was full, and the primary focus was my own seat, I hadn't noticed the care of the shape. The very floor over which all the worshipers walked was a cross. The last bits of morning sun glided in through the tops of the windows behind the altar. It faced the east, the sunrise. A secret care had been built by the architects to infuse the room with meaning even if no one noticed. Cohesion added to the awe, but it was quiet that made the details more acute.

Sweeping the bristles over the worn-in floors, small piles of debris formed like little volcanoes. In taking the broom over the ground, it revealed what had been hidden by immobility and camouflage. With each sweep, I became better acquainted with the corners of the church. I stood in new vantages and considered how my ideal church would look. If I had total control, people would be encouraged to wander the grounds and the halls before the service. The doors would remain open like an invitation's envelope. Churchgoing didn't have to be so rigid. If the congregation could be given some freedom, some time to settle in and appreciate what they were doing, wouldn't they grow to love it more? It felt awful to think of a church that opened its door twenty minutes before the service like some sort of stadium and then had ushers clearing people out like cattle. A good church should have everything in common with a good library.

I swept the entirety of the floor. Even with the high and wide ceilings, moving around on the sun-warmed floors was enough to sweat. Not in a dripping way, but with the kind of sweat that crept and sat as if hiding in intimate places. There was a small garbage can in the supplies closet and I took it around the room to each pile of dust. The dust formed a respectable heap that pulled the edges of the garbage bag down from the can's rim. It looked heavy even though it wasn't, and I felt as if I had cleared a great deal of weight under which the church had been sitting for months. Putting the can back and looking through the closet, I saw some rags and a polishing spray. With all the gold and other shiny adornments around the altar, surely they needed a light buffing. Just as I approached the front, rag and spray in hand, Father Rogers emerged from his room.

"Hello there! How's the work coming along?"

"It's been good so far. I've swept the place and now I figured I'd polish up some of the gold and things at the front here."

Father Rogers had a new expression on his face that first showed gratitude but then a joyful kind of misunderstanding.

"Don't worry about the gold, Declan, it never tarnishes."

"Oh?" I thought this may be some kind of religious test. As in, since these were blessed items they weren't to be touched or maybe, since they were so special, they stay shiny forever on god's word.

"Yes! It's one of the things that makes gold so valuable and interesting to people—no matter if it gets bumped, scratched, wet, or anything else, gold never loses its lustre. Isn't that something great? And I think it's bronze, but I may be wrong on this, that self-disinfects as well. There truly are some great wonders around us, eh?"

I agreed but did feel a bit foolish.

"I suppose so," I said. "Then if that doesn't need to be done, what would you like me to do next?"

He put his hands on his hips for a moment before speaking.

"There are a few things around here that need fixing.

I'd have you take a look at one of the confession boxes but I just got off the phone with a handyman that can come sometime in the week. The pews could use a staining but that's a bigger job than we have time for." He paused again while his thumb spun circles on his chin. "You know what, there is something you can help me with. That is if you still have some time today."

"This is literally the only thing I have to do today."

"Splendid! I was doing a bit of archiving in my study last night and there's a letter I seem to have misplaced. If you'd like, we go back up to the house and look for it. Would that be alright?"

"I'm here to work, so why not?" I said with a shrug.

"Thank you and, I know it's not much, but after that you can probably head home unless you spot something else that needs doing. I'm sorry I don't have much at the moment, but even I lose track of all there is to do around here."

"Then it's like something my Dad always says: there's always something to do on a boat. Maybe that applies to more workplaces."

With no cleverer remark, Father Rogers and I walked out like we had so many times before towards his home. The walk was silent between us but loud in the world. Cars and birds both competing for the right to claim most of the sonic dome while our footsteps blended in unheard. Father Rogers welcomed me into his home and we began our search.

Chapter Eighteen

In the mornings, Father Rogers encouraged me to stand in the entrance room and talk to the people that passed through. My first day had been a bit of an anomaly with no one to see the space. In the subsequent days, small collections of visitors walked through the doors. Some were tourists taken in by the impressive building. Others were retirees that were out to savour the last gasps of summer. There were also those who may have believed but, primarily, sought a place to take them in, even if for a little while, to get out of the relentless sun.

When I was in that room, my role was simple: be a gracious host. Engage with the people coming into the building, ask them how they are, and be there for their questions about the building. Father Rogers told me about a bookseller in Paris that he had seen decades ago who had a saying painted on the inside of his shop. It read: Be Not Inhospitable To Strangers Lest They Be Angels In Disguise. He said that's how he hoped to treat everyone that came into his holy home. I thought it was wonderful, even if the teenager in me would have gagged at the invocation of the angelic. The grown-up in me saw it for all it was: a metaphor. A harmless attempt to connect two even ideas.

Talking was how I got to know the passersby. Cleaning was how I got to know the church. When I arrived, Father Rogers and I would chat and then I took to my broom and pan to start on my work. No matter how well I had done the floors, by the next day or the day after that, a new layer had invisibly returned to be found and compiled. Over and again the work proved its worth, not by its presentation in the beginning, but by its result in the end. I learned how to cover ground quickly, found an art in passing the bristles back and forth like a pendulum, and allowed my mind to wander across the walls to better understand what was there.

On the wall near the confessional were three images. They were hung near each other, but not so near that a person could see all three clearly at once. It took attention to focus in on each one first before stepping back to view them as a whole. These images, which formed a sort of comic strip, each depicted a different stage in the crucifixion of Christ. His falls, his rise, and his ascension. I only knew the newspaper reader's version of the story. Jesus had been arrested and sentenced to death in a manner common with other criminals of his day. He would be affixed to a cross and left on display as a deterrent against further similar action until exposure to the wild sky killed him. Looking at the images again and again, I noticed how many other people were up on the mount that day. It seemed odd that there was no special method reserved for Christ's killing, no separation from the rest of the thugs that had committed much graver evils than he. Perhaps that was part of the story's power.

He could be treated like us and still transcended us: that was his paradox. Through lashings, spitting, and hate he could become stronger for them. This ran antithetical not only to being human but to the idea of punishment for which he gave his life. All over this religion were irreconcilable pieces that were fascinating. Nevertheless, he was tried as a man and condemned as a man. He slogged his cross through the streets, leaving behind a trail that must have carved deep into the sand. Yet not so deep that the wind could not blow it over and hide it from latecomers. The thorny crown on his head cut into the thinnest parts of skin and bled down his face with the grace of a waterfall. With stinging sweat, he walked through toil and ridicule, drank vinegar, and then was placed in open view of the hot desert sun. And yet, once he was up there, as the bottom of the third image had written under its frame, it is reported he said, "Father, forgive them; for they do not know what they are doing."

It was an admirable quality to think of the lives of others while in such a state of suffering. After staring into a representation of the crucifixion, a strange opinion began requesting my mind's best chair. What if, even for a moment, when he stared up into the blankness of heaven, nothing stared back? Was it written that he had heard the word up there? Could it have been possible that even Christ faltered in his faith? After all, there was no action shown by god that this man was divine at that moment. Or was there? The images only displayed some of the story and if I wanted to know the rest, I had to search the text.

After I finished sweeping, I went to Father Rogers to ask where in the Bible the crucifixion story was. He grinned while meaning well.

"Declan, it's not that simple."

"What do you mean? Is it not actually in the Bible?"

"No, no, the story is there, but there is more than one account. Here, let's take a look together."

He took me over to the altar where his largest and most ornate Bible was left.

"Usually, I don't use this one, but it's easiest to show another person. Now, I know you'll be honest when you answer, but I must ask anyway. Have you actually read the Bible before?"

I shook my head. There were parts that I knew and stories I could cite, but if I was asked whether Romans came before or after Numbers, I would have had to guess.

"Few have," he said, "and when they do, they aren't always sure how to read it. You see, when we come to the New Testament, there is not one account of Jesus's life but four. We have gospels according to Mark, Matthew, Luke, and John. There are others, of course, but these are the main stories that tell us about the life of Christ. But they don't all say exactly the same thing. In fact, in some places, they outright contradict each other."

"Doesn't that make them hard to believe? I don't mean to reveal my true beliefs again, but how do you, or how does one, come to grips with the differences?"

"I'll put it like this. You have four other people in your family, correct?"

"Yes."

"And if I asked them to write a full account of who you are, what you've said, and why you matter, do you believe they would turn in identical reports?"

He had me trapped in an inescapable logic. So well tied that I didn't need to respond.

"That is what I believe has happened with the life of Jesus. Yes, it can be frustrating at times to not know exactly who he was. And it may be that there is not a consistent person on the planet. We all must assume different roles and create different impressions depending on who we happen to be with. It seems Jesus is just like us in that respect."

It was in contradiction that reality was established.

"Too many in this clergy," he continued, "learn the stories because they feel they have to but without any direct purpose. I want you to learn the stories because they can be applied to our lives as we live them now. The faults and the pleasures of these people, in this book, have never stopped being relevant to us in some way. Perhaps that's true of all books that last. But not everyone can make those connections fully on their own. Part of our job is to relate the information with a kind of wonder and then tie it to something current people can understand."

He made his role sound more like a storytelling therapist than preacher.

"Do you think it's our job to tell the people what the stories mean or why it's important to follow them?" I asked.

"No, I don't believe that's our purpose. I think what

we are meant to do is help the people find their own way through this material. For people in the world today, coming to Church and studying the Bible is not always realistic. They have families or jobs or other more immediate obligations. It really is a shame that our society doesn't make very much time anymore for the still reflection that this place offers. But, when they are able, and they can make the journey, we want to provide them something that will nourish them until they can come back next time."

I thought of our family while he spoke. We, who had been so spotty in our attendance and yet, for four out of five, retained the same strength of faith was perhaps testament to Father Rogers' methods.

Father Rogers turned through the pages until they began on the gospel according to Mark. Instead of turning the page to exactly the spot of the story I wanted, he left me to discover it within the bounds he had established. He showed me that the other gospels all come after it and with those directions, he left me to my reading. It took some passes, and in doing so, my eyes passed over the life of Jesus, not as though it was a biography but a photo album. Brief sentences about the life of the man called Christ were sparse in their detail but resonant in their meaning. It was like reading an account of a great friendship recorded with all the inaccuracies of human memory.

When I found the four versions of the crucifixion story, I saw how correct Father Rogers had been. As Mark remembered it, the event was an act of mob bullying as they pelted Jesus with insults up until the moment of his death, when suddenly they were convinced of his divinity and the women of Jesus's life came forth through the crowd. For Matthew, all the graves opened and with them, the town's lost loved ones walked freely, which was enough of a link to prove Jesus was indeed divine. Luke's approach also laid in the crowd when their recognition and interpretation of the event clothed Jesus in his power. But they had understood too late, having failed to do so during his life. As I went through these accounts, I failed to find what I thought. They all took a distanced view of Jesus, as if his cross was so out of reach that he could no longer be identified with it. That in seeing his divinity, he was inherently separate from the people below who would now have to spend their lives looking up at him like hungry dogs. But for John, desolate John, there was vindication.

In his last image of the living Christ, John made no mention of the holy, recorded no final private whisper of worship. He wrote that Jesus had cried out to the sky above and when nothing came back, he did not plead and he did not persist. Instead, he appeared to have accepted the end of his life, his human life, and chose silence. In silence, I read renunciation. With his mother and his dearest friends curved around his bleeding feet, Jesus made no effort to console them. They huddled and stared and when Jesus did speak, he said only this: "It is finished." Then John wrote: "With that, he bowed his head and gave up his spirit." In that moment, Jesus did not give his spirit up to a higher cause. No, on his cross, he gave up the need for a spirit. That was his atheism.

Hovering above everything, Jesus lost his faith in his final moment. He had been let down by his god and at the end of his life came to know something for certain. When he needed help, and none was present, that was enough to be stripped of his faith. He had given up the requirement to believe in a spiritual part of himself and when he saw the wondering faces of his life, he could think of nothing else to say than it was all over. His mission, his conviction, his purpose, it was his example that could now be shown as erroneous. Christ, then, was the great liberator of religious belief as no one else came as near to its full embodiment as him, and if he could falter, how could anyone else survive? The death of Christ should have brought about the death of god. Unfortunately, he was loved too much. In that love came the childish refusal of death and the confusion that what had been dreamed could be true. Perhaps I had more in common with them than I thought.

I brought my interpretation to Father Rogers and he considered it. While he didn't believe my version, he understood how I got there.

"One of the reasons why I believe this book has lasted for so long is because it is perfectly vague," he said. "I remember reading about these ideas years ago and whenever I'm working with new members of the clergy, I ask them if they've noticed that as well. So often in this book, we are given few details about what happened. We are rarely told what it was like to be there, what people looked like, how they worried, and yet due to the absence of such passages, we are free to invent those details for ourselves. You mentioned the crowds of people that formed around Jesus at the moment of his death, but how many were there? Ten? One hundred? We never know for sure, and in our imperfect understanding, our minds fill in whatever will satisfy us. Those who come looking in this book for consolation will find it on every page. And those who seek fear will see it equally. What you have found is, to my knowledge, unique, and perhaps it will lead you to a kind of understanding that would be wonderful to share."

"Perhaps I could believe someone without believing in them," I said.

"Perhaps indeed."

The phone rang from one of the secret rooms. Father Rogers left the altar to answer it. Without anyone else in the church, it was easy to hear what he was saying but difficult to understand what was being said to him. His side of the call was decorated with yeses, okays, I sees, and thank yous. He clicked the receiver back into place and stood near the phone for a moment.

"Is everything okay?" I asked.

He walked back towards me as he spoke.

"Oh, it's nothing. That was the man I had booked to come and look at the confession box. The company said he's fallen ill and won't be able to make it today or tomorrow."

I looked at him as he puzzled over his solutions.

"I could take a look at it, if you'd like. Do you know what's wrong with it?" I said.

"Thank you, Declan, but it'll be alright. I'll just have to call again some other day."

"Please, Father, I'm here to work and to help. I insist."

He thought for a moment then shrugged.

"I suppose it couldn't hurt. There's a problem with the hinge on the right side door. It must be stuck or rusted—I'm sorry, I took a look at it and I'm not totally sure why the door is jamming. What's happening is that when the door is fully closed it's taking more and more force to open, and when it's open all the way, it's just as stuck."

"I'm not going to say I definitely know what the solution is but if you've got some tools, I'm sure I can hack away in the right direction."

"Thank you very much. That is quite nice of you."

He collected a small roll of tools and pointed me in the direction of the box. If I couldn't figure it out today, he mentioned, then he might have me put up some kind of curtain for privacy's sake. That was a task that I could do tomorrow after I'd done my sweeping.

The confessional sat in a tucked-away corner of the church like a misbehaved child. It wasn't as big as I thought it would have been, but it wasn't minuscule either. Instead it was like a precisely carved capsule meant to hold precisely one sinner and one priest with no room for anything else.

The door was open, and from the exposed side, the hinge looked to be in working order. After stepping inside, I closed the door and, again, I couldn't locate anything glaringly wrong with the hinge. True to Father Rogers' assessment, the door did stick when shut. I thought he meant I would have to put my shoulder into it, but when I pressed with all my weight the door held as if it was solid. The wood looked old and precisely carved so it was possible I was holding back. I certainly didn't want to kick it, so I returned my attention to the hinges, seeking a problem if none was obvious.

At that moment, when I stopped moving, a noise floated in from the other side. It was faint and damp, punctuated by quick swipes of breath. Someone was crying to themselves. It sounded like desperation.

Chapter Nineteen

She was there. A woman crumpled into herself as if a stitch that ran across her stomach had been pulled. All her reservoirs, all her dams, had failed to hold, and now she was leaking out in personal distress. Through the obscured partition and behind the leaves of hair drooping down, I couldn't see her true face. Not that I looked long enough to study. Instead, my instinct was to try and sneak out and find Father Rogers. He would know how to handle this situation. There would be some anecdote or parable that he could relay in order to quell the rising turmoil on the other side of the bench. I fidgeted with the door again, moving with the perfect combination of speed and silence, only to reveal a small gap of light in the top corner. When it closed again, the door whacked against its frame clumsily. The woman paused her sobs and looked up.

"I'm so sorry," she said.

"It's alright, no, it's fine." I paused and she didn't speak. "Is everything okay?"

"Forgive me, Father. I didn't know where else to go." Her words broke through tight mucus. Did she think I was Father Rogers or did it not matter to her?

"It's perfectly alright, you're safe in here," I said in an attempted impression of my mentor. "Please, take your time. I will listen whenever you are ready. Okay?"

The woman coughed out dregs of phlegm in her elbow before making an effort to compose herself. I listened to her correct the positions of her clothes as she ran her hands across all of their surfaces. They made for quick, whooshing noises that seemed as repetitive as they must have been compulsive. It was as if she was trying to smooth the ocean but, after every smoothing wave, the tiny mountains of water continued passing, rocking her vessel.

"I'm sorry, Father, I really am. This is not how I wanted to appear in Church. When I came in, I thought I might be able to find you walking around, but when no one was there, this seemed like the best place to wait. I haven't committed any sins—at least, I don't think—and I'm not here to make a proper confession but I… I just didn't know where else to go. There's no one I can think of to talk to right now and I just really need to talk to someone."

Her voice strained through the partition like clay through a press. She wanted so much to be well-presented and mannered like I was sure she had appeared in childhood photographs. The kind of photographs that existed of me and my sisters on our way to church. Her reality was at odds with her history.

"You are welcome here for as long as you need," I said, still in imitation.

A few more breaths tripped over each other, sounding

nearly like hiccups, before they relented to an even pace. I heard her legs as they nervously shook which caused the old wood on the bench to creak. Bounces reverberated through to my side but without the same force. She coughed again and tossed her hair out of her face. With one deep inhalation, she primed her shoulders for a drop that accompanied an exhale strong enough to puff out her cheeks.

"Maybe if I just start talking, I'll figure out what I need to say," she said.

The silence I left was like an open, unturned hand, gesturing for her to continue. She exhaled one last great gust.

"I have had a very busy life. There was school which was always so hard for me, and then I went away to study, but I could never get settled. I grew up in a really nice family too, so being separated from them felt like being away from myself, you know? It was all so hard, so hard when it shouldn't have been. And when I was there, I couldn't seem to do anything right. My professors all hated me and I had no friends and I just wanted… I just wanted to quit and never be seen again. But I couldn't just quit because I didn't want to show up back home as a quitter. So I let myself fail. That way I could come home without the bruising of having to tell my family that I couldn't do it. If it was done to me, then everything would be fine, we could blame the place, and I could get on."

She paused and shuffled.

"But it wasn't all just fine. I moved back in like a loser

when I was supposed to be out on my own. Listen to me, 'supposed to,' what are any of us supposed to be doing? I stayed put for what felt like years and took a path that no one expected that was as far away from the life of a good girl student as I could think and I finally began to set up my own life. And yet, I couldn't get away from my family. I don't need to be around here to do my job and yet I feel compelled to be stuck in their gravity. And they're not even bad! But because we're supposed to be so tight, if I went away it would feel like I was betraying them. I'm sorry, is any of this making sense?"

"Yes, it can be hard. But I'm sure they mean well." I had to stifle the thoughts of my own parents and my potential defences for them. She wasn't attacking them, of course she wasn't, but still I had a shelling response.

"Sure, they have their intentions and that's fine—until they permanently curve your spine so you can never stand up straight again." She paused after snapping that remark so reflexively. "I'm sorry, Father, I don't mean to be so snarky. It's just… it's more than just my family that's got me here, but they're at the heart of this."

I thought about asking her to continue but instead remained without words, letting her fill the emptiness when she was ready.

"So I go out and I get a job and it's a real job. I have real clients who've never heard my last name and it's something none of my siblings want to do. At least, I don't think they do. Anyway, at work, there's this guy that I can see likes to look over at me a few times a day. I'm sorry, don't worry, I'm not here because I've been violated by him or something—

quite the opposite in fact. He and I started seeing each other, casually at first, but then the meetings became more frequent and the love began to grow, he started accompanying me to everything I went to and, within a few years, I think it was in this Church, we got married."

"Weddings in here are always so lovely." I was thinking about the architecture and the music.

"Always? Must be nice to be that consistent. Anyway, we were so happy on the day of our wedding. It wasn't anything crazy expensive and we agreed that the event should be small and intimate so everyone would know who they were dancing with. It's not like I would have wanted all of my family to attend even if they were available. At home, nothing changed. People kept telling us that, after the rings went on, things would be different. I'm sure I'll have to come back for this, but we were living together before we got married and, afterwards, it was mostly the same as before. Our routines didn't change, all of the blessings and ills that we had before we were married carried over. But, now that it was legal and sanctified, there was hope for something. Something new."

Any confidence or momentum she had gained in her story slowly halted over those final words. It was as if she was doubling back in her recollection to assure that what was coming next was so close. By the poison of her remembrance, she must have been reinfected with the original illness of her soul. My palms and feet went damp as her story inched closer to its revelation. What would pull a person to such secrecy for comfort? With nothing to relate, I swallowed any potential judgements before they emerged and, left without replacements, the inside of my throat felt black and sticky.

She wiped her face and took a few measured breaths. Both sounded like scrapes of sandpaper.

"We tried for months to months to get pregnant and start our family. That was going to be our salvation. We were going to correct any and all mistakes from our parents with our little one. In her, there would be something blessed. But, for whatever reason, it just wouldn't take. I tried taking classes and tracking my cycles and I read every book on the subject. All of the things we were supposed to do, we did. And, still, every test was negative. I am thankful that my husband was so consoling on those mornings when I was seated and huddled in the bathroom. As much as I would have loved to stay curled in there forever, I knew it could never last. I would have to go to work and I'd have to walk around, wondering how the world was still turning.

"IVF was our next option. I couldn't agree to a surrogate and not to adopt either because, while I'm sure those are right for some parents, and I don't want to seem prudish or possessive, I wanted this child to be ours and wholly ours. When we looked at her, there wouldn't be any flickering thoughts of anyone else. She would have eyes that matched ours. I wanted her to be unique and personal, not something someone else dropped off that we would pick up. God, listen to me, I'm sure I sound like some kind of puritanical elitist and, yes, I don't feel great about it, but is it so wrong to want to be the mother, the full mother, of your child? I mean, of all the people in the world, can it be bad to want just one of them to be yours?"

I thought about answering, but my mind was dry.

"At first, of course, it didn't work. But my husband wouldn't let me give up. At times, you know, I thought he wanted to be a father more than I wanted to be a mother. So he kept taking me back to the clinics and we kept trying again and again and, just under a year ago, it worked! I was pregnant and we were going to be our own family!

"Each day was its own twisted miracle. Most of the time, it hurt. The baby would turn and writhe—one day her hand reached out around my ribcage. I swear I saw her knuckles on the edge of my skin. It hurt so much. I was sick and irritable—especially in the mornings. But sometimes, at night, there was this glowing calm that settled over me. Like the baby was asleep, my husband was asleep, and I was there, half awake, but knowing it all. In those times, there was no pain. I would lie there aware that I was finally doing something noble, something I was in control of. It made dealing with the cramps and the cravings a little less painful.

"We went in for our regular check-ups and everything was fine. It was all fine. It was all supposed to be fine. We had our ultrasounds done and, looking into the murky screen of black and white, I couldn't believe I was looking at… at my daughter. I know my parents were always advising us to not know until the birth day, but we couldn't hold it. It was a girl! I was going to have my own daughter! On the screen, I could see her nose tipped up like mine and I imagined what she would get from me and what she would get from him. How would our blend put her together into something both old and new."

Her voice trailed down and my eyes were on the floor. I knew she wasn't looking over at me because it felt like an absence. She took a few more laboured breaths and continued.

"So last week, or I think it was last week—I don't even know what goddamn day it is anymore. Oh! Sorry! I probably shouldn't say something like that here."

Dad would have yelled.

"It's quite alright," I said. "Don't worry. I don't take that kind of thing personally."

"Sorry. Anyway, we were just over eight months into the pregnancy and we went in for our last of the routine check-ups before, you know, the birth. I was checked out and everything looked fit and fine. They did the first scans and the baby… the baby looked to be alright. But then there was this serious look of concern on the doctor's face. It didn't last long, but I caught it for what it was. He asked if I could stick around for a little longer, apologized for the inconvenience, and explained he wanted to run some more tests. He left the room to go get some more equipment and my husband took my hand instinctively. I remember he held it very tight.

"When the doctor came back, he brought some other specialist with him. They hooked me up to more machines and took more looks in and around me than I had ever had before. The whole thing was violating but, worst of all, was the silence. Never did they address me, only each other, and if I asked something simple like

'What's wrong? What's going on?' they waved me off and continued their search."

She paused again.

"I think I knew. I think I had known for a few weeks. I had woken up one night in a full sweat and I felt this kind of drop inside me. I went to the bathroom and, when I looked at myself, something was missing from my eyes. Like they were looking from deep in the ocean, past where the light can reach.

"But even if I knew, I still didn't believe it. There had to be something they could do, anything to keep my thought from becoming true. But they couldn't. There was nothing. Not a shock, not a surgery, nothing at all. A doctor came in after all the others had left and told my husband and I that... that our baby was gone."

An anvil wedged into my throat. She wasn't crying anymore, she was momentarily frozen. On the blank brown door wall in front of her must have been the exact projection of that memory. A projection which, if she closed her eyes, only played clearer on her black eyelids. It must have ended before she spoke again.

"If my scream could stain, the room would never be clean again. She had a name. SHE HAD A NAME! She was going to be Angelina-May and she was going to live in our house and we were going to love her. And 'gone,' what could the doctor mean by that? If you saw me, Father, out of here, you wouldn't think anything was gone from me. I still look pregnant, I still feel it, but now instead of walking around with life... I'm full of death and I don't know what to do about it. I just... I just need something more than the earth can offer. Father, why did this happen to me?"

It felt like my heart and stomach switched places and were now crawling back to where they originally sat. I was rightly uncomfortable and now needed to act. But how? What amount of culture or critique would apply to her situation? Panic flooded through like rats from a fire. I didn't know why this had happened, no one could, it just did. And now its impact would remain unfilled forever. The great pain from which she was suffering begged for a balm that belief could provide. But in the confines of that box, I was assured there was nothing to believe in. If there was, and it could intervene in our lives, how could it be so merciless to not only this mother but to all the others before and after her that have been damned to the same experience. The crowds of the lost, the confused, and the hurt, why did their god not show up for them?

She was waiting for me with the patience of faith, the ever-enduring hope that things would turn out according to some secret yet pleasant plan. I couldn't lie, but I couldn't be totally honest.

"I'm so sorry," I said, "I wish I knew why these things happen too."

She sniffled at that answer.

"Father, am I going to be punished?"

"No, no you're not going to be punished. Never."

She deflated from her shoulders. With one word, I had reassured her of her faith. She would leave the confessional believing she was absolved from punishment, that nothing more would hurt her. Perhaps because she was suffering now it meant she would be liberated from suffering later. I didn't mean it that way. I said no because, even in that moment of extreme crisis, I knew that there couldn't have been anything to punish her. No outside force pulling on the strings of life that would continue to harm her beyond her days.

I listened through my heart for some kind of message. Ones like Father Rogers and Dad had heard that settled themselves into their beliefs. I put my hands over my ears like shells and, hunched, waited for the sound of god to arrive.

Nothing did.

Suddenly, I was back in the memory of being a teenager, rocking on the floor in front of my locker. Then I was in argument, then at the inlet, then walking through the world on the way to the church. The sounds of life had covered and invaded the world, filled it completely with vital power. A plunge of a heron's beak, a soft swirl of a mother's hand—even the sounds next to silence stood out with their unique and resonant noise. What was the sound of god? Even in silence, there were reminders of beating hearts and flying winds. The world as manifested by its materials arrived to intervene and called out their names in answer. There was no room for god, no need for him, because he did not have a consonant sound to add to the world. It played on in his absence. Sometimes beautifully, sometimes cruelly, but clearly without his intervention.

I looked back towards the woman, unaware of how long it had been since my last word. She wore a look of unsatisfactory consolation. Her posture tilted forward to-wards the partition. I should have said more, I should have told her not to worry about the influence of any god on her situation because I could assure her that no such entity existed. But then I thought about what that might mean to her. If her faith was the last line of gold through her cracked pot, who would I be to tell her anything else? Her lie, as I saw it, was her truth, as she lived it. I had already lied by being in my place, by impersonating a priest, and now all of my innards thrashed about like fish on land.

"Is there anything else I have to do?" she said in a hushed tone.

"No, no, there's nothing more. I'm so sorry. You are free to be and go back to people who love you. Just be with them. Hold them."

"It's okay, Father, thank you. I just needed someone to listen."

That, I thought, is where god failed.

We sat together on either side of the partition like sprinters after a race. She closed the door on her way out and I left myself inside, immobile. I felt like I should rot. Remain still in a dim place and allow the mould and fragments to take my body until I could be blown away like so many chips of paint. Looking up to the top of the booth, I saw no light extending my way as I seemed hard-ened to my seat. There was no need nor desire to move. But a thought, which was obvious, came through me: I couldn't do this and retain my honesty. I thought I was cleverer than the profession, that I could escape something so central to its needs. More than the stories, more than the relations, the guiding line of true faith was insurmountable. That woman needed someone sincere who could use their mutual belief to provide for her a touching service of mercy that I, holding to a different kind of compassion, could not. Sincerity, authenticity, honesty—these were the virtues I had felt I had violated by imitating them. I had falsified myself. It had been so easy to flip over the paradoxes in thought. When I arrived in reality, suddenly what was true and real straightened out.

Something akin to an illness slid through me and I had to get out of the booth. The door remained stuck in its corner. I twisted, pushed, then slammed the wood until, with one final hit, I screamed to be let out. Jaws wide and fluids dripping, I screamed and screamed again as if this booth was a mouth devouring me alive. With a hurried pace, I heard Father Rogers dashing across the hall and, when he got the door open and saw my strained and exhausted complexion his eyes lost their twinkle to instead fill with horror.

"I... I... I can't do this, Father. I'm so sorry. I'm so sorry."

I left him behind as I hurried out of the Church with one clear sentence imprinted in my mind: I needed to get home.

The light of the world outside was shockingly bright and the noise of day had become one unnavigable clump. Everything that passed did so with indiscriminate streaks and the sounds piled on each other like wet leaves on a gutter. This was not in unity or with purpose but a blend of the world that told me to only focus on the essentials: my heartbeat and my thoughts. I crossed streets without consideration and assumed I was walking the right way home. Persisting through hardening guilt, I bounced off of streetlights on my way along the sidewalk.

In one rushing torrent, I saw the phantoms of Mum, Dad, Hélène, and Céline. They cruised calmly through their faith as I stood on the side, immovable. How could we have been so separate? We were mixed with the same blood, lived in the same places, and yet I grew up to drift differently. The influences of my life had been away from the tangible, removed from the personal, and still they had shaped who I became. Yet I had never met them. Those people, those ideas, that corrupted me most thoroughly, that had incited my mental runnings, had come from people who lived long and far away. What did they know of their influence and how much responsibility could they take for my confusion? Fry, Kierkegaard, Caravaggio, Christ, all of them had altered a secret part of me that lay hidden beyond the influence of my family, my immediacy. They who had poured their pestilence of various truths which mixed with my chemistry beyond reform. I believed in what they said, in how they portrayed themselves, even against the personal influences of all my relations.

And then there was Father Rogers. A man of compassionate service—why couldn't he have been in any other profession? His influence, his care, had he also eclipsed my two parents? Or did I unknowingly grow up with three? I thought of how I left, how stunned he must have been to see me tear out of his meditative space, surging with torment. Would he have run after me if he could? In the last gully of my hopes, I was sure he would have.

Why couldn't I go along with the stories like a good little parishioner? It wasn't just that they were untrue, but they weren't enough. This god, this Christian God, was still too small to oversee all the aspects of life. It missed out on the quietude of life, the creativity of the problems people face, and the continuing wonder of new discovery. His obsession was with servility and punishment, of making something once and then expecting eternal praise afterwards. What about the toil that maintains the world? Those who have seen the inevitable effects of entropy and still decide to work against it. This ever-reticent figure had left his creation with no clear evidence of his existence and then commanded that they believe anyway. What was more, his system had been created so that he would be immune from all responsibility as he left no way for his creation to usurp him. It just could not be and I could not see myself participating in it, even ironically.

Amidst the dreamlike environment that was this walk home, where the trees brushed together in broad lines, the occasional parked car popped out in recognition. The same cars that had been parked in front of the same houses for years were in my view. Home must have been within a few blocks. Home. That safe place which had also become dreadful. It was a living statue to my past. In those rooms was where I had had my first free-thoughts and my first declarations. Now it was a cursed shell that no longer housed a creature looking for safety. Without such a being, its shadows looked endless.

All of me burned with a fiery secret that would soon blaze through my mouth with irrepressible vengeance. I would have to tell them I quit, but I wouldn't have to tell them why. Holding back was not dishonest, was it? They had been harmed enough by my ideas that, perhaps, it was nicer to leave the world simple.

I found our block and I started towards the house. The cars were in the driveway, which was odd. My parents shouldn't have been home until much later. Didn't they have to keep working all day? Passing the front window, I saw more than two outlines in the house. I didn't want to peer and risk being seen before I was ready so I ducked my face and focused on the driveway. It was full of unique stones that gave the impression of a solid piece of concrete. With each heavier and heavier step, I approached the door, my hands and forehead hot as a skillet. My hand lunged slowly towards the knob and just as I was about to touch it and radiate through all of my heat, it opened with the speed and power of an eagle's wing.

It was Céline.

"Hey, Uncle Declan."

Chapter Twenty

"Is he here? Is he back?" Dad said, his words easily heard from the back of the house.

Hustling past Mum and Céline, he threw himself towards me at the door. While he was not a distant man, this kind of gripping hug was an unusual act of welcome. It was something his mother might have done but never him.

I shoved my head out from his chest to the top of his shoulder. Céline stood, arms folded against the wall, with a look of sarcastic reflection. I hadn't seen her in so long and she wasn't as I remembered her. In the light of the passing day and amongst the positions of the shadows, she looked like a skeleton of her former self. I wondered if she had been able to afford much since she moved to Montréal. It had been her distance over time that had made her a version of a stranger now. I still knew her voice but, when she opened the door, I had forgotten her height. If I had been asked to place the height of her eyes, I would have been wrong. What a shame that such a fact could have disappeared so easily. Seeing her move through three-dimensional space made her seem like someone else's photograph come to life. Her face looked back toward the regular street we had grown up on as the edges of her frame contoured with silhouettes.

She had called me Uncle Declan. Had Hélène already delivered? Mum came down the hall like a neighbour approaching a fence to see what our commotion was all about.

"Is everything—" she started to say before she looked at me. "Declan! What's wrong?"

Dad and I separated. At arm's length, he lowered himself to my eye-level. I saw reflected in his dark eyes jagged cracks that looked like black lightning leading towards my irises.

"I'm sure he's all fine," Dad said. "Did you take an allergy pill this morning? I know the cottonwoods have been absolutely brutal this year and have hung around way longer than normal."

He patted me on my shoulder and led me to the heart of the house. Mum and Céline remained still, looking me over like vegetarians watching a lamb being led to slaughter. Everyone else smoothly reentered the imprints they had left while I was gone. Sitting centrally, in the most comfortable chair, was Hélène. She was safe and hadn't yet given birth. One hand was constantly rubbing the curve of her bulging torso in a dress that was too fashionable to have been a hand-me-down. I had a brief but untraceable wave of relief roll through like when a breeze picks up for a moment on a flatly hot day. She looked at me with recognition and care.

"Here you go," Dad said at my shoulder with a water glass and a small white pill in hand. "This'll clear up those eyes of yours."

The family took up positions like posing statues. Hélène faced me from her throne. Céline had turned at the neck and was looking out the window. Mum, leaning on the doorframe, had one hand covering the bottom of her face with her elbow resting on the upturned hand of the other arm. Dad had retreated and now had his arm around Mum's waist with a look of considered pleasure on his face. It was like he was looking out over a kingdom. I couldn't place myself in this arrangement, not with the spirit of my sisters, nor with the pride of my parents. Drifting between them made me feel seasick. When that rolled over, I went back to my instincts. The lesson from my childhood was to look for the stationary horizon if the boat rocked too much and the stomach started to quiver. Its firm line was always constant and helped regulate the body's systems in such times of liquid turbulence. When there was no horizon, because the fog had taken over the sea, the only place to look was down. My head dropped and I looked into the tile of the floor. With a spine curled into a hook, I ran my eyes in repeated patterns through the lines separating the tiles.

"Hello, Declan," Hélène said with patience. "How was Church today?"

"You're still going?" Céline interrupted, turning back to the room, "I'd've thought you'd be in cinders by now after crossing the threshold that much. Although, come to think of it, I thought I smelled something scorching when you walked in."

Dad snapped a look in her direction before answering for me.

"Your brother has been working very hard at this job and it sounds like it's been going quite well. So I don't want to hear any more cranks about it, especially so near to the birth. We've got to make sure this baby is born into a nice family."

"And then it can learn snarkiness as it ages?" Céline said.

"Depends how often you take care of it," Dad retorted.

Amidst their back and forth, I glanced up to see Mum and Hélène looking steadily at me. Their faces were blank but their gazes were not absent. It was a light burn, the kind given by an old spotlight. I was inventing what was in their minds, how they were scanning my head, and seeing all the details of my morning. But they said nothing. Instead, they allowed the natural need to confess to swell and push against my skull. My skin tightened. Words began to boil in my throat and bubbled over when I picked my head up. I didn't know what I was interrupting.

"If you'll all excuse me, I've got to go get out of these church clothes," I said

"You sound like our Father. Gross. Dad, are you aware that Declan is slowly stealing your personality?" Céline said.

The two of them fell back into banter while I awkwardly sidestepped out of the room. From the second floor, the meaning of the conversation was lost, but its tune carried on. Its tones were happy and quick, with each voice overlapping the others.

I went first to the washroom to douse my face with all

the water it could surface. Plunging my cupped hands into the small pool once, twice, three times before I firmly gripped the edges of the sink, slowly exhaled, with only the continued hiss of the faucet to provide sound relief. I tilted my head up towards the mirror and locked my eyes on my reflection. They were still slightly red, the jagged cracks had melted to a streaky pink which fit in fine to the general hue across my face. In that reflection was exhaustion, disillusion, and worry.

"Are you just about finished up in here?" Hélène said from the other side of the door.

"Pardon?"

I opened the door.

"Sorry, I didn't mean to scare you. It takes me a little longer to get around right now. I was wondering if you'd be much longer?"

"You didn't want to use the washroom downstairs."

"You don't want me using the downstairs washroom. Not for the next few days at least."

I held back on further questions. Of course she wanted some privacy. I quickly dried my face with one of the hanging towels. We scooted around each other in a strange square-dance as she closed the door behind her and I went to my room to change my clothes. After I had put on more comfortable pants and a simple striped t-shirt, I heard the voice of my eldest sister again.

"Since when do you have such severe allergies?"

I didn't feel like inventing a lie, but I also didn't have the endurance for the truth.

"I don't know, I never used to get them. But I think I

heard somewhere that every seven years or something a person's responses can change enough to give them allergies they previously didn't have. Or something like that. They can also go away too."

Hélène looked down and across my room. One of her hands floated to her stomach and it didn't look like she knew.

"You know, I never would have considered seven years to be a long time, but just think about how much bigger she's going to be in that time. How much she'll change."

"She? Dad and Céline have been calling it an it."

"They don't know. And, well, I don't know for sure either, but it feels like the right thing to say. Mum said she knew with each of us before we were born. Maybe I'm wrong but that'll be its own adventure. Can you believe I'm really going to be a mom?"

"No, I really can't."

My eyes glanced quickly to her stomach before moving back up to catch hers.

"Anyway," she continued, "I just wanted to check in about your allergies and make sure you're really okay."

"Yeah, I'll be fine."

"Will be?"

"Yeah."

Hélène looked like she was about to hug me. We stood there, away from the noise of the family, for a moment. There was compassion in her. Even if she didn't say anything, it felt better to hold on to this time away from everything.

"I think I'll teeter my way downstairs again," she said. "I can't wait to hear about how your work at

Church has been going. You know, Mum and Dad are really proud of you for trying."

She turned away from the doorframe and made her careful way down the stairs, one hand on her back, the other on the railing. I stood alone in my door frame as the sounds of cheery reunion tangled downstairs.

As the sun dropped into the gullet of the horizon, there was a knock on the front door. It was feeble but rang with intent. Back in my spot on the couch, I made no attempt to move. Dad, after asking if anyone was expecting company, took to his usual rolling gait on his way to the sound's origin. The door revealed the intense orange of the late summer sunset and standing in its way, but somehow blocking none of the power of light, was a plump and hunched outline.

"Father Rogers!" Dad exclaimed. "How's things? How's the old Church? I trust Declan isn't working himself into too much trouble down there, eh?"

"Good evening, Alan, it is so nice to see you. Please excuse my intrusion. I was wondering if Declan was around? May I come in for a moment?"

"Sure, sure. Please." Dad stepped back from the door and swung his upturned palm in an arc that mirrored it.

"You'll have to excuse the sense of the place right now, Father, you see our Hélène is due to become a mother any day now so we've got the whole group together again! First time in too long of a time."

"Oh, well isn't that just wonderful. It is such a special thing when a family can be together to welcome its newest member."

"Thank you, thank you, it really is. Here, everyone's in the living room. Hey! Everyone," he clapped his hands, "we've got a guest in our midst, no doubt here to make some blessings on our next Murphy!"

The family shuffled around a bit as Father Rogers greeted each of them personally with expected grace and attentiveness. Céline curtsied when it was her turn and Father Rogers bowed as best as his body would allow. Mum's arms tensed, briefly, anticipating a fall. But, true to his spirit, he remained upright and forthright, holding himself in earnestness.

"Will you take some tea, Father? Or perhaps something stronger?" Dad said.

"Oh no, thank you. I wouldn't want to put you in any inconveniences." Father Rogers said.

"It's no inconvenience, really," Mum said as she was already moving towards the alcove that separated the main room from the kitchen.

"Then I'm grateful. Thank you, Jacquline."

I had sunken away from this reception like schoolchild from a principal. A speckled sweat emerged, first on my forehead, and then down the line of my spine as I looked for a place hidden from the only lights in the room. Mum passed me with a glance that wasn't intruding but spoke enough to tell me to go into the room. It would have been rude to be so reticent with a guest.

"Hey again, Father," I said. "How are you?"

"Ah, hello!" he said, turning his entire body in the chair. "I hadn't seen you yet and worried you hadn't come home. I'm glad to see you're here, safe, and with your family."

I smiled without meaning and took a space on the couch next to Dad and Céline. Hélène was back in the room's central chair with Father Rogers in another. She had offered him her place, but he gently patted the air and took comfortably to what was available.

"Father, what can we do you for? Are you here to set a date for the baptism?" Dad said as I was settling.

Hélène looked down with tenderness, along with Father Rogers, as both their faces bloomed in equal time with the thought of new life.

"It is so wonderful to see," Father Rogers said. "To think, that girl, of such great manners and mind, is now about to become a model of a new member of our community. What a treat it is to be in the presence of this kind of ordinary miracle. Please, do let me know when the little one arrives and I would be honoured to help it begin its spiritual life."

There was space for a collective nod of thanks before Father Rogers continued.

"But perhaps we can discuss that matter more at another time. Actually, I'm here as a bit of a follow-up. If I may take some of your time to relate what happened so we can all know why I dropped by. You see, Declan here took it upon himself to try and fix the confessional box today. It had been broken for some time and, you know, I don't much have the body for that kind of work any more. In fact, that's been one of the things that's made me so grateful about having him around. The Church is sparkling again in a way it hasn't in a long time. Anyway, he told me he was going in to fix it and, after I don't know exactly how long, I couldn't find him anywhere. I heard a slam and then something like pounding and wailing so I went as quickly as I could to the booth."

The tea cried out in interruption.

"Is everyone going to have a cup?"

"None for me, thanks," said Hélène.

With no other points of dispute, Mum made the careful clinks of five saucers and cups on the counter.

Dad turned to Céline. "Do you think you could go and help your mother deliver?"

"With pleasure. Please, Padre, continue."

"Such a lively spirit, that one. Anyhow… where was I?" Father Rogers said.

"You had said something about a racket coming from the confession box. Is that what you're calling it now? A confession box? Confession booth? Confessional? The altar boys I knew as a kid had less flattering names for it that, unfortunately, are much easier to memorize." Dad said.

"All will do. Thank you for the reminder. Yes, there was quite a noise coming from that corner of the Church and so I went over to see what it was. It's not often that there is anything to hear in there during the middle of a workday so perhaps it only seemed loud amid that quiet. I thought I might be able to pull the handle from the other side but when I got there, it broke open and standing inside was our Declan, drenched and out of breath. He looked like he had been through some terrible experience.

Before I could ask what was going on, he apologized so sincerely and ran out of the Church. I'm so sorry about my delay as I was held up by a couple of visitors who had come all the way from Germany and wanted to know everything about the place. They moved at about my pace so it took a while to cover all of the grounds and, mercy, did they have a great many questions. Once they were gone, I got in my car and came straight over. My apologies for my delay. I had to make sure Declan was okay."

He turned his gentle face to me as he finished his recounting. The eyes of the room were upon me. Dad shuffled through a few expressions before finishing on one that balanced both acceptance and confusion.

"Declan," Dad said, "care to fill us in on your side?"

I stammered through a series of vague starters, each beginning with less authority. Father Rogers appeared relaxed, but Dad leaned in to anticipate the story. His forehead was a wave of creases. What if I just started talking? What if I let go of all planning, all worry, all restriction and let loose in whatever fashion first arrived? I opened up to free my first thought.

"Tea's ready!" Mum said. "And we found some crackers as well."

Mum and Céline floated through with the five cups of tea, each followed by a tight tail of steam. We four, even Hélène, were unmoving, showing only a minimal display of gratitude—except for Father Rogers who took the tea with both hands and bowed his head sincerely as he possessed it. Céline lost her seat to Mum and stood over everyone else in the room.

"I sense we've missed something," she said, her eyes hovering over the edge of her teacup, taking in the stone-faced room.

Dad provided a terse summary of Father Rogers' account like he was frantically cleaning a room before company arrived.

"Have we considered the possibility he's actually allergic to religion?" she said.

"Céline, please," Father Rogers said with a slightly raised hand.

I plunged my head into the air of the room and no one seemed to notice I had been drowning. The floodlights of stares were aimed at me and there was no escape.

"This all was so much simpler in my head. You know that dream I had, the one with the huge figure and the armoire. I guess you don't all know, but maybe you do. Anyway, at the end of it, there was this woman and we were able to relate but without words. I don't know why she was there or who she was supposed to be in real life but when it felt like I had helped her, I don't know, it felt fulfilling. It was like having an amount of food that was so perfect it was satisfying. When I woke up that morning, it was like I was illuminated from inside and I wanted to know how I could share that."

Father Rogers looked at me with increasing satisfaction while Mum's chin was on the edge of her knuckles. She wasn't looking to pry but she did look the most interested.

"Throughout this attempt at a career, I've been in

search of that feeling again. Trying to find the thing that makes me feel lit from… not my spirit but my core. The place that's tucked behind my heart. Or, you know how sometimes when you're really happy you dance without noticing? I wanted to feel like that in my work and I thought the church could give that to me. It's an idea that kept me from the contradiction in what I've been trying. If I could just get around that base fact, and connect to something, then it wouldn't matter where I was. But it did.

"I can kind of explain it like this: there was this guy we read about in my last year of university who said something like every invention invents an unforeseen disaster. So the invention of the train also invents the train-wreck or the train delay. Something no one else had experienced but now had come to expect. Today, at work, I was met by my train-wreck. What Father Rogers is saying is true. The box was broken and I went in there to fix it. When I got in, I heard there was someone on the other side, someone who was there for a reason."

My throat lumped like a boxer's fist as I knew what the words had to be.

"I really tried, I really, really tried to be the person that she needed me to be. The person I had thought myself to be. But her pain was too much and…"

"What was her pain?" Mum asked.

My eyes instinctively went to Hélène.

"She… she, uh… she had miscarried," I said.

There was a collective gasp. It wasn't huge, but it was enough to show each of them processed that final word uniquely.

"She had been so far along too—something like eight and a half months—and then the baby was just gone. Just like that. No accident, no fault—just gone… and I couldn't relate to her. I couldn't do my job. The one thing I had gotten into this line of work to do: help other people. Instead, I pretended. I sat there like I really was who she needed to hear and when she asked me a simple question, I responded with the truth and a lie. And I'm not sure which is which anymore."

"Declan," Father Rogers said lightly, "it was never your job to know everything. You did what you felt was right and I'm sure you still helped that woman, even if in a small way."

"I know, I know, but it wasn't anything to do with knowledge that stopped me. If she had come in for Sunday School homework help, then we would have been fine. But she came in bearing the worst offence of this world and do you want to know what she was most concerned about? She was terrified that this pain wasn't the end. That, for the innocent death of her child, she might be punished in eternity. And I realized then that I couldn't do this job because, while I could pretend to give her answers, it's made me feel sick ever since. I failed her by insisting on being myself. The part of myself that cannot be made to believe. Even in that place, in those circumstances, I wasn't moved to god. By refusing her the consolation that she required, and instead putting in its place a copy, I've gone against the thing I do believe in. Against the thing that ruined my place in the church in the beginning. Honesty, and what I understand that to be.

I failed today. I failed her and I failed me."

Mum's face drooped as she said, "Declan, no, you're never a failure, never to us."

"Yes," Dad added, "that's not what a failure is."

"If not, then what, Dad? Then what is it?"

"A failure," he took a serious pause, "is someone who goes through hard times and stays there forever. Now you've never done that, not once, so you'll never be a failure. Failures cannot change and, trust me, I've worked with a bunch of them. They sit in bitterness and constantly blame and reimagine, but that's not what you do —it's not what any of you do," he motioned to all of us. "We raised you all to keep going when things are hard because we know that that's what matters the most in this life. That you always keep trying."

"And if I don't make it?" I said.

"Then you adapt, you shift, you change something and go for it again. But you never, never stay put where you are."

I didn't know if it was the severity of the story, but now Dad's faucets were really opening.

"I watched too many of my brothers and sisters become like barnacles to that old Rock and live each day in anticipated hatred of the next. That's what a failure is and I don't think you're stuck there yet, Declan. You can still move on."

"What makes you so sure?" I said.

"Because the people who are stuck don't realize it until they're much too old to change it. You're still able to make a transition out of yourself, believe me."

A transition out of myself. There was a statement of wanting from the old man.

"But I can't, at least I don't feel like I can," I said.

"Why not?" Mum asked.

"I'm so tired of saying 'I don't know,' but that's all I've got. Maybe it comes down to time. I've been away from the church longer than I was ever really in it and when I look around the world, it's not part of my perspective. It's like I see everything as complete in its own way without the need for a starting force or someone who meddles in every shaking leaf. The things of the world make their own impressions, leave behind their own sounds. Just where exactly is god supposed to fit?"

It was not what anyone wanted to hear. Even Céline was quipless. We sat in the silence of that thought for an uncomfortable amount of time. It was the first time they were all forced to reckon with the sincerity of my unbelief. I looked across the faces of my family and then to Father Rogers as his lips kept circling like he was chewing. His mouth spun, and in anticipation of his next remark, I spoke out.

"Why didn't you make me believe?"

The attention of the room was united as everyone turned to his chair.

"I'm sorry?" Father Rogers said without a threat.

"Years ago, when I first went to see you and told you I was having trouble with my faith, you didn't force Catholicism on me. Instead you gave me books about the world, scepticism, and wonder. Why didn't you just revert me to the faith of my family?"

He didn't answer right away but took time to recover

from the question. His fingers interlocked for a moment and then he brought one of his hands up to his chin. He twisted his thumb as his gaze drifted out of the presence of the room.

"You know, Declan," he began, "I remember very much about those days when you came to visit me. They were such welcome days. And I remember having a conversation not only about you but about people like you; young people who were more and more inclined to throw away their faith and abandon the Church. Some did it by hiding, others were nastier, calling their parents and grandparents by bad names. It was a hard time to be a representative and there was much discussion amongst those in the profession as to what we would do about this. How we could combat it and such. Many of them suggested exactly what you have just suggested. That is to say they believed we had a duty to make everyone believe as we did, that retention was a word to become obsessed with. I had immense trouble with that notion."

"But you are the authority," I said. "Isn't that your job? To force people into doing what you want?"

"That's just the thing about it. I don't believe I can. Perhaps if I share a few influential words, you may well see what I mean. I heard of a conversation once in which a priest and a professor were talking. The priest asked the professor if he too was a priest. The professor said no, Father. Then he asked if the professor was a Catholic. The professor said he was. Finally, the priest asked him 'Do you believe in a personal God?' Once again, the professor said 'No, Father.'"

I glanced at my parents and flashed them an expression of reassurance that Father Rogers would, eventually, have a point.

"So then the priest says to the professor 'I suppose there is no way to prove by logic the existence of a personal God.' And the professor replies 'If there were, Father, what would be the value of faith?'"

"You know," Father Rogers continued, "that's always been one of my favourite stories about faith. Do you know why that is?"

We all shook our heads.

"Because it suggests that this thing called belief cannot be forced nor nurtured nor faked. That it simply is and that is good enough. With logic or with belief we can imagine everything that is possible. From that, and with a touch of practice, we can discover what exists."

"Am I just broken?" I said, too quickly. "I was born without a faith gene and now I'm going to miss out on this huge section of my community and culture?"

"No, Declan, that is not what I believe."

"But if a person can't prove by logic what it is they believe, why was logic and argument at the base of what I believe?"

"I'm not so sure it is. You see, when you came to me, I didn't just see a boy; I saw a tectonic plate. One that was sliding away from a firm and genuine belief into an area of nothingness. A place where instead of being anything, there was only nothing. I worried that the harder I pushed to bring you back, the quicker you would slide away, and that the rift between yourself and all the things you knew would be too wide to overcome. So I decided to help you become who you thought you were. And you did. If I recall correctly, the thing that mattered to you most wasn't any of the arguments or the words themselves, but how they were presented. It was the rhetoric more than the content. Not only that but also the images and the paintings depicting Biblical scenes in a human way. There was no logic in that, rather experience. You didn't have to think about what it was you responded to, you merely responded and then, later, you could do your thinking, when you'd had some more time to let perspective bloom. Believing can be such a troublesome thing to think about and so can living. The people that do believe find it either necessary or useful and, once they have it, they can't imagine a life without it. What mattered to me most then, and what still matters to me now, is that you have something you're connected to. Something to keep you away from disengaging with the world of life. We can call it belief if we like, but we don't have to."

"That is certainly a new perspective, Father. Maybe I'll have to think more about it later, but whether or not I find belief useful or necessary, I still need to work and—"

"Maybe you could still find some work in the Church?" Dad interrupted. "Keep studying the scriptures and all that? You could be a great scholar of religion because you come from outside of it, eh?"

"But it was never about the scriptures, Dad. Those are stories like any other. It was about the connection. That's what brought me back."

"The connection to what?" Mum said.

"To an institution, to a particular place, to the passersby, to everyone that came in. I wanted to know more about them, to engage with them."

"Isn't Hell supposed to be other people?" Céline said.

"I disagree," Hélène said.

"Come back to me in a few months," Céline said. "When the young one doesn't believe in sleep."

"Girls," Mum said, in French, "this is not the place for that kind of talk."

"What's she saying?" Dad asked the room.

Mum shook her head like she had a chill before looking back at me. She narrowed her eyes for a moment, then began speaking in English.

"From the time you were small, you've always had this huge imagination. Sometimes, when I drove you home, I'd look back in the rearview mirror and see those huge eyes and wonder, 'What could he be thinking about?' You always looked so… preoccupied with what was going on in your head. When you said you'd had this dream, I sort of understood how it could be so real to you. I get that part of it, because I've seen what it can do to your eyes, but there's more to life than what's in your head. You know, it can be so easy to think of something then it's entirely different to actually do it. I know it happens with me all the time with my English. Yes, I've been speaking it for years, but my mind is still in French. If I really want to express myself perfectly, I have to do it in my mind's language. I don't know if the same thing happens to the rest of you because you were raised on both, but maybe. What I do believe is that you believe you had a genuine experience that was just misplaced. Your idea was in the wrong language. That doesn't mean you can't translate it or find out how to express it in a way that feels natural. It takes great strength of character to have the courage to say 'I think I made the wrong choice' and then change rather than sticking it out in stubbornness." Mum said.

I sighed out in agreement.

"I think I made the wrong choice. It was wrong of me to think otherwise. I'm so sorry, Father."

"Please, please," Father Rogers said. "The path through one's life is tangled. I appreciate your apology but I'm afraid it isn't necessary. In your attempting, you have done enough."

"But you have your faith, all of you," I said. "It binds you together, literally. Can't you see how I'm outside that? Doesn't that bother you that I'm not the same? How, in every category, I'm the exception of this family?"

"Not every one," Dad said, after a moment's break. He leaned forward, placing his forearms on the edges of his thighs and assumed a storyteller's posture.

"Even in the old days when we started dating, your mother worked harder than a factory to try and get some French into me. We tried immersion, we tried children's books, we tried films, we tried talking to her relatives, we even lied once about her abilities so we could take the same entry-level course at a community centre. Sorry, Father, I'll be sure to atone that one someday."

Father Rogers tilted his head and held his lips in a neutral smile.

"But for whatever reason, the words just don't stick to me. I mean, according to some people at work, I have a hard enough time with English! Then we had you three and the question of language came up again. I was so nervous to raise you all bilingual, thinking I'd lose some connection, some piece of you in the confusion of languages. That you'd side against me, if you could. Those years of watching your mother become a mother, holding and swinging her young children, comfortable in her mother's tongue are some of my most troublesome memories because I wished, and this is something selfish, that I was in control of what was going on. Everything I was seeing was against everything I was thinking—like two separate oceans battering opposite sides of the same landmass.

"You all grew up and took to the language so brilliantly. And the speed at which you could switch was nothing other than astounding. It was like you three all had two brains in your head that were in good relation to each other. You didn't even carry an accent so it must've felt like being spies when you were kids. Sneaking around the world a secret code that, in these parts, nobody was wise to. Meanwhile, I felt the fool for having to constantly ask for translation or correction since I knew I had no connection to the heart of the words."

Mum took her hand to his upper back and began rubbing small circles on it. Céline's eyes were downcast, and with her hushed presence was most noticeable.

"But without you, there would be no us," I said.

"That's true," Mum said.

"It is, you're right," Dad said, "and it's something I've had to contend with forever. You see, Declan, this thing called connection doesn't have to be total to be strong. Whether two things are tied together by one rope or one hundred, what matters is that the knots are tied well and wet, that they are strong enough to resist the pulling of other forces, and that even when they feel slackened, they're still there."

"Always the fisherman to understand his ropes," I said.

"I think it's been the hardest for me to understand your beliefs. Or are they beliefs? You see, I'm not even sure how to talk about them! And maybe, like the French thing, I'll never fully understand how you can go through life claiming there's nothing divine in it. When I see the world, God is as present as rain. He's like a layer that covers all and holds it in place. Letting things shine and hide as they need to."

Mum's glance was shifting, becoming slightly more stern, but her hand remained gentle in its consolatory work.

"How you can see the same thing, the same world, and not give up on it without that firm shroud is lost on me. But I know that you don't take this thing lightly and wouldn't hold on to it if you didn't think it was right. Declan, I'm sorry if I, or we, have made it feel like you have be a perfect copy of something you can't. That's not what a family is about, that's not what being an adult is about. You are a Murphy, that's indisputable, and even if you sometimes feel like you're an island," he paused, turning his chin into his shoulder before regaining eye contact with me. "Even if you feel like you're an island, just know that you are part of an archipelago."

No one spoke for a minute, letting the words crash and drift their way through the ears of the room. Even Father Rogers appeared impressed.

Dad took a more relaxed seat on the couch with the posture of a tired athlete, a pugilist at rest. I looked to my sisters and to my parents, and they were all doing the same. It would be my silence to rupture.

"So you don't care that I'm an atheist?" I said.

He paused before a grin crept up his cheeks.

"Well I'd say I forgive you but that might not mean to you what it does to me."

Céline let free the loudest, quickest laugh—catching Dad's wink for being first. But I knew too what he meant, I knew how important that word was for him. Even if its meaning only lived in a dictionary for me, I saw in the same degree where his meaning came from. We found each other's glances and didn't say anything more on the matter. The understanding was there as the feeling of an invisible string tugged at my wrist.

"Sound carries the message of its creator," Father Rogers said. "Excuse the interjection but this does remind me of what I have considered to be the difficult call from the scriptures."

"Is it the one that says you'll go to Hell if you wear fabrics of two different materials?" Céline asked.

"No, no, it's from the Philippians. In that text, it says 'Wherefore my beloved, as ye have always obeyed, not as in my presence only, but now much more in my absence, work out your own salvation with fear and trembling.' I must say, I've spent a long time churning through that line because of its inherent affirmation of choice. It's daunting but it may be the truest expression I know."

I wanted to retreat, to analyze, to make some internal sense of what was being said and felt. But then I looked at the people sitting around. We were not physically tied together, nor compelled by anything to be where we were. They had assembled to celebrate a new life and, when met with a crisis, acted to aid. There were no debts, no clinging obligations. Just love and the recognition that one kind of consolation doesn't have to work for everyone.

"My water is breaking."

le travail continue…

ACKNOWLEDGEMENTS

I don't know if I'll ever get to do this again. Not because
I'm ill or anything, or even because I feel I only have one
novel in me. I just know that publishing is a capricious
beast whose feeding times and appetites no one has been
able to predict to satisfaction. As such, you're going to
have to indulge me with I assure that those who made me
into a now-published novelist get their due.

Novel writing can be a long and lonely enterprise,
especially a debut, since the novelist may be unsure as to
whether or not they want to tell anyone ahead of time of
their project. Which is a shame because support is often a
helpful thing when the revisions are becoming tedious
and the rejections numerous. In my case, I had support in
the woman who, at the beginning of this work, was my
girlfriend and now is my wife, Jes Perry. When I thought
this book was going to be published (by a group that
turned out to be scammers) and told her, she came racing

over to my apartment so we could celebrate as if I had just won the Giller Prize. Even when that turned, and it was years before I had another bite, her interest and belief that I could become a real novelist was unwavering.

These kinds of books aren't her usual reads. Nevertheless, she wanted to see it published. While that may seem like something one spouse does for another, I see it a bit differently. For her to be as encouraging as she is, as excited as she can get, without a personal attachment to the genre, it must mean that those reactions come from a place of pure love. Love for seeing the success of another, unrelated to something of interest. This has been a profound insight for me. It makes me want to do the same for her, to be as unconditional as she is, and provide for her the same growing warmth that comes from someone else being so selfless. Not only that, but the cover of this book was designed by her as if plucked from my own mind, and when I asked her how she knew, she said what all spouses hope to hear as often as possible: "I just listened."

Next, this novel would not exist without Anne-Marie LaMonde. Not because she lived the events or led me to the best dens of research, but more the meagerest bit of inspiration. It was in one of her classes in which I pretended all her assignments were Letters from the Editor and wrote them with all the passion, reference, and verve of someone who loves to imagine himself as an already established literary presence. While I had always done well in writing in school, she was the first not merely to say "You're good at this" but that I should seek publication, that she believed my work was full enough to deserve

a place amongst those I loved. It was a miraculous suggestion. Since then, she read every draft of this book, being
kind when she could and critical when it was warranted.
Now I get to put her name atop this pile of gratitude because it was her initial belief that has made this dream
possible.

Speaking of those who read the drafts, the names
Aaron Barry and Dylan Leonard must also be put in
print. The former is a formidable poet whose love for literature often curves into the sarcastic. Of everyone I
know, he has been my most reliable critic, never fearing to
cut around the problems of a story or a sentence and
serve them to me in a bright manner. Without his input,
this book would lack a maturity I expect from myself but
that I am not always capable of catching. Mr. Leonard,
another creative, this time from the world of acting, kept
this book honest. His inputs came from the place of the
kind of reader I imagined would benefit from this book.
Someone who is working, and working diligently, on being well-read. When he came back with a section that
worked, I knew my spell was effective, and when he needed to use words like pacing, I knew I was in real trouble.
If this book was only for those who read all the time it
wouldn't be worth reading. Thanks to his advice, the story
and the characters never lost their guide.

Finally, before I get to those who filled the blood of
this book, there is one last believer who needs naming:
Alanna Rusnak. A novelist can have an amazing idea,
outstanding execution, and a style worthy of imitation,
but unless they can find their space in an industry already

covered in a variety of talent, they will never be read. I had submitted this book out in full and in parts for a long time with some rejections coming in fifteen minutes. When Alanna's magazine, *Blank Spaces*, picked up the opening chapter, I thought that might have been it. The topic was too strange, there weren't comparatives in the market, and I was an unknown. Once the magazine went to print she did something writers think will never happen to them: she requested the rest.

When I looked around at what she had written and the size of her business, I thought I had a shot at this being the real thing. Never did I expect to see her on Instagram promoting the book before we ever signed a deal! I believe that any good relationship on any scale must be circular. The parties involved must be in a kind of exchange of hope and interest and benefit. When it was clear that she not only wanted to put this book out because she thought it was good but because it was something she wanted to participate in, there was no other answer than yes. Alanna, your vision and your championing have turned people into novelists and your care and enthusiasm deserve to shoot out as fireworks all over this business which can be so dishearteningly impersonal.

I also believe that writers are essentially conduits. Conduits of experience, knowledge, questions, reflections, and the seemingly imperceptible. As this was my first novel, it served as a channelling of everything I've ever known since it is unknown whether I will again have the fortune to publish another. As such, the people and minds to whom this text must acknowledge are too long for this text. Details that could not have been imagined came from novels, of course, but they also came from one-time university professors, former managers, lifelong friends, and a couple of birds that hypnotized me one perfect day at Spanish Banks.

However, those that need naming in their acknowledgement are simply and effectively my family. This novel was about doubt; but doubt, if trying to give a definition, is an amorphous quality of being. Anger is spiky and sadness is heavy, but doubt floats along through life suspended. What it needed to create not only drama but interest and worth were multiple lives all joined together by an unbreakable mixture of duty, history, kindness, and love.

I am one of immense fortune to say that I live in a family like that. They, the Perrys, the MacDonalds, the Curries, and Landrys, and now the Naskes, all believe in family lore. It has not only formed us, shown us the spherical sides of character and narration, it has anchored us to people we may have never known but feel like we do. They get repeated at gatherings with details shifted around depending on who's at the table and how much they think they know. That is the brilliance of stories, and anyone who claims that such tricks of verisimilitude are somehow cheap or exploitative is simply too sour to be enjoyed. If I have done my job with more than competence, if you have now left this book feeling like you know the Murphys and Father Rogers with some degree of clarity or even intimacy, I want you to know it has been because the families I come from are so vivid they deserved a place in literature. I could not have imagined all of this on my own. To them, there will never be enough thanks for instilling in me such a love for story and for being there, hovering over when my mind needed them, for encouragement, for inspiration, and for their belief.

You are all loved.

- Nick

ABOUT THE AUTHOR

Nick Perry is a classic combination of schoolteacher and writer from Port Moody, B.C. His work has appeared in publications from Canada to Iceland and the first excerpt of this novel was published in *Blank Spaces Magazine*. He lives his life as if he's already on television. Instagram: @nickperrynovelist.